GOING CRAZY
IN PUBLIC

GOING CRAZY
IN PUBLIC

A MAC FONTANA MYSTERY

EARL EMERSON

WILLIAM MORROW AND COMPANY, INC.

NEW YORK

It is the policy of William Morrow and Company, Inc., and its
imprints and affiliates, recognizing the importance of preserving
what has been written, to print the books we publish on acid-free
paper, and we exert our best efforts to that end.

Library of Congress Cataloging-in-Publication Data

Emerson, Earl W.
Going crazy in public : a Mac Fontana mystery / by Earl
Emerson.— 1st ed.
p.   cm.
ISBN 0-688-13750-4 (acid-free paper)
1. Fontana, Mac (Fictitious character)—Fiction.   2. Fire fighters—
Washington (State)—Seattle—Fiction.   3. Seattle (Wash.)—
Fiction.   I. Title.
PS3555.M39G65   1996
813'.54—dc20   96–4910
                                                                CIP

Printed in the United States of America

First Edition

3   5   7   9   10   8   6   4   2

BOOK DESIGN BY CLAIRE VACCARO

SPECIAL THANKS TO ERIC LARSEN

FOR THE CHAPTER TITLE.

Whoever gossips to you will gossip about you.

—SPANISH PROVERB

GOING CRAZY
IN PUBLIC

ONE

♦

ONE COLD SISTER

Fontana was standing on the roof of the elementary school with his hands in his pockets, thinking that when it came to mouth-to-mouth resuscitation on dogs you could just count him out.

It was June and warm and windy, and below him people were jogging toward the scene of the shooting on the playground. Because he would have to cross the roof and descend the ladder and then go around the front of the school, he would be one of the last to arrive. It would give him a few moments to review what he'd witnessed.

He had been standing on the Staircase Elementary School roof waiting for his firefighters to begin their next drill when he'd noticed a tall woman below.

Although she had heavy legs and portly hips, she moved smartly, as if her disproportionate build was only in other people's imaginations. The boy alongside her carried a sack lumped with groceries from the nearby QFC. When he was halfway across the playground, the boy glimpsed something over his shoulder and began running. Stumbling on the groceries he'd shed, the woman glanced behind, then ran too.

Sleek chestnut hides shiny with sweat and corded with strings of drool, two massive rottweilers galloped after them, zigzagging and shouldering each other in their zeal. In the almost empty parking lot at the west end of the school, their owner emerged from a small sedan and ambled nonchalantly behind, smoking a pipe. By the time the woman and the boy achieved the monkey bars and climbed to the top, the dogs were only yards behind.

Fontana'd had the urge to yell at the dogs or the owner, but the wind ripping down the valley from the direction of Mount Rainier would have robbed his words of force.

The monkey bars formed a sort of hollow igloo the dogs raced under, snarling and snapping, occasionally at a swatch of drifting cottonwood fluff, mostly at the boy's feet. One of the dogs circled back and rooted through the spilled groceries, shaking a sack of cookies the way he would a rat until gingersnaps wheeled across the pavement. Ferrying the shredded bag around on his snout, he trotted in a posture that, under different circumstances, might have been comical.

"You want us to do it again, Chief?" At the edge of the flat roof a female firefighter had stood at the top of a fire department ladder tilted up against the school building. "The drill. You want us to do it again?"

"Yes. Reverse positions and run it again," he'd said. "This time bring a hose line up with you." Ordinarily Fontana would have been observing the drill from the ground, but Roger Truax, the town's safety director, had come with them to watch the drills and was leaning against the flagpole in the center of the traffic circle in front of the school. Having just that week discovered Truax was afraid of heights—an unheard-of trait for a former firefighter—Fontana had decided roofs, ladders, and tall trees could be useful strategies for avoiding the man.

From Fontana's aerie, it was hard to tell whether the woman and the boy were in danger or just thought they were. When the dogs' master approached the monkey bars, he and the woman had spoken for a moment or two, the woman waving her arms and gesticulating, upset and angry. The man seemed remarkably unconcerned, packing his pipe for another smoke, grinning and laughing, chest puffed out in a show of power as the dogs raced around his feet, snapping at the boy.

Moving so quickly Fontana was stunned, the woman pulled a gun from her purse and fired three shots. Both dogs dropped to the pavement. The man raised his hands straight over his head, the pipe clenched in his teeth.

She pointed the pistol at the man as shiny crimson pools fattened under the dead dogs. When the contingent of firefighters came into view from around the school in their bulky yellow bunking coats, the woman put the pistol back into her purse.

"Jesus," said Fontana to himself. "You are one cold sister."

"Staircase Elementary School. Gunshots on the playground," Roger Truax whispered over his portable radio, as quietly as an announcer doing a professional bowling tournament. Fontana listened to the report on his radio, as well as the loud apparatus radios in the traffic circle in front of the school. "Gunshots on the playground. Two down. Repeat. Two down. Get some help in here now!"

The evening breeze died down, and the tar and gravel roof under Fontana's feet continued to let off heat from the June day as he jogged to the ladder. The position of fire chief in a small town brought one surprise after another.

TWO

◆

ELECTROSHOCK THERAPY
ON A TOILET SEAT

By the time the police arrived, several locals had converged on the schoolyard: children with half-eaten Popsicles, ballplayers from the fields at the far end of the schoolyard, one resident from a nearby house shuffling around the bloody puddles in moose-hide slippers. One boy used his mother's automatic camera to snap close-up photos of the pop-eyed dog cadavers. Eleven firefighters, three full-timers and eight volunteers, stood in a half circle watching.

Arriving just in front of Fontana, his inherited German shepherd, Satan, limped over and sniffed at the first dead rottweiler with an air of disdain. Satan fancied himself superior to every dog on earth, and this was only added proof.

Fontana recognized the dogs' owner now, a hatchet-faced man named Joshua Clunk, who stood with tears in his eyes, looking suddenly shriveled and deflated while the June evening mothered the last of the daylight.

Clunk was a former volunteer firefighter who had been expelled from the ranks earlier in the year when Fontana caught him with a trunk full of soap cakes and enough toilet paper rolls to last five years, all of it copped from the station supply locker. An individual who'd always had difficulty making friends, Joshua Clunk had relied on the fire department for companionship, so that when he was ousted for thievery, he was also cut off from nearly all his social affiliations.

The evening skies were measled with cottonwood fluff wafting along, sticking to people, clogging gutters, and sinking into windshield wiper slots, bestowing on the township a snowy look. Fontana spit a piece of fluff out of his mouth and approached the congregation around the dead dogs.

Roger Truax tended to take all things seriously, and a pistol still hot from firing was serious indeed.

"I need that gun," Truax said to the woman. "We're talking public safety here. You have a weapon you've discharged on public property, and I'm the city's safety director. That makes *your* gun *my* problem. *Capiche?*"

"Are you a police officer?" the woman asked.

"I'm the safety director."

"If you're not a police officer, I'm not giving it up."

"Tell her, Mac. Tell her you're the chief of the fire department and I'm the safety director. Tell her who we are."

"It's a true story. He is the safety director."

Keeping his distance, Clunk wailed, "Why'd you shoot my dogs, lady? Why the hell'd you shoot my dogs?"

Fontana knew Clunk had a volatile temper and thought a quiet talk with him might help calm the situation. "What happened?" Fontana said, walking Clunk away from the others where they wouldn't be overheard.

"I dunno." Clunk brushed tears out of his eyes. "She's crazy. First she tells me I owe her six bucks. I says, 'You talkin' to me, lady?' Then she says the money's for them cookies and a broken jar of grape jelly. I tell her I ain't paying for no groceries they threw down. Then she says for me to remove my dogs. Orders me to."

Tears still rimming his eyes, Joshua Clunk surveyed nearby Mount Gadd, which had a rain cloud hugging the top of the sheer rock face almost four thousand feet above them. Clunk wore logging boots, tattered jeans, and a checkered flannel shirt with longjohns crawling up his forearms—as near as Fontana could tell, the only getup he owned. He loosed a stream of spittle onto the pavement and fiddled with a tobacco pouch.

Clunk continued his narrative. " 'Pretty scary lookin', ain't they?' I says. And then I told her they wouldn't hurt her. She says her son is scared and for me to get them away. Like I take orders from some dumbass broad. I says, 'Lady, rottweilers got a bad rep, but they don't hurt nobody don't hurt them first. And them cookies ain't wrecked. You can dust em off. Thing about these here rottweilers is, you rile em, they'll rip you up. See that deal in the paper last week 'bout the little three-year-old got her face half chewed off? Riiiled a Rooooott-weiler. Her parents taught her some manners it wouldn't'a happened. Chalk that one up to the folks.' That's what I told her."

"So then what?" Fontana asked.

"She says, 'I am asking you again to put those dogs on a leash.' She must'a thought I'm one of those assholes carries a leash around. I tell her my boys is voice-trained. I tell her to just stick her hand down in there and let em sniff. She claims her kid has bite marks on his shoe. She wouldn't make no effort to be friendly. Then she says she's going to count to five and I better get my dogs outa there. You know that ten-year-old got mauled down south? They proved he was teasing them dogs. Proved it. I told her that. But she just a'kept count-ing, real slow like. Then she shoots em, no warning."

"Why didn't you get the dogs away from there?"

"Hell, I didn't know she was crazy. At first I can't believe my eyes. Then I come to my senses, and I say, 'You bitch! You stupid bitch! You shouldn't'a shot my dogs!' 'You're right,' she says. 'I should'a shot you.' That's when she aims the pistola at my brain."

When the first arriving officer, a woman named H. C. Bailey, ap-proached the group, the shooter walked over to Bailey and gave up the revolver, picking it up out of her purse with two fingers.

"So who shot em?" Bailey asked, unloading the gun, bagging it, and swiveling around in her bulky bulletproof vest.

"I did," said the woman. For the first time, Fontana recognized her. Back in April there had been a fire behind her house in the woods. Her son had started it.

"You want to tell me about it?" Bailey said, taking the woman aside.

"Sure." A relatively new cop, H. C. Bailey was short, bull-jawed, intense, and career-oriented, liked by most who knew her, though she had no sense of humor at the best of times and little regard for fun at any time. For the past six months she had been working out of the King County substation in Staircase.

Fontana realized the boy was still on the monkey bars, but in the bad light it took another gander to see why. A stain the size of a football had developed at his crotch. He was thirteen or fourteen and seemed not to know whether to come down or to stay on the bars and hope nobody noticed.

Fontana removed his heavy bunking coat, walked over, and held it out to the boy, who climbed down the bars backward and slipped into it wordlessly. Fontana turned the boy around and latched two of the metal clasps so that the long coat concealed the stain.

In April the boy had set a small fire in the trees behind his house, which was a couple of miles up the middle fork of the Snoqualmie River. Engine One tapped it with a tank supply and six hundred feet of hose before digging out the remaining embers with shovels. Afterward Fontana sat down with the terrified boy and had a long chat about setting fires and the consequences of same. Fontana had taken two things away from that conversation. One was that the boy was fascinated with fire and everything surrounding it: firefighters, alarms, sirens, smoke, ambulances, crowds. The other was that although the boy was fourteen, he spoke and behaved as if he were seven or eight.

When Fontana had finished buttoning his bunking coat, he noticed one of the boy's shoes had tooth marks on it, that the boy's pant cuff was torn, his sock bloody. "The dogs bite you?" Fontana asked.

"I was scared," he said.

"But they did bite you?"

"Twice. The man said I was teasing them, but I wasn't."

Fontana examined the wound and found it superficial. He looked across to where H. C. Bailey was interrogating the taller woman. Although the woman was not pretty, for some reason she was hard to look away from. Her name was Sally Culpepper. She was in her thirties, perhaps as much as ten years younger than Fontana but probably less than that, and she had a certain confidence in the way she carried herself, as much confidence as a woman could have while fleeing dogs, balancing on playground equipment, firing guns, and bickering with city officials.

H. C. Bailey stooped and studied the wounds on the first dog. When the officers from the second and third patrol cars arrived,

Bailey conferred with them, then walked over and handcuffed the woman's hands behind her back. She was read her rights and frisked while Roger Truax watched, a look of personal triumph in his cold blue eyes. Near the monkey bars, Sally Culpepper's son stood as if his feet were cemented to the earth.

When it came to light that the dogs had been attacking the boy, and when Clunk testified to what had transpired, it seemed unlikely to Fontana that they could charge her with anything more than discharging a firearm inside the city limits.

One of the longtime volunteer firefighters, Ken Valenzuela, shouted, "Get up from there, Josh! You look like some sort of idiot."

Everyone within earshot turned toward the monkey bars, where Clunk was on his hands and knees giving artificial respiration to one of the dead dogs, blood and dog snot smeared across his hands and the cuffs of his frayed longjohns.

"Somebody help me, for Jesus' sake," Joshua Clunk said, tears streaming down his face. "I can't bring him back myself."

Roger Truax ventured, "Yeah. Somebody help out here. Somebody?"

"Hell, you can't bring him back at all," Valenzuela said. "Not with a bullet in his skull. Get up from there, Josh. You look like a damned idiot."

"Yeah, get up from there," said Truax.

After one more feeble pass at the bloody dog, Clunk came out from under the monkey bars in a low stoop, the unwilling focus of the crowd. He spit a stream of tobacco onto the playground and said, "I was always afraid my boys'd be running around out in the woods and get caught by Cambodians. Turn into dinner for them illegals. I never thought for a minute some hysterical bitch would plug em."

As the small crowd slowly dispersed and the principals made their way to the patrol cars at the edge of the playground, H. C. Bailey sidled up to Fontana and, pretending to look the other direction, spoke at his chest, which was how high her head reached. "Isn't this Clunk fellow the one who kept stealing that lady's beagle?"

"That's him."

"Oh, crap."

Not content with his disgrace in the fire department, Clunk had forfeited the goodwill of everyone in town when he was discovered repeatedly kidnapping Meaghan Spinners's beagle and returning it for the reward. Nowadays there were few people who did not think of him as the town scumbag.

Without the dogs, Clunk was about as dangerous as an old man listening in on a party line, and Fontana realized Clunk had most likely detained the woman and boy on the monkey bars because they were somebody to talk to. It was doubtful he'd intended the dogs to harm them. Eventually Clunk would have put the dogs back in his Datsun and left. His downfall and the dogs' demise were due to the fact that he didn't read people well enough to know the woman had run out of rope almost immediately.

Walking back to the boy, Fontana put an arm on his shoulder and said, "Come on, son. It'll be all right."

"Is my mom going to jail?"

"I don't think so. Let's go to the substation and sort this out."

The crowd had been divided equally between dog fanciers and dog haters, or at least rottweiler haters, and the dialogue as they decamped had been animated and somewhat misguided, as people who hadn't seen it tried to re-create the scenario. Sipping from brown beer bottles, two baseball players hypothesized that looking in the dogs' gullets for fingers might be the only way to straighten things out for sure.

Clunk, who had been shouting threats behind the handcuffed woman, returned to his dogs and dropped across the body of the nearest. Ears pricked up, Satan, who still had not left the corpses, backed away warily. A volunteer firefighter and one of the police officers walked back and pulled Clunk off the dead dog, but they couldn't get him to entirely release the animal, so he ended up dragging the dog's body across the tarmac by a hind leg as he in turn was dragged by the volunteer and the officer. It was almost funny.

Lieutenant Pierpont, Fontana's second in command, who had come back with the volunteer but had remained clear of the struggle, whispered to Fontana, "Man needs electroshock therapy to bring him out of this."

"Wiring up a toilet seat would be about the best," said Fontana.

Pierpont laughed, and when Clunk heard it he let go of the dog's hind leg, broke away from the two men, ran over, and fronted Fontana. "You can look smug, but how'd you like it if somebody shot *your* dog?"

"Somebody did shoot my dog," said Fontana, referring to an incident that had happened the year before. "He still limps. Josh. Your dog bit that kid. He's bleeding."

"My dogs don't bite."

"No, he bit him. The kid's bleeding."

"My dogs don't bite." Before he could reply again, an alarm came through on Fontana's pager.

"Smoke in the building," came the dispatcher's report. The address was a ten thousand number on Hays Road, and as soon as the volunteers heard it, their eyes lit up and they began running for the fire engines. Even rookies knew about Hays Road.

Roger Truax jogged over to Fontana, who hadn't budged, and, being careful to keep his voice low and controlled, said, "You're not going? Smoke in the building. It could be a real fire, Mac."

"That's always a possibility."

"Look at them. I've never seen them move that fast."

"They don't want Fall City or Preston to beat them in."

"Fall City and Preston didn't get dispatched."

"No, but they'll be responding." Fontana grinned.

"What? What's so funny?"

"I were you, I'd go with them, Roger."

Truax eyed Fontana suspiciously. "If *you* don't think it's anything, I don't see what I could do."

"I didn't say it wasn't anything. I just don't think it's a fire."

THREE

◆

FIRE DRILL IN
A NUDIST COLONY

The town of Staircase contracted its police duties to the King County Police, who worked out of a substation in the same building that housed the fire department and, upstairs directly above the substation, the mayor's office. The substation was on the first floor and consisted of three tiny holding cells and six desks.

After they'd all gathered in the substation and the principals had given their versions of the events, Culpepper and Clunk essentially agreeing on what had been said, for they had argued only a little over the wording, H. C. Bailey looked at Sally Culpepper and said, "I'm not going to charge you at this time. Just don't do anything like this ever again on my watch."

"Thank you," Sally Culpepper said. "Thank you."

"Damn bitch." Joshua Clunk shook his fists. "She tried to kill me."

Sally Culpepper looked imploringly at Roger Truax. "Where's my son? Earlier you said he was okay."

Truax's face went blank. It was clear he hadn't given any thought to her son in spite of what he might have told her.

"He's next door at the fire station," said Fontana. "I brought him back with me."

"Thank you." She looked around the room. "Jesus, this whole thing didn't even have to happen. Now my life is ruined."

"It's not that bad," Fontana said as they walked out of the substation together. "You have a concealed weapons permit. You perceived you and your son were in danger. They may fine you, but more than likely, if you have a clean record, they won't even do that."

Clunk was one of those men who looked at all women through a veil of longing, so that the looks he threw at Sally Culpepper as he followed them out the door were a synthesis of hatred and ragged lust.

"You whore! You dog-killin' whore!"

"You better just move on out of here, Josh," Fontana said.

Grinding his teeth, Clunk tried to give Fontana the evil eye but noticed Satan watching him intently. "Fuck you and fuck your dog too. My boys could've eaten your mutt alive."

"Get out of here, you sorry Mother Hubbard," said Fontana. Clunk turned and walked unsteadily back toward the elementary school. He was so skinny that from behind it looked as if his pants were walking by themselves.

"Don't worry about him," Fontana said. "He's a twit." Then, to the dog, whose presence and obvious lethal potential had the woman mesmerized, he said, *"Fuss!"* Satan came and sat beside him.

"Is there a place I can freshen up inside?" Culpepper asked. "If there is, I'll get Audie and get out of here. He'd hang around a fire station all night."

The rear of the station next door reverberated with boisterous talk as Fontana led her through the watch office to a small rest room in the hallway across from the officers' rooms.

Wandering down the narrow hallway toward the beanery, he heard someone in his office on the left, then saw Culpepper's son sitting dejectedly in a chair in the far corner, head lowered, still clad in Fontana's bunking coat. The toes of an enormous pair of boots poked out from behind the partially open door. Only one man around the station had feet that huge—Roger Truax, a man who looked as if he might have played football in school and then gone to seed, but who, in fact, had never participated in any sport more rigorous than walking across a parking lot to a Pizza Hut.

Truax looked far taller than his six feet and heavier than his two hundred pounds. His pale complexion burned at the least touch of sun, and he had a large, unexpressive face that combined with a very small mouth to make him look like a cartoon character. Truax had once, in a rare fit of drunkenness, confided to Fontana that in his former department he'd been called Baby Huey behind his back, and, though it hadn't yet, he was deathly afraid the name would track him to Staircase.

"You know what we do to arsonists in this town?" Truax asked softly, addressing the boy. "Do you?"

"No."

"They go to jail. You know what happens in jail?"

Fontana stepped into the room. "You look good in that coat, Audie. I see the crew got your foot bandaged. You want a tour of the station? Go on out and wait in the truck bay. I'll show you around in a minute."

Glancing from Fontana to Truax and back again, the boy dashed out of the room. Truax said, "We were just—"

"I know what you were doing." Fontana closed the door.

"I would appreciate it in the future," Truax said, combing the long strands of hair across his balding pate with his left hand, "if you would not interrupt an interrogation. I think that boy has been starting the fires we've been having around town. You could see what sort of an influence his mother was. What d'ya want to bet, they run some checks, she turns out to be a jailbird?"

"Roger. I'd rather you didn't use my office to interrogate a fourteen-year-old retarded kid about a felony."

"He's retarded?"

"If anybody around here is going to investigate the arsons, it's me. I don't want any potential suspects questioned by you."

"You think he's our firebug, don't you? Mac, I heard he set that fire last April. Doesn't that give you any hints?"

Fontana sat in the chair Audie had vacated and crossed one leg over the other. "I'm surprised you're even in here. I would have thought you'd be in the beanery finding out about the nudists. I would think, as safety director for Staircase, you'd want to know."

"What are you talking about?" One of the misfortunes of Truax's life was that he blushed easily, and right now his face was flaming.

"That alarm they just had was to a nudist colony."

Trying to conceal his excitement, Truax exited the room without another word.

Formerly a captain in the Tacoma Fire Department fifty miles to the southwest, Truax seemed to relish the fact that technically the safety director ranked above the fire chief in the city's hierarchy, even though the practicality of the rankings had never been tested. But then, Truax cherished any morsel of power. Since he'd been placed in charge of stamped envelopes for the city, it was next to impossible to obtain one.

Fontana had always suspected Truax was one of those people who'd never quite been a part of any crowd, and who had adopted the fire service because it established an automatic rapport with a group, a rapport he'd clearly never enjoyed anywhere else. In fact, Truax and Joshua Clunk probably had a lot in common.

Fontana found Audie in the apparatus bay and took the boy on a tour of the vehicles: Engine One, Engine Two, the tanker, the air truck, and the aid car in the far bay. Instead of laughing with the others in the beanery, Heather Minerich was busy in a corner of the garage refilling a pump can with water and Wet Water. As it turned out, the alarm to Hays Road had been for light smoke in the building, and they never found the cause, even though they'd worn down the better part of an hour looking.

Audie asked questions about everything. "Do you guys have a fire every day? What do you do on days when you don't have a fire? Do you ever get to set them?"

"We have a couple of good fires each year. And we never set them, Audie. I hope you don't either."

"No. No. Never. Well, that once. Have you ever been burned?"

"A little bit. Not bad."

"Did it hurt?"

"It hurt." When Fontana chaperoned Audie back into the beanery, Truax, listening to talk of the nudist camp, appeared almost at the point of collapse.

"You'd think they saw a bunch of horny old firefighters coming through the gate, they'd all jump into T-shirts or something," Ken Valenzuela said.

"Showing off," said Lieutenant Pierpont. "Pure and simple."

"That old geezer?" Valenzuela said. "What the hell was *he* showing off?"

"It was gross." Heather Minerich came into the beanery and began rinsing coffee cups at the kitchen sink, aligning them in the dishwasher rack.

Though he had been with the city six months, Roger Truax clearly had not realized there was only one occupancy addressed off Hays Road, a private club called Sun Country, a nudist colony. The more graphic the descriptions of Sun Country and its occupants, the pinker Truax's ears got and the more frequently he fingered the long strands of hair on the side of his head, pulling them across the bald spot on top.

"Gee, Roger," Fontana said. "As the safety director, I thought you would have wanted to respond up there. You know the chances of burn injuries are greater in a nudist colony than anywhere else." Everybody in the room laughed. All four full-timers were in the room now: Fontana, Kingsley Pierpont, and the two rookies, Heather Minerich and Frank Weed.

"I thought about responding," Truax lied. "But I was the only one who saw the shooting. I had an obligation to testify for the man with the dead dogs."

"I saw it," said Fontana. "I told you I saw it." Truax ignored him.

"Just about every volunteer in Preston and Fall City showed up in their cars," said Lieutenant Pierpont, the only black man in the room. "Must have been twenty-five cars. Too bad the gate man only opens it for the first-in engine company unless it's a confirmed fire."

"That's why you were laughing when the alarm came in? You knew it was a nudist farm." Looking at Fontana, Truax tried not to show his anger. "Why didn't *you* go?"

"I've seen naked people before."

"Yeah?"

"When I was married I got a peek at my wife maybe once a week, sometimes twice." Everybody in the room laughed. Audie, not quite getting it, looked up at Fontana and smiled, pleased to be around so many firefighters. Life was good.

FOUR

◆

DANCING WITH
A STRANGER

A late and curiously weak dusk had muted the town, painting a
dull gray wash over the buildings and trees and streets and
drifting cottonwood fluff. Mount Gadd's sheer rock face reflected
pinks, purples, and flaming oranges, mirroring the sunset. It would
be their only report from the sinking sun, since the low foothills west
of town blocked a direct view. To the east, the Cascade Mountains
bisected the state on a north-south axis.

In Seattle it rained thirty-seven inches a year, but because it was
pressed up against the mountains, Staircase blotted up anywhere from
ninety to a hundred fifteen inches a year, a virtue most newcomers
found hard to comprehend until they'd survived a season of grayness.
Every once in a while, generally in the winter, somebody grew depressed enough to commit suicide before thinking to move away.

"Who was that pompous ass?" Sally Culpepper asked when the
three of them were on the sidewalk in front of the fire station, Fontana
relieving Audie of the bunking coat.

"Joshua Clunk?"

"No. The self-righteous dandy with the mop strings on his head.
Calls himself the safety director."

"Roger Truax? He's on a disability from the Tacoma Fire Department with a bad back. Safety director's only a part-time job, but
he takes it pretty serious."

She was almost as tall as his five-ten, and watching her in the
dimming light he thought he knew her from somewhere.

"You know," said Fontana, spotting Joshua Clunk behind the

wheel of his idling Datsun on the other side of the intersection, "I was just headed out your way. You want another ride in the chief's buggy, Audie?"

Sally Culpepper glanced over at Clunk and nervously fingered her hair, hooking it behind an ear. "We've got the Bronco over by the school."

She would have to walk past Clunk to reach the school. It was hard to know for sure in the growing darkness, but Clunk seemed to be watching them over his steering wheel while he played with an object that could have been his elk-horn hunting knife. The dead dogs were jammed into his trunk, the lid lashed down with twine, a pair of brown feet sticking out at one corner.

"Before you two head out, let me go across the street and have some words with that Dugan."

"I'd rather you didn't speak to him on our account."

"I won't be long."

"Okay then, if it's a choice between talking to him and accepting a ride, we'll accept a ride. I don't want to be the cause of any more trouble. I feel bad enough as it is. Thank you."

Fontana opened the rear hatch on the new Chevrolet Suburban and let Satan jump onto a scrap of carpet reserved for that purpose, then unlocked the doors for Sally and her son. Clunk drove away in a haze of blue smoke and screeching tires.

Riding in the backseat, Audie Culpepper machine-gunned questions at Fontana so rapidly he had to answer in batches. When the boy's mother attempted to deter the onslaught, Fontana waved her off. "Is this your truck? Are you the chief of Seattle? How come your coat was so heavy? Do you guys keep dead bodies at the fire station?"

"The truck belongs to Staircase," said Fontana. "I'm the fire chief of Staircase. Seattle has its own fire chief. I was, at one time, a captain in the fire investigation division in a pretty big department back east, but I got tired of that. When I came out here a little over a year ago, I was the sheriff of Staircase, too, but I didn't much like that part. The county does all that now. The coat is heavy because of all the liners. It's waterproof and nearly flameproof. Also, it has tools in the pockets. A wrench. Some keys. A knife. And my gloves. That flashlight. Some door wedges. There's fifty feet of rope. Back east we carried rope to rappel down from a building if we got trapped in a fire."

"You ever get trapped?"

"Couple of times. I never really needed the rope, though."

"What about the dead guys?"

"We don't keep dead guys around."

"Are you married?"

"Audie," his mother admonished.

"I *was* married. My wife died a couple of years ago. But I have a son. His name is Brendan and he's starting third grade next year. We live on the same river you do, about two miles down."

"How did your wife die?"

"Audie," said his mother.

"I don't mind any of this. She was in her car and got hit by a drunk driver."

"Maybe your son can come over and play some day?"

"I'm sure he'd like that."

One of the reasons Fontana had been attracted to Staircase was that it was so backward. It had its own post office, a handful of beauty parlors, service stations, and barbershops, a county library, two golf courses, and an Italian restaurant that changed ownership regularly and where Fontana had once requested water without ice, only to see the flustered waitress scooping the ice chips out of his drinking glass with her fingers.

In some respects it was a strange little burg. The area most travelers thought of as the town contained only about a quarter of the population, the rest residing in outlying neighborhoods incorporated willy-nilly into the city limits.

Land in the region was costly, even though much of it was on floodplain and unbuildable. After heated debates with the local conservationists, developers were getting ready to plow up the golf course at the east end of town and plunk down three hundred seventy new houses along with several low-income apartment buildings.

None of the accelerating growth made Fontana happy. In fact, it was one subject guaranteed to piss him off, and he wasn't alone in his disgust. City council meetings had become hotbeds of debate. Only Mayor Mo Costigan and one elderly council member had weathered the strife, the most contentious council members having been run out of office by one coalition or another.

To Fontana it was reassuring to live in a town where the mayor directed traffic with a flashlight when a windstorm put out the lone stoplight. He almost liked waking to find deer eating the lettuce in his garden. There was something endearing about an escaped pig running down Main Street.

Sally and Audie lived in a densely wooded area along the river two miles east of town. The property consisted of a large house with twenty-five acres of adjoining trees and pasture. Pulling great clouds of dust behind them, logging trucks rumbled down from the hills in front of their home during the week. Farther into the mountains, there were abandoned gold and crystal mines and a hot spring first discovered by the Snoqualmie Indians.

When Fontana came to a stop at the gate, Audie leaped out of the Suburban and eagerly asked to see the emergency lights, which Fontana turned on. Without any prodding from his mother, he came back to the window, thanked Fontana for the ride and for the loan of the bunking coat, then pulled open the gate far enough to squeeze through and ran toward the house in a kind of shambling gait that resembled a duck Fontana had once seen after it had flown into the side of a moving car.

A gray-haired woman in a flame-blue housedress opened the front door for the boy and remained in the doorway with her hands on her hips. Fontana remembered her. The grumpy housekeeper.

Sally Culpepper said, "By the way. I forgot to thank you properly when you were up here for that fire last spring. I've often wondered what you said to Audie. He hasn't touched a match since."

Fontana smiled. "I'd tell you if I could remember."

She kept her gray eyes on him for a moment. "Most men . . . well, a lot of people wouldn't have been so tolerant." She gazed off into the dark maples and alders. From the truck they could see a fragment of the river which was mostly white water, this stretch a magnet for kayakers and canoeists. "You think that man will cause any trouble?"

"Clunk's a coward. He was all het up tonight and he had an audience, so he had to act tough. After he goes home and changes his britches, I wouldn't be surprised if you never see him again. You do, call H. C. Bailey. Or me. Don't wait around."

"Thank you. I hated those dogs. I guess that was a dumb thing to say. You have a dog."

"Inherited. Besides, Satan's not like other dogs. Sometimes, late at night, he reads to me and my boy. Mark Twain mostly. Proust a few nights ago."

Not knowing whether to laugh or to ignore the feeble joke, she surrendered the smallest part of a smile.

Until he'd acquired Satan, Fontana hadn't had much use for dogs either, but after living with the beast for almost a year, he believed he understood the connection between people and dogs. Joshua Clunk, for instance. Clunk had elected to acquire the most vicious animals he could, training them in the harshest manner possible. Clunk spent a lot of his life wondering who was going to take advantage of him and how he was going to get even when they did, and he believed brutal dogs were a necessary part of his armory. His greatest fear was that thieves would back a tractor trailer up to the gate of his junkyard and rob him blind, as if, except for the dogs and a ficus plant his mother had left him, there was anything worth taking.

Fontana reached into the backseat and handed the woman a large paper bag.

"What's this?"

"Your groceries. They looked a little sorry in the schoolyard."

"Thank you." She smiled now, the first unadulterated smile she'd allowed herself. Her teeth were perfect, and her widely spaced, large gray eyes and dramatic bone structure gave her a model's face. Yet her hair was a blackish-red swatch and there was something unsightly about her thick, untended eyebrows. For a moment, he felt a fondness for her he hadn't been anticipating. He knew she was single from his visit in April. "You ever been to the Bedouin?" he said.

"The dance palace? No, I haven't. Is this . . . are you asking me out?"

"Dancing. That's all. Nothing serious." When she hesitated, he added, "I like to dance, and I prefer not to go alone. No hidden agendas."

"Is that a warning or a promise?"

He smiled. "Whichever you want it to be."

"I haven't been out for a long while. Can I think about it?"

"You've got a rain check. Anytime."

The day of the Culpepper fire, Kingsley Pierpont had voiced what they'd all been thinking about Sally: "What a mess." It was true. The hair. The eyebrows. The extra weight, sloppy clothes. Yet she dressed her son impeccably. It was funny because she could have been attractive if she'd lost a little weight and tried. He wondered now why he'd asked her out. He hoped it wasn't because he admired the way she'd shot those two dogs.

FIVE

◆

WHAT MAXINE LIKES

When the fire came in, Brendan was asleep in his bedroom. Mary Gilliam, their neighbor and landlord, was propped up with five pillows in the hideaway bed on the far side of the knotty-pine living room where she'd been sleeping off and on for the past few weeks.

It was one A.M. Saturday night, and Fontana's pager had just gone off. He hadn't been asleep anyway. He rolled out of bed, stepped into his bunking boots and pants as a unit, and looped a suspender over either shoulder while heading for the front door.

Mrs. Gilliam's short white hair was sticking out in all directions, making her look like an elderly punk rocker or possibly the Three Stooges' grandmother. She wore two sweaters over her flannel night-dress, each a different shade of pink. In her pudgy hands was a pulp novel. Mary's reading glasses had slipped low on her ruddy nose. "You go on, Mac. I'll hold the fort. Aid or fire?"

"It's a fire. Two fires in the past hour."

"You think it's him again?"

"Gotta be."

It would be the town's fourth visit from a serial arsonist in three weeks, thirteen fires in all.

The previous calls had been on a Thursday, a Friday, and a Saturday night. Whether through luck, vigilance, or the design of a timid firesetter, each incident had been minor, turning up in clusters that commenced after eleven-thirty at night and terminated before four in the morning, although one smoldering fire, slowed by an unexpected rain shower, hadn't been discovered until dawn.

Staircase's arsons in the past month were overshadowed by a series of arsons that had terrorized the greater Seattle area. All told there had been forty-eight hostile fires in the Puget Sound region. It was not known whether Seattle's arsons and Staircase's arsons were attributable to the same person, though Fontana had his suspicions. He preferred to think they were all the same individual—because then, when the county investigators caught their boy, they would have his too.

Lying on a mat in front of the cold fireplace, Satan whined as if to follow Mac out the door. When Fontana said, *"Bleib!"* the dog laid his head back down.

Without bothering to switch on his siren, Fontana sped down the wet, two-lane road into town. Most of the township, certainly all of the central portion of it, was dead flat. In the rainy season, the three forks of the Snoqualmie River often rampaged over their banks, and in the sixties a fallen tree logjammed the south fork, flooding the downtown area before army engineers could dynamite the jam. When not overpowered by the smell of chewing tobacco and adolescent underarms, the movie theater still smelled like mildew from the flooding thirty years earlier.

The fire was in the alley behind the Bedouin, a beer and dance joint.

When he drew close, Fontana spotted a column of white smoke over the roofs of the buildings on the south side of the street. White smoke usually meant steam, and steam meant they already had water on the fire. In the mouth of the alley, Fontana kicked a kink out of Engine One's preconnect hose line as he walked past it.

The alley was full of do-gooders from the Bedouin, some drunk, some disheveled, some dolled up in their party clothes. The fire had been in a garbage bin, the lowest seams of which were now pissing water, and the bin had been up against the wall of the building, so that an inverted arrowhead of black char extended fifteen feet up the wall above the alley. The char was deep enough in some spots that

Frank Weed and two volunteers had put up a small ladder and were whacking away at it with axes.

Sandusky, a professional firefighter in the Seattle department, had been volunteering in Staircase since his late teens and was directing the operation tonight. Besides being experienced and aggressive, he was also the most accomplished athlete in the volunteer ranks.

Heather Minerich took a pick-head ax from the side of Engine One but, because of the horde of volunteers, couldn't get close enough to help on the wall. Looking for something to do, she reached into the Dumpster with one gloved hand and began pulling out wet paper. Sandusky stopped her, explaining that they needed to keep the evidence as intact as possible for the fire investigators.

Wearing rubber boots, heavy yellow bunking pants, a bunking coat, and a yellow helmet with the red rubber band around it signifying that he was an acting lieutenant tonight, Sandusky approached Fontana. Well over six feet tall, Sandusky had dark brown eyes, unkempt hair, and an endearing, face-crinkling smile. He was a handsome man but didn't seem to realize it. Known to have one of the foulest mouths in town, he displayed a brand of raw humor that probably wasn't appreciated as much in polite society as it was in the firehouse.

Sandusky was thirty-six, and although he had a position with the Seattle Fire Department and his father had retired out of Seattle, he had applied for the vacancies in Staircase last year when two regulars were killed in separate incidents not related to fighting fires. Fontana never had figured out why he wanted to work in such a small department except that he had resided in Staircase since he was fifteen and must have harbored a special fondness for the Podunk department.

Although everyone had expected him to do well, to possibly score in the top two or three and get a job, Sandusky had scored only sixty-seventh on the hiring list and, after being turned down, had stopped volunteering for the next six months. It was only in the past couple of weeks, since the arsons started, that he'd been responding to his pager at his former pace. Fontana assumed that like most firefighters, he couldn't resist the action.

"Chief," Sandusky said. "Second one tonight. About forty minutes ago a Dumpster out behind the Texaco went up like a bag of shit on Halloween. Somebody saw it and drove 'round to the station to tell us. By the time the fuckin' dispatcher called us, we were already tapping it."

"Anybody see anything?"

"At the service station, no. But one of the women over there thinks she was out here smoking a cigarette right before this one started."

"Thinks?"

"You gotta talk to her." Together they walked over to the crime scene ribbon stretched across the alley.

A redheaded woman flirting with two rough-looking men in cowboy hats saw the firefighters and after a moment came over to the sagging crime scene tape. "Why don't you tell the chief what you saw?" Sandusky said.

She was a blowzy woman in a polka-dot dress and ankle-high cowboy boots festooned with silver geegaws. Her eyes were bloodshot. The muscles of her arms wobbled slackly as she waved them around.

Her name was Maxine, and she lived with a husband Fontana didn't much care for in a double-wide trailer on a weed-filled lot not far from Joshua Clunk's junkyard east of town. Her husband's parents had left him the property.

"Oh, hello, Chiefy," Maxine said, batting her eyelashes and making what she must have thought were provocative movements with her hips.

"Tell me what you saw, Maxine," said Fontana.

"I was out here in the alley with one of my friends having a cigarette. Which friend I cannot say." She gave Sandusky a suggestive leer. "Do I know you? You're kind of cute, honey. Anyway, I heard that Dumpster rollin' across the alley. It made a fearsome racket."

It was an unremarkable alley, single-story businesses on one side, a strip of slant-in parking on the other. Beyond the parking lay the railway station at the end of the block, used only on weekends for the tourist steam train. "You see anything else?"

"Me and my friend were mutually occupied."

"Where were you exactly?"

"In the backseat of a Dodge stretch cab about halfway down the street there."

"You mind telling me who you were with?"

Maxine lowered her head. "Why do you need to know?"

"I was thinking he or she might have seen or heard something more."

She broke into gales of laughter. " 'He or she'? Chiefy, you ain't been listening. I ain't climbin' in the backseat of a truck with no *she*. And *he* is even more shitfaced than I am. *He* didn't see shit. Hey, cutie." She was looking at Sandusky. "You know how to dance?"

"I'm working."

"Well, hey, don't get your shorts all lit up. That wasn't an invitation, honey. Just a question."

"Let's keep a guard posted," Fontana said, as he and Sandusky walked back to Engine One. "We'll have the county fire investigators dust that Dumpster for fingerprints. Maybe we'll get lucky. By the way, I think Maxine likes you."

"Maxine likes anything she suspects might have a pecker hidden somewhere on it." Turning to a regular who had been helping one of the volunteers stretch out and drain hose lines, he said, "Heather, I want you to stay here until the county investigators show up."

Heather looked pleadingly at Sandusky. "Why? He won't come back here. I'm going to miss some fires."

"It's the chain of evidence," Sandusky said. "We let this out of our sight, it won't hold up in court."

"Chief? Please. I don't want to miss any fires," Heather said.

Even as she pleaded, another alarm came across on the apparatus radio, the dispatcher calling for a full response to Nedley Avenue. "House fire. Flames visible."

"Chief?" she said.

Fontana collared a volunteer, an older man who worked at a shake mill up the river, and asked him to guard the Dumpster. "Thanks," Heather said, running toward Engine One, where she leaped into the jump seat opposite Frank Weed.

As soon as somebody disconnected the line from the rear of the apparatus, Engine One roared up the alley, scattering bystanders and blowing torrents of black diesel smoke out the tailpipe. Fontana followed in his Suburban.

After eighteen years in a big-city department in the East, eight as an arson investigator, the last three as a captain in operations, Fontana believed he'd stumbled onto the perfect job: fire chief in a one-horse town where the tallest building was the hose tower on the fire station.

Staircase averaged one house fire a year, two or three in a bad year. During the winter months they had the occasional overturned 4×4 on nearby Interstate 90. From time to time a summer brushfire in the hills. The odd run to Sun Country. One year a chicken farm burned to the ground, the air saturated with roasted meat, scorched feathers, and bad jokes. The largest incident Fontana could recall was a church fire shortly after he accepted the job.

Like most fire departments in the country, 85 percent of their alarms dealt not with fires but with medical emergencies, and for that they used the engine and an aid car, as well as a medic unit staffed each shift with two medics from the city of Bellevue twenty miles away. Most volunteers had qualified as emergency medical technicians.

When he had moved to Staircase a little over a year earlier, he decided the people were the friendliest and sometimes the dumbest he'd known anywhere. It was a town that tried to be charming and didn't quite measure up. Half the downtown building owners had nailed up a Bavarian motif across their facades, the other half refraining on the basis of politics, personal prejudice against Germans, financing, or ennui.

The pace of life was generally slower here than most places, and that suited Fontana just fine. A dog could sleep in the middle of any road and traffic either went around or patiently waited for him to amble away—usually without so much as the honk of a horn.

The downside was that since Fontana had lived here, there had been three murders, several scandals, and some suspicious sexual activity by the mayor.

And now he had a full-blown arson spree on his hands.

SIX

◆

FLAMES VISIBLE

Nedley Avenue was on the wealthy side of town and bordered the north end of the golf course in a neighborhood where many of the houses had small dents in their south-facing outer walls. The yards were spacious and lacked fences, farm animals, abandoned appliances, or other eyesores; almost none of the homeowners parked on their lawns. Mayor Mo Costigan lived here. So did Roger Truax, along with his wife and child.

Trailing Engine One, Fontana sighted a column of gray smoke a few hundred yards away, beneath the smoke a low glow that brightened as he drew closer. This was a garage fire but not much of one.

When Fontana pulled up amid red lights, the neighbors standing around in robes, the flames slapping rouge onto the night, he tried not to think about how much he loved the spectacle.

As always with these recent fires, Fontana couldn't keep his mind off the possibility of fatalities. The garage was attached to a house. Another twenty minutes and they could have been hauling charred bodies out of the ruins. It was the reason he hadn't been asleep when the alarm came in. In fact, he hadn't slept well in three weeks. The town had too many easy veins for this fire junkie.

He glanced around quickly at the spectators in their pajamas, their bare feet, their underwear, at the volunteers arriving in bunking clothes, and wondered whether the firebug was here among them. It was not uncommon for a thrill-seeking arsonist to mingle and watch the commotion he'd caused. For some reason he found himself scanning the onlookers for Joshua Clunk.

As Engine One pulled up directly in front of the house, Sandusky gave a radio report, the key points of which were repeated by the county dispatchers, while Frank Weed and Heather Minerich raced to the rear of the vehicle, together pulling a two-hundred-foot section of inch-and-three-quarter hose line from its slot. Frank grabbed the top section with the nozzle, which relegated Heather to hooking the other end onto a side discharge port on the engine and backing him up.

It took less than thirty seconds to purge the flame and send a barrage of steam and black smoke skyward.

On any other night, Fontana would have told his volunteers to crawl back into bed with their wives and dogs, but tonight he gave a code green to the backup unit from Fall City, sending them home, and a code yellow to the Staircase units, which meant they were to continue on in without lights and sirens.

A silver-haired man in a monogrammed silk bathrobe approached Fontana, his face screwed up with rage. A handsome, younger woman with hair down to her waist followed behind. Jesse Rothem and his wife, Kim, were vocal foes of the plan to turn the golf course into a residential community.

"You see anything?" Fontana asked.

"Not a goddamned thing," Rothem said. "My neighbor's kid just got home from a date and found it. Jesus Christ. If he hadn't come home when he did we might have lost the whole kit and caboodle. You move out here to the boonies and you figure you're safe from all this bullshit. Where'd it start? In the garage? Why can't you people do something about this shit? You're the goddamned chief!"

"Calm down," said Fontana. "We're doing everything we can. See the inverted triangle where the flame went up? Started off pretty hot. You have something lying there in the grass? What did that metal handle belong to?"

"God. The bastard burned up my lawn mower!"

"You're lucky you got away with your lives," said a barefoot neighbor who had thrown on shorts and a backward puce top, the tag flapping under her chin.

"Why would anyone pick on us?" Kim Rothem asked.

Before Fontana could reply, Engine Two called on the radio, their transmission constructing a tinny stereo as it traveled across both Engine One's apparatus radio and the radio in Fontana's pocket. Fontana recognized the imperturbable voice of Ken Valenzuela, a long-time volunteer. "Engine Two to Nedley Command."

"Nedley Command," Fontana replied, using the mike clipped to his collar.

"We're at the entrance to Nedley Road here, but we see smoke out behind the QFC supermarket. Do you need us at your location?"

"Negative," Fontana said. "Nedley Command code green all units except Engine One out of service at the location. Engine Two, check out the smoke."

"Two, okay."

Fontana spoke to Sandusky, who was walking toward him. "You know what to do here?"

"Sure."

On his way out of the neighborhood, Fontana spotted a small pickup parked crossways in a dark driveway, engine idling, headlights framing a man and woman in bunking gear as they performed what looked like an Indian war dance. A blur of light smoke rose as high as their pockets.

When Fontana pulled into the driveway and let his headlights wash over the scene, he recognized Opal and Les Morgan, but it took longer to figure out they were stomping on a section of smoldering wall panel in the grass.

"We just now saw it, Chief," Opal said. "It was leanin' up against the house here."

Looking more like brother and sister than the married couple they were, the Morgans had brown hair—his limp, hers curly—and round faces, and both walked with their feet pointed out like ducks. Their pale, doughy flesh was the result of twenty-seven years of Opal's deep-fried cooking. They worked hard at fires, were dependable, and almost always showed up together.

"Nice work. Look around the property and make sure there aren't any other ignition points."

"What the devil is going on?" The voice came from behind the screen door of the house: a man with a shotgun at his side.

"Fire department," Fontana said, climbing into his Suburban. "These people here just saved about half your house and maybe all of your life. I were you, I'd put that scattergun away and thank them."

Before Fontana reached Engine Two's location behind the QFC supermarket, the dispatcher reported a paper-shack fire on Baldachi and Fourth. Heading toward Baldachi, Fontana notified the dispatcher and Engine Two that he was responding. Sounding winded on the radio, Ken Valenzuela replied, "Bunch'a cardboard boxes out here behind the store. Some employees using fire extinguishers on them or it would'a gone up bigger."

"You need help?"

"No. We'll have it in a minute."

At Baldachi and Fourth, Fontana left the motor running, sent out a code green to all units on this response, got a pressurized water pump can from the rear of the truck, and carried it to the eight-by fifteen foot paper shack. A film of smoke hung in the air, but it wasn't until he got close that he found a small circle of charred paint where somebody had tried to ignite the base of a wall. He stood up straight and surveyed Fourth. Then Baldachi Way. The houses were dark. No pedestrians. No moving vehicles. Along Fourth he could see several lots with newly laid foundations. Framing had begun in one.

Moments later a souped-up Mustang raced up Baldachi from the direction of the river. A young man jumped out and gaped at the paper shack in sleepy-eyed disbelief. He was short, twenty-one years old, and had a shock of flaming red hair. One of the more excitable volunteers, Jim Hawkins had already caused two accidents responding to alarms in the past year. Fontana told him it didn't make any sense to kill people on your way to a Dumpster fire, but for Hawkins the advice was never as seductive as the speed.

"Jim. Ride with me."

Grabbing his keys and bunking clothes out of the Mustang, Hawkins climbed into the chief's truck and, words slurred with sleep, said, "Was that even a fire? I didn't see a fire."

"It wasn't much. But there were five others in front of this."

"Christ on a crutch. How come I always sleep through my beeper? I had it under my pillow, but with all these fires and the way I sleep, maybe I should tape it to my head. What do you think?"

"Tape it to your head. Definitely."

When they reached Staircase Way, the street scene was about what Fontana expected to find. A dozen customers from the Bedouin were milling about on the sidewalk in front of the dance-hall doors. In the Dairy Queen parking lot across the street, two cars crammed with teenagers idled next to each other with their windows rolled down, although the hand-painted SHUT sign had been displayed in the darkened window of the greasy spoon for hours. An old man walked up from one of the neighborhoods strangling a kitten on a leash. In the distance, pedaling toward Fontana from the east on Staircase Way, a spindly figure approached on a bicycle. He waited until the cyclist was within hailing distance.

"Audie. What are you doing out this time of night?"

"That's the kid set the woods on fire," Hawkins whispered.

"My scanner reported trouble," said Audie. "I came to see if I could help."

"We've pretty much got it under control. Don't you think your mother'll be worried?"

"She thinks I'm in bed."

"That's the kid who set the woods on fire," Hawkins whispered again.

Fontana studied the boy, who in turn cautiously studied the two cars at the Dairy Queen. It occurred to Fontana that other youngsters probably made sport of Audie and he undoubtedly had a long list of individuals to avoid. "It said on the scanner somebody set fire to the QFC."

"Don't worry. It's out. Audie, you'd better go home. Your mother's going to be upset."

"She's been upset ever since those dumb dogs. Could you talk to her and tell her we don't have to move?"

"She's going to move because of the dogs?"

"Yeah. Hey. Did anybody get burned?"

"No."

"How many fires have you had?"

"A few."

"Who's doin' it?"

"We don't know," Fontana said, realizing that Audie was looking a lot more bedraggled than a mere two-mile bike ride would have left him. He wondered how long he'd been prowling. Before he could say anything else, Fontana's radio crackled and the dispatcher barked out another full alarm, the address only four blocks away.

It was a house fire, flames visible.

"Can I ride with you guys?" Audie asked excitedly. "Can I?"

"No. And stay on the sidewalks. There's going to be some fast traffic."

It was a vacant house on Main Street directly behind the fire station, and the flames lit up the night. Debris and paper had been piled below one wall in the dry grass and ignited. A police car was already on the scene, parked in front of the hydrant.

With a sound reminiscent of flags rippling in a high wind, one wall of the structure was aflame, thin tongues of orange licking the eaves on the second story. Next door, the limbs on a thirty-five-foot plum tree smoldered. Under the tree a slow ragged circle of burning grass spread outward.

Using a CO_2 extinguisher, Fontana knocked most of the wall fire down while Hawkins attacked the grass with a pair of pressurized pump cans, one after the other, but then, as they waited for Engine Two's crew to stretch lines and get the pump operating, for more volunteers to show up, the wall flared back up, as did the grass. Volunteers dragged hose across the overgrown yard, but not before the wall was burning almost as fiercely as it had been on Fontana's arrival.

Two firefighters hauled a four-inch line across the street and hooked up to the hydrant with the help of the cop who'd finally moved his vehicle.

Gabbing animatedly, four women in dresses and high heels stood across the street in the dark. They had to have walked over from the

Bedouin. In the shadows behind the women, Audie Culpepper watched. The street was soon filled with gawking neighbors, wide-eyed children, and weepy tots clenched in their parents' arms.

By simply walking up to a less experienced volunteer and asking for it, Hawkins took control of the pipe, smirking as he did so. No experienced firefighter ever willingly gave up the nozzle, and most firefighters riding the tailboard competed for it, as had Weed and Minerich back at the Rothem fire. Everybody wanted to be the hero who put out the fire.

Blacking out the house, the grass, and then the plum tree, in that order, Hawkins continued to pour water on the burned areas on the side of the house and in the grass. Another crew took a line inside and a moment later could be heard drumming the walls with their hose stream. Because it was a vacant house, water damage was not a consideration, so their nozzles were wide open, water eventually running out the front door in a stream. By the time Engine One arrived, the dispatcher said a county fire investigator was on the way.

When Engine One pulled up, Heather Minerich, who had missed the action and the pipe at each of her fires, tipped her helmet back on her head and said, "Crap! This was the best yet."

Sandusky and Valenzuela, the two acting volunteer lieutenants, conferred with Fontana away from the others. Valenzuela, who had a slash of soot across one cheek as well as the smell of smoke rising off him, said, "Seems like we got a lot of curious people cruising around tonight—a lot of strangers. I'd feel better if I recognized more people. A few years back, you'd look around, you knew everybody. Any one of these guys could be starting these fires."

"The sonofabitch is probably standing right here," Sandusky said. "I knew who he was, I'd kick him in the nuts."

"You think maybe he comes to the Bedouin and goes out and lights fires when he can't get any babes to dance with him?" Valenzuela asked.

"That's a new one," said Fontana.

"But you know what else?" said Sandusky. "Look who lives directly across the street. Since when've we ever had a fire where Claude Pettigrew didn't show up? Why isn't Claude out here?"

One of the few workers who hadn't been laid off at the wood mill, Claude Pettigrew was an inveterate fire buff as well as the station mascot. He spent more time at the firehouse than any other individual and would have volunteered if it weren't for his bad knees, ankles, and feet, all of which were crippled from carrying his three hundred pounds around. Whenever there was an alarm in the center of town, Claude hobbled over and watched, his jaw jutting, a twinkle in his eye. Tonight they'd fought a fire a hundred fifty feet from Pettigrew's front door and he hadn't cracked a blind.

"It *is* suspicious," said Valenzuela.

"He's probably drunk," said Fontana. "It's Saturday night, and you know Claude."

"Being stinko has never stopped him before," said Sandusky.

Valenzuela took his helmet off. "Hey, Chief? I just thought of something. This arsonist, whoever he is, was maybe three minutes in front of us. Right? I'm surprised we didn't see him driving out of that cul-de-sac by the golf course when we drove in."

"You're right. He doesn't usually corner himself like that," said Fontana. "I wonder if he set that one from the golf course side. Walked in."

"I wonder if somebody else set it." Sandusky banged his helmet against his knee to dislodge soot. "Maybe we have two creeps now."

Moments later, Roger Truax arrived from one direction while Jenny Underhill, the only female arson investigator on the King County staff, arrived from the other.

Sandusky said, "You think Roger knew she was working tonight, or did he just wake up and sniff and say, I gotta go see that fire location, there's going to be some poontang?"

"Come on, Sandusky," Fontana said. "Be nice."

"Watch this. First thing, he'll put those canoes of his in some dog shit."

SEVEN

♦

COPYCATS

Fontana walked over to the fire building with Jennifer Underhill, who said, "It's too bad we always have to meet under these circumstances."

"That's what firefighters do. Meet at fires."

"Don't be so reasonable. What've you got?"

Fontana took her to the side of the scorched house and directed a flashlight beam at the base of the wall. Rivulets of water dripped from the burned boards. Here and there, wisps of steam danced off the building. Jenny squatted in the blackened grass and poked around with the tip of a pocketknife, gouging boards on the side of the house and sniffing for the odor of flammable liquid.

A large-framed woman, Jenny had a softness about her features and manner that made Fontana wonder why she'd entered the fire service. In her early thirties, she was sunny of disposition, blue-eyed, wide-hipped, gangly, pleasant to look at, and clearly had a minor crush on Sandusky, who hadn't seemed to notice.

She had a manner of enunciating that placed her tongue between her teeth so often Fontana found it hard to not stare at her mouth when they chatted. Because she was unassuming and quiet, most men tended to dismiss her. Tonight she wore bunking boots that came almost to her knees, jeans, a T-shirt under a light windbreaker, and a tiny hard hat that not only made her look taller than her six feet but made her chin-length brown hair flair out like a clown's.

"You know, Mac," she said. "We're not getting any closer to find-ing this person. All these fires in Seattle, Tacoma, and out here. We're not even sure if we're chasing one arsonist or five."

"It's rough on everyone."

"We realize it isn't your responsibility as local fire chief to inves-tigate arsons in your area, but this thing has us so jammed up we're asking all the local jurisdictions to do whatever follow-ups they can."

"Fine by me."

"Good."

Walking like a shy boy about to greet an award, Roger Truax shambled across the dried grass of the yard.

"Hello there, Jenny," Truax said.

Underhill, who had been crouched at the base of the building poking through debris, looked up, mumbled a reply, and went back to work. Truax's interrogation of the boy the night of the shooting still stuck in Fontana's craw. It must have been bothering the boy too, because as soon as Truax showed up he climbed onto his bicycle and pedaled off into the night.

"You know, Jenny, as safety director, I'm going to have to take a more active role in these fires. You think it's one person working western Washington? What would be the motive?" At times, watching Truax try to keep a conversational ball rolling was a little like watching a poodle trying to open a door.

"I'm not at liberty to talk about it," Underhill said.

"After all, you are working with the new Arson Task Force."

"There's an Arson Task Force?" Fontana said. It was upsetting that Truax knew about it before he did.

"I was about to tell you," said Underhill.

"The problem is," Truax said, "any of these fires could take out half the block, half the town. We don't have enough fire suppression equipment, and we don't have enough firefighters. Lives could be lost. What would you guess, Chief? We might lose five people? Eight?"

Fontana ignored him.

"What else have you had tonight, Chief?" Underhill asked.

Truax interrupted before he could reply. "What about that fire they had in Tacoma the other night? I read where it was a ten-million-dollar loss. I had occasion to talk to the chief's office down there this past week, and they're a little distraught. So give us the real skinny, will you?" Truax laughed the laugh of a man in the know, glancing once at Fontana but mostly trying to make eye contact with Jenny Underhill. Fontana was beginning to feel like the third person on a blind date gone wrong.

"Okay," Underhill said. "As you know, we've got an arson spree going on in the north portion of King County and some parts of Snohomish County. We're pretty sure that our primary arsonist is responsible for about forty fires. Unfortunately, Staircase seems to have become part of this guy's stomping grounds. In addition, Seattle has three copycats. Three that we've recognized. There's one on Capitol Hill, and we think we know who that is. An inmate in the King County Jail ratted on him. There's one operation in the Rainier Valley that we think is a couple of kids. Fourteen car fires. And then there's the one in north Seattle.

"Already one businessman torched his building hoping we'd think it was done by our arsonist. A lady in Lake City set fire to her own apartment complex and then played hero pounding on doors and warning people. She might have gotten away with it if she hadn't done it again four nights later. She'd been having family problems and thought she needed some attention."

"Ho, ho, ho," Truax said. "I guess she got some attention all right."

Underhill and Fontana exchanged looks. Fontana said, "I'll have Sandusky write you out a list of tonight's fire locations. By the way, Jenny, has anybody spotted this Dugan? You folks have any sort of description?"

"There were a couple of witnesses who saw a businessman type driving a dark sedan around the time of some of the fires. But that's a real long shot."

Truax cupped his chin in one huge mitt and held the elbow of his supporting arm. "Supposing the primary arsonist set a few fires out here and then got tired of it, for one reason or another, and another person took over. Couldn't it be a kid on a bike?"

Underhill rose from her work, and she and Fontana made their way across the yard. Truax might have followed them, but he'd discovered something on his shoe and was scraping it off.

EIGHT

◆

THE MAN IN THE
WHEELCHAIR WATCHING

Sunday at nine, Fontana woke up to the sounds of Brendan fumbling around in another part of the house. Fontana had gotten home at four and for a long while hadn't been able to sleep. He didn't know whether it was from having his sleep patterns interrupted or from worry.

After the house on Main Street, there had been two more fires, one in a stack of weathered lumber in a field between Staircase and Truck Town. It occurred to Fontana that this particular fire, having been set more or less in the open, was dissimilar to the others in the string, all of which had been structure fires, or attempts at structure fires. It also occurred to him that this fire might have been lit around the time Audie would have pedaled past on his way home.

Half a block from the vacant house on Main Street, a garage fire was discovered by Les and Opal Morgan, their second discovery of the night. Afterward, like pigeons on a ledge, Opal and Les strutted through the fire station so pleased with themselves neither could think of a word to say.

After the fires, sleepy volunteers stood around the beanery chewing the fat, hashing over war stories, gossiping, sipping coffee, unsure whether or not to go home.

Sandusky noted that five of the fires had been within walking distance of Claude Pettigrew's house, including the one directly across the street in the abandoned building both Pettigrew and his mother had been bitching about for years.

Witnesses from the Bedouin came to the station and said they had spotted a well-dressed man in slacks and a sport coat hanging around near the service station prior to the fires, and of course the service station was only across the street and down a few buildings from the Bedouin where Maxine had, from the backseat of a parked pickup truck, heard the garbage bin rolling across the alley.

In the neighborhood next to the golf course, one resident remembered having seen a man riding a bicycle prior to the Rothems' carport fire. The cyclist, she said, had been a rather small man, an observation that spurred Hawkins to ask if he might have been a boy.

Firehouse scuttlebutt, which had already digested Claude Pettigrew, now swallowed Audie Culpepper too, although most of the participants didn't know the boy's name, only that he had set a fire last April and that Thursday night his mother had murdered two dogs.

In the morning when he stumbled into his own kitchen in his sleeping shorts, his sandy hair rumpled, Fontana found his son reading the Sunday funnies. Mary had gone home.

Small for an eight-year-old and favoring his late mother, Linda, Brendan had large gray eyes and freckles spattered across his nose.

"Been up long, kid?" Fontana said, ruffling his son's chestnut hair and gazing out the kitchen window at the river, which had gone down a foot in two days.

"Mary said you had some fires."

"Yeah, we did. Thanks for not waking me. You had breakfast?"

"Nope. But I let Satan out."

"Good for you. What're you in the mood for?"

"I guess pancakes. It's Sunday, isn't it?"

"Blueberry okay?"

"Yep." Brendan returned to the funnies. Outside the window, the sky had cleared. The wind had picked up. Wispy clouds clung to Mount Washington to the south. It would be at least another hour, perhaps longer, before the sun climbed over Little Gadd and tagged their home. Farther upriver, mist rose slowly and whirled like misshapen apparitions.

The house on the river where Fontana and his son lived was owned by their neighbor, Mary Gilliam, and sat next to her house on a small promontory of land directly under Little Gadd, a ridge that had slipped off Mount Gadd some ten million years ago.

In front of their house was a pool in the Snoqualmie River, fed from two directions where the river blasted through channels on either side of a small island. The water in the pool was green this time of year. When it got hotter, youngsters would trek down to it and catapult into the water from a rope swing.

Fontana had arrived in town with a crackerjack reputation as a former arson investigator, and now his town was being riddled with arsons. Was it a hot-fingered local parodying the Seattle arsonist? Or were they one and the same? Analyzing it, Fontana realized there were a number of hard-to-find neighborhoods surrounding Staircase, and so far they had remained unscathed. In four nights of fires, not one had been set anywhere an outsider wouldn't have been able to locate easily. If it wasn't a non-local, it was somebody trying to make it appear to be a non-local.

What angered and worried him was the possibility that somebody was going to get hurt. His tiny department was a pastiche of professional firefighters and volunteers from all walks of life—students, homemakers, mill workers, loggers, hardware-store clerks, a carpet layer, a physical therapist, even a dentist who wore latex gloves to keep his hands clean while working around the station.

Having finished the funnies, Brendan looked up from a map he'd been making, a map of a mythical island he said he would buy and develop after he grew up and became a famous inventor. "Mac? Is that arsonist back?"

"I'm afraid he is, Brendan."

"I thought he was going away."

"So did I. You know that old vacant house behind the fire station? He lit that. We'll swing by and look at it today if you want. The fire roasted a bunch of green plums on that big tree in the lot next door."

"Did anybody die?"

"No. They were all little fires. Relatively little ones."

"Is he going to burn our house down?"

Fontana started to smile but thought better of it. "No, Brendan. We've got a surprise here."

"Satan would start barking, wouldn't he?" Fontana nodded. Brendan gave his father a brief smile. The dog had saved both their lives last summer. "Mac? What happens if you take Satan with you when you go out to fires?"

"I'll leave him here with you and Mary."

"Promise?"

"He's getting too old to drag all over the countryside anyway."

Talk of arsons and arsonists had stirred up memories of an incident that had happened years earlier during an arson spree in his former department back east. It was something Fontana had feared from the moment he'd taken the Staircase position: losing a firefighter. It had been a warehouse fire. The fire had been out when they'd changed shifts. Fontana had helped turn command over to the oncoming chief, a crusty, overeducated man who disliked details but who liked to think he was some sort of legend in the fire service, a man who spoke endlessly about himself in the mistaken belief others were as interested as he was.

Knowing the chief paid little attention to particulars, and knowing also that there were several large holes in the warehouse roof that had loose pieces of tar paper obscuring them, Fontana made a point to explain the situation thoroughly. It wasn't until he was home from work and stepping out of the shower that he heard a radio report saying a firefighter had plunged twenty-seven feet to the floor of the burned-out warehouse. The man had broken both legs as well as his back in two places, would spend the remainder of his life in a wheelchair. The chief in charge never accepted responsibility and several weeks later publicly denied having been warned.

If there was one thing Fontana couldn't accept, it was the burden of another man in a wheelchair watching him from the sidelines. Or worse: a widow.

At noon they went to the fire station, where Fontana had appointments with three separate news crews. After the interviews he returned calls to local radio stations while Brendan watched cartoons in the beanery with a pair of volunteers who made a habit of shucking their wives and shirking church by volunteering on Sundays.

Fontana and Brendan walked to the arson site on Main, where Brendan tossed cooked plums to the dog, who caught them in his mouth and then spit them out. Every time he spit one, Brendan convulsed with laughter. Between efforts, Satan cocked his good ear forward and looked from boy to man, trying to figure out what was so amusing.

NINE

♦

PASSING FOR NORMAL

At eleven o'clock Monday morning, when Fontana walked into the station with Brendan, he found Lieutenant Kingsley Pierpont conducting a drill on the apparatus floor behind the rigs. Kingsley claimed he had to be twice as conscientious as the next man because everyone was watching him since he was black—and for the most part he *was* twice as conscientious. On the floor in front of the group were four MSA face masks with compressed air tanks on backpacks.

"Heeeey, there's my little buddy." Brendan and Kingsley went through a complicated ritual of handshakes.

"You missed a doozy of a Saturday night," said Fontana.

"That's what they been tellin' me."

"Listen, we're going to have to start working night shifts, bringing volunteers in during the day. I don't see any way around it. Can you work up a tentative schedule?"

"Sure. By the way, Bailey's been looking for you all morning. Mr. Truax too."

"Chief, I got him by half a second," Frank Weed shouted. Weed was an exceptionally tall, thin specimen with black hair, what was left of it. Fontana could have lit a match off his smile.

"And it'll be the last time," Kingsley Pierpont said. "Sheeeeit."

"That's what I'd say too," Fontana joked, "if my rookie beat me masking up. I'd say my spastic colon got loose or I forgot to take my medication. Didn't you once hold the station record, Kingsley?"

"What do you mean *once*? I *still* hold the record. I had a bad day. Records? He didn't break no records."

Frank Weed said, "By the way, Chief. We saw you on TV. You looked real good."

"Thanks."

As luck would have it, Weed had been out of town the first few times the arsonist had struck, and it galled him no end, being the type of firefighter who paced the floors like a caged cat, dreaming about all the catastrophes that weren't coming his way: house fires, train wrecks, factory amputations, home hangings.

A few minutes later, H. C. Bailey came through the front door and buttonholed Fontana. She wore her brown King County Police uniform: a short-sleeved shirt, trousers, spit-shined brogans, a Sam Browne belt jangling with equipment, and a bulky bulletproof vest under the shirt. Bailey had penetrating brown eyes, a short mop of hair with blunt-cut bangs, and a prominent jaw she unsuccessfully tried to play down with makeup. Whether she was or not, the jaw made her look stubborn. When they spoke, she had a habit of standing too close, but backing away from her only caused her to step forward, so Fontana normally stood his ground.

"Chief? You're never going to believe this. Remember that shooting we had the other night? The woman killed those poor little rottweilers? Her real name is Aimee Lee Culpepper."

"I must be missing something."

"*Aimee Lee* Culpepper. The actress? She was in that movie *Weird People*. Aimee Lee?"

"So?"

"Sooooooo? The whole world has been trying to find her for three years. And all the time she's been right here in Staircase passing for normal."

"Maybe she *is* normal."

"But she's not. She's famous."

"If that was Aimee Lee, why didn't any of us recognize her?"

"She was wearing a disguise. Her teeth are different. She's not a blonde anymore. Sandusky kept saying he thought he knew her from somewhere. And there's something about her eyes. Maybe she's wearing tinted contacts. She used to have these icy pale-blue eyes in the movies. Remember all the rumors about her being in a mental hospital? Chief. Aimee Lee lives in Staircase." When Fontana disengaged himself, Bailey followed him and Brendan into his office, her utility belt rattling as she moved. He found a couple of phone messages and tucked them into his pocket.

When he looked up from his desk, Bailey's brown eyes were ten inches away. "She's been spotted in Memphis, New York, the Southwest, even Russia; and for a while it was rumored she was living underground in some caves in France. Think about it. I had her in cuffs."

"Maybe you can put her in leg irons next time."

"If I'd put her in a cell, they'd screw a plaque up. Japanese tourists would stop in every Tuesday. I'd be in the papers."

"Japanese what?"

"She's really hot in Japan. And *you* drove her home."

"Who told you that?"

"Clunk. He came back and claimed you were backing up her story because she'd promised to have sex with you."

"Clunk's a half-wit. You don't believe that, do you?"

"Of course not. Tell me what happened?"

"What do you mean, tell you what happened?"

"What haaaapppeeennned?"

"I took her and her kid home."

"What's that house like? I drove by it, but I couldn't tell much. Did you see any other celebrities out there?" Before he could reply, Bailey got a call on her portable radio and bolted the station in a haze of electronic chatter.

Brendan looked up at his father and said, "Who's Aimee Lee?"

"An actress."

As they were leaving, Roger Truax and Robinson Jeffers showed up in tandem at the front of the station.

"I believe you know Mr. Jeffers," Truax said, touching the knot of his purple and yellow tie. "He's a reporter? He has a few questions. And then you and I need to talk."

"This is my day off, Roger."

"Oh, yeah? This won't take long."

TEN

THE VICE PRESIDENT IN
CHARGE OF EATING CROW

Truax went to the rear of the station, where Kingsley Pierpont and the others were shouting good-naturedly, leaving Fontana and Brendan in the watch office with the reporter.

Relaxing against the edge of the desk, Fontana looked at Jeffers, a freelance reporter visiting the Puget Sound area to cover the arson spree. He had been hanging around Staircase since the fires began. Jeffers was in his early thirties and was so quiet one automatically assumed something was wrong with him. He was a tidy little man who carried a notebook and always wore the same khaki pants and gray windbreaker zipped to the neck. He had a bush of unruly brown hair, horn-rimmed glasses, and a manner of speaking that was so slow it made Fontana suspect he was ill. He kept to himself and was taking his lodgings in one of the seedy motels on Staircase Way, a man who probably didn't leave footprints.

"Chief Fontana. On the tube yesterday you called him a firebug. I was surprised you said it was a *him*. I'm wondering if you might elaborate."

"What paper are you with again?"

"It's a national feature article, an overview of the arsons and how they've affected one small town." Jeffers began to look nervous. He'd interviewed Fontana before, but his inquiries tended to drift off-center, as if he were not certain what he wanted or how he wanted to attain it. And apparently he wasn't with any paper.

"These types of fires are usually set by males."

"Do you think he might be a professional arsonist?"

"Not likely."

"Why not?"

"An amateur firebug sets fires for the hell of it. For fun. For reasons he often doesn't even recognize himself. A professional generally has a traceable motive. Maybe it's insurance. Revenge. Maybe it's to cover up another crime."

"Like what? What might the other crime be?"

"A burglary, for instance."

Jeffers was sitting in a chair across the room, and every time Fontana spoke, he scribbled in his tiny notebook, head down, pen clenched so tightly his knuckles were white. "Were there any burglaries here in Staircase?"

"Not associated with the fires."

Jeffers flipped back through his notes rapidly and said, "Saturday night there were two fires a block south of here. Then there was that house a block north. And I understand there was another fire set in a paper shack? You'd think it would be a little embarrassing to have all these fires so close to the station."

Fontana shrugged. "It's not a particularly large town. Everything is bound to be close to the station."

"You don't think he was thumbing his nose at you by deliberately setting fires in your own backyard?"

It was exactly what Fontana thought. "You'd have to ask him."

"But he is getting bolder?"

"These types usually run in a pattern. Debris and Dumpster fires in the beginning. Then abandoned buildings and garages. Then they graduate to inhabited occupancies. Saturday night, he lit the Bedouin with over a hundred fifty people inside, and then a private residence where two people were sleeping. This is not a welcome trend."

Without looking up, Jeffers adjusted his glasses with the thumb and forefinger of either hand. "Maybe I'm not supposed to know this, but I understand you have two suspects."

"There are *no* suspects. And the primary arson investigation is under the jurisdiction of the county. They're who you should be talking to."

Jeffers flipped back through the curled pages of his notebook and looked up at Fontana. "What about Claude Pettigrew? Quite a few of the firefighters I spoke to yesterday seem to believe he may be implicated. Wasn't there a fire directly across the street from his house? And he's been having problems as a volunteer?"

"Claude's never been a volunteer. And he's not a suspect."

"And the other suspect is a man named Audie Culpepper, reputed to be a brick shy of a full load."

"Who told you about him?"

"Then he is a suspect?"

"I didn't say that. Who told you about him? Truax?"

"I can't reveal sources. You probably have some sort of code in the fire department too, so you know what I'm talking about. He's mentally retarded, isn't he?"

"Truax?"

"No. Audie Culpepper."

"We don't have any suspects. Thanks for the interview. It was great. Let's go, Brendan."

"Just a couple more questions?" Robinson Jeffers sprang to his feet. Brendan opened the front door so the cowbell jangled, wagging the door to and fro, working the bell. Fontana would have told him to quit, except he could see it annoyed Jeffers. "Aren't you romantically involved with the mother of one of the suspects?"

"Good lord. Pettigrew's mother is in her seventies."

"I'm talking about Audie Culpepper's mother."

Roger Truax walked into the room and said, "Everything okay in here? I can probably be of help too, Jeffers. I'm not entirely unfamiliar with the case."

Jeffers ignored Truax and stepped around so he had a better view of Fontana, though he kept his eyes on Brendan who continued to work the cowbell. "Do you think she moved to this isolated town because she knew her son played with matches in a big way?"

Ignoring Jeffers, Fontana took Brendan by the hand and stepped out of the station onto the sidewalk. Sunshine glinted off Rattlesnake Mountain south of town, but it was cloudy overhead. He could feel warmth off the sidewalk and off the front of the building.

"You heard?" Truax said, following Fontana toward his truck. "About our guest?"

"Jeffers?"

"That was her Wednesday night butchering those dogs. Aimee Lee's a dog killer. A goldanged dog killer. Wait'll the papers hear. They'll go berserk."

"It was Thursday night."

"Pardon?"

"The dog thing was Thursday night."

"Yeah. I guess it was. But listen. A deal like this could put our town in every newspaper and magazine in the country. It wasn't just that she had it all, the money and the glamour and the status. What boggled everybody was how she gave it up. Even her Hollywood agent, for godsakes, didn't know where she was. There's never been anything like it. People are dying to hear her story. And we've got it. You and me and this town. Hell, Mac. You've been dating her. What's she like? And how do you think she got so fat?"

"Where did this I've-been-dating-her business come from? I haven't been dating her."

"Just sleeping with her?"

"Damn it, Roger. I don't even know the woman."

"Can you get me on her good side? I had the feeling the other night she and I might have been at cross-purposes."

"Cross-purposes? Roger, she hates your guts."

Truax looked imploringly into Fontana's blue eyes and took a step backward. "Really? Did she actually say she hated my guts?"

"That wasn't exactly how she put it."

"How about if you and I and Helen and her have dinner one night this week?"

"Roger. You tried to get her arrested. You put the screws to her about the gun in her purse. Your version of the dog affair was different from hers. And that doesn't even take into account the way you cornered her boy and grilled him."

"I thought she and I got along okay."

"Does that reporter Jeffers know who she is? Did you and Bailey tell him about Aimee Lee?"

"Didn't think of it. Mac, if you could arrange it so Helen met her I'd be a hero at home. Can you manage that?"

"She obviously moved out here for privacy."

"Why would she want privacy?"

"That's what some people want."

"It's going to put us slap-dab on the map, Mac. We'll have reporters from all over the globe trotting right here to this town. TV crews. Robin Leach. We'll be interviewed."

"I've *been* interviewed."

"But we're all going to be famous. Me, Mo, this whole area. Property values are going to skyrocket. Are you sure she hates my guts? 'Cause I was thinking of calling her up myself and maybe having lunch with her or something. And I'll lay off the kid. Just because he started a few fires doesn't mean we have to be all over him."

When they had climbed into the Suburban and pulled away from the curb, Brendan said, "Why doesn't Mr. Truax just go over and be friends with her if that's what he wants?"

Fontana said, "Things are never that easy for someone like Truax."

ELEVEN

I BE LEGEND

"We'd better leave Satan outside," Fontana said, when he and the boy got out of the truck in front of the Culpeppers' estate. "I have a feeling they aren't partial to dogs."

"*Bleib!*" said Brendan. "*Bleib!* Sit!" The dog looked at Fontana and sat obediently next to the front wheel of the truck. Together, father and son squeezed through a small opening in the black wrought-iron gate.

It was a two-story house, white, with a circular driveway, a new Bronco parked near a huge garage, behind the garage a stable. Through a stand of alder, he could see a white fence, a good-sized pasture, and two grazing horses. He remembered reading somewhere that Aimee Lee had practically grown up on horseback. At the far end of the driveway was an older Chevrolet, which Fontana assumed belonged to the gray-haired woman running at him from the front door. She stopped running with a bone-jarring maneuver and stood breathing heavily with her hands fisted on her hips. She wore the same flame-blue housecoat she'd worn the night he'd brought Sally and Audie home.

"You can't come in here," the woman said, distracted momentarily by the sight of his Suburban with its fire department insignia. "Oh. It's you. Well, you can't come in either."

She had curly hair cut close to her scalp and the bluest eyes Fontana had ever seen, her slack face hanging off the eyes like pizza dough barely hanging off hooks on a wall.

"I need to see Sally."

"I'll go see if she wants company. Don't move."

"Was she the actress?" Brendan asked, after she'd left.

"She's the housekeeper."

A few minutes later, muttering under her breath, the woman appeared once more at the front door. "Go on. Go on. Go on."

"Pardon me?"

"Oh, for godsakes. She's around back."

She wasn't anything like the woman he'd met Thursday night. On her hands and knees in dirt-stained jeans and a baggy gray sweatshirt, Sally Culpepper wore thongs on her bare feet. Her close-fitting jeans didn't reveal an ounce of fat—all bone and sinew like a fashion model.

She was weeding a flower bed that ran along one side of the house, the soil freshly spaded, tomato seedlings sitting nearby in small boxes. The bright green grass in the backyard looked new and flawless, as if it had been trucked in only last week. The yard was enclosed by trees, and sunshine stroked the wall where the woman weeded.

Rolling off her knees, she sat on one haunch, her free leg bent up so that she rested her chin on a grass-stained knee. Fontana was trying to figure out what sort of fat-lady getup she'd been wrapped up in Thursday night. Her makeup was different too, her eyebrows no longer looking like the front end of a bug-stained Kenworth truck. Her hair had changed color. In April when they'd had the fire in the woods, she'd worn a huge raincoat, probably in lieu of climbing into the padded pantyhose.

When she saw Brendan eyeing a rope swing on a maple tree, she said, "Sure. Go ahead. Go swing on it. That's what it's there for."

Brendan sprinted across the yard.

"Good morning," Fontana said.

"He's a cutie."

"Takes after his mother."

"To what do I owe this visit? My son hasn't set any more fires, has he?"

"Not that I know of. You know, you're a little late with those tomatoes."

"So I've been told."

"You look different." Her eyes had even changed color.

"I know. The disguise was a lot of trouble to go to, but I don't go out much, and it was worth it to me. I found out a long time ago, nobody looks at an overweight woman very closely."

Fontana put his hands in his pockets and glanced across the yard at Brendan, who had one foot in a loop at the bottom of the rope swing. "I understand you were an actress."

She moved a trowel to her right hand, using it to loosen the soil in the flower bed, pulling weeds with her gloved left hand. She didn't look up. "I figured people would know before now. Where did you hear it?"

"One of the police officers from last week found out."

"How many people have you told?"

"You."

"On your way to tell who?"

"You're a little paranoid, aren't you?"

"You get that way."

"So why'd you let me in when you weren't in disguise?"

She shrugged. "Are you kidding me? I got arrested. There's no way I can keep it a secret now."

"And you wanted to know if I was part of the ruination?"

"Something like that."

"If I wanted to tell people, I wouldn't be out here warning you. My guess is you moved here for some peace and quiet."

"Two years," she said. "It was bliss. I suppose that was more than I could have reasonably hoped for. And then the other night. Audie told me how you saved him from Mop Strings. Thank you."

"You mind telling me why you went into hiding?"

"You ever in your wildest dreams think people would lie about you on the cover of a tabloid magazine?"

"I guess not."

"I wanted to do my job and go home and have a normal family life. But they won't let you do that. My mother called me up once in a panic and wanted to know why I'd moved to Belgium. It didn't compute that she'd reached me at this number."

"For a while you lived a pretty high-profile life."

"I socialized with some famous people. They were the only ones who didn't act peculiar around me."

Audie had come out of the house and was pulling the rope swing back and releasing it so that Brendan arced through the air, shrieking. Audie laughed in a voice almost as deep as a man's.

"By the way," said Fontana, "did you know Audie was in town on his bicycle Saturday night during the fires?"

"That stinker. You'd think a fourteen-year-old would listen."

"It might be good if you kept him away when we're having fires."

"Why do you say that?"

"Well, because it's pretty general knowledge now that he set a fire out here. He's set other fires too, hasn't he?"

"That little trouble in April was more of an accident than anything else. He's a good kid . . . a little confused at times . . . but a sweet kid."

"I believe you. But the feeling among the crew the day we came out here was that he must have worked pretty hard to get that damp undergrowth going the way it was."

"I'll keep him in at night."

Fontana looked across the lawn to where Brendan and Audie were playing. Brendan said, "What two words have more letters than any other in the alphabet? . . . Post office!"

Culpepper scooped up the weeds and dumped them into a plastic bucket, scooted over a few feet and began loosening more soil with her trowel.

"There's already a fair amount of excitement in town about finding you," Fontana said. "I can't imagine what it'll build into."

"I can."

"If you need anything, I'd be glad to help."

"Thank you."

He knew she would never go to the Bedouin now. In fact, the town had probably seen the last of her and her son.

TWELVE

◆

THE

DEFROCKED PLAYTHING

Never one to squander words, in her dotage Lorraine spoke even less than before, often going hours at a time without uttering a sound. Several times a day, Mary Gilliam would snap her fingers as she passed in front of her mother, who sat hunchbacked on the sofa in front of the television. "Mother? Are you alive? Are you alive today?"

Because she had been nursing her ninety-three-year-old mother for over twenty years, Mary felt entitled to macabre jokes and made them not only with impunity but with disconcerting frequency. "Nobody should live that long. She changed my diapers for two years, and I've been changing hers for twenty."

When Brendan visited, he sat on the opposite end of the sofa from Lorraine, almost as a symbol that they were at opposite ends of life. Of all the people in her minuscule world, Brendan was the only one Lorraine treated as an equal.

"What do you think?" Lorraine would say, when something of note occurred on the television. Brendan would answer and the old woman would nod, neither of them looking away from the tube.

Mary Gilliam would stand behind the sofa in the opening to the kitchen, ironing or working a crossword puzzle, or more often, glancing through her tabloids. Mary collected gossip rags and often referred to her old issues for vital scraps of trivia.

It was Thursday night, and Fontana and Brendan had been invited next door for lasagna. Mary was planning to keep Brendan for the next three nights, sleeping him on the sofa in the living room. Besides making Fontana's fire responses easier, the venture had turned into a holiday for the boy, who didn't have access to a TV at home. Since Mary's TV was never off and it was summertime, he and Lorraine would watch television together late into the night.

Mary had driven into Seattle to purchase a biography of Aimee Lee penned by a man who'd produced inflammatory works on Jackie Kennedy and Michael Jackson. Reading from the open book while she prepared a salad, Mary said, "It says here that after Lee's first two movies she became the hottest property in Hollywood. Her relationship with her long-term boyfriend, James McAlees, fell apart and she went on a whirlwind spree of dating every big name in Hollywood, as well as the governor of the state and a bunch of rock 'n' roll singers." Fontana washed his hands, took a large bowl from the cupboard, and began chopping green onions.

"It says here that two movie executives left their wives for Lee before she dumped both of them for Victor Visconti, the Italian actor. What do you think it's like, Mac, to be wanted by everyone?"

"Just a little piece of hell," Fontana said, rinsing a tomato and slicing it, then laying the slices down and chopping them into chunks.

"It says a billionaire head of a software computer company who was courting her bought her a new car every week until she broke off the affair. A Lamborghini. Ferrari. DeLorean. Can you imagine?"

"We didn't see any exotic cars in her garage."

"Of course you didn't. She drove them all into the ocean. Not only that, but she apparently was taking eight hundred milligrams of Thorazine a day. 'Her mental problems have been kept secret from the public and some are still secret even from this writer.' "

"I suspect a lot was kept secret from that writer."

"And get this. She took the Thorazine in suppositories because she didn't want anybody to know."

"Mary, you don't believe all this, do you?"

"When you see her, ask if it's not true."

"You want me to ask about the suppositories?"

"I'd like to know."

"There are already film crews camped out in town waiting for her to show herself. I was her, I'd be running through the hills like a wounded antelope."

"Oh, Mac. Don't be silly. It would be so much fun to be famous. Think about all the people you could meet."

"Are we going camping?" Brendan hollered from the other room, having picked up on the "running through the hills" comment.

"You want to go camping, Brendan?"

"Does Mount Rainier still have snow?"

"Oh, yeah, even in June."

"Let's go camping."

"Okay."

"Listen, Mac," Mary said, as Fontana finished the salad. "It tells here all about that big catfight she had at the Oscars."

Fontana recalled the occasion. They'd lived in the East and Linda was still alive and they still had a television set and Linda, who never missed an Oscar telecast, had popped a batch of popcorn. Arriving on the arm of Harrison Ford, with whom she'd recently completed a film, Aimee Lee had been poured into a dark-green sequined sheath with a slit from ankle to Alaska and a décolletage that had even Hollywood talking.

Aimee Lee had been nominated for best supporting actress in *The New York Jungle,* and the talk was that her part should have been included in the Best Actress category and that she should have been the hands-down winner. She did not win.

Later, she was on the podium to hand out a lifetime achievement award to a beloved aging foreign actress, and the camera came back early from a commercial and caught her on mike telling Nick Nolte, "I can't believe I'm in this. It's so cheesy." She also mumbled a phrase that was widely quoted on the major networks and in newspaper headlines as "She's such an old cow."

Thousands of editors across the country had a field day with the upstart actress. Radio commentators, television anchorpersons, gossip columnists, even psychologists hosting radio call-in shows, expressed scathing opinions. Overnight, Aimee Lee was dethroned, defrocked, branded a superbitch.

Fontana thought it a peculiarity of the American psyche that the public could set her up as a goddess, worship her for two years, then suddenly take such delight in her public disgrace. The Aimee Lee jokes going around the country were mordant when they weren't juvenile.

While her public persona took a bashing, Aimee Lee's personal life felt the consequences as well. She was in New York City, with the mayor as her date, when three women ambushed her outside a trendy restaurant and tossed cow blood on her. Spurred by misguided teachers attempting to impart a lesson in virtue, seven hundred schoolchildren wrote admonishing letters to Ann Landers about her, some of which were collected and rushed into a book by a major New York publisher. Her acting, her talent, her personality, even the way she walked, were lampooned in every paper in the nation.

Aimee Lee's mother's house had a cross burned on the lawn. In New Jersey her brother was beaten up in a park. Around that same time, her son was kidnapped and reclaimed by police a few hours later. A worker at a dry cleaner's slashed her garments with a razor and was applauded by the media.

It didn't help that Lee insisted she had been talking about her dress when she said, "I can't believe I'm in this. It's so cheesy." And no one wanted to believe her claim that she had actually said, "I feel like such an old cow." Nick Nolte confirmed the remarks had not been directed at the aging actress, but his support invited comment only in the back pages of the papers that had already blasted Lee in their headlines. It was widely thought Nolte was gallantly lying to help Lee, and this, of course, raised his stock with the public. Some commentators offered apologies, taking advantage of the airtime to lambaste her once more for being bitchy. Lee couldn't win.

Repercussions on her career were puzzling. Weeks after she became once again the most talked about actress in America, a bidding war flared up for her next picture. Hollywood Casanovas fell all over themselves attempting to be seen with her. The tabloids ran amok. And then, in the midst of the hoopla, Lee vanished.

The paparazzi thought they'd located her in Paris, and a few weeks later, American tourists claimed to have seen her in Southern Italy.

And then she was gone.

"You know what else it says here?" Mary said. "It says the reason she went into hiding was because a magazine reporter discovered she was a lesbian."

"Mary. Are you sure you want to believe all that?"

"Well, of course I don't believe it *all*. You have to read between the lines. But this must be based on something. They're not calling her a lesbian out of the blue."

When they sat down to eat, Lorraine remained on the couch as was her custom, an untouched TV dinner tray in front of her. In her yellow nightgown, with a pink rose in her disheveled hair, Lorraine looked as if she might already be mummified, a fact that didn't escape Mary's notice. "Mother, did you run out and get yourself embalmed just to surprise me?"

As they ate, Fontana thought about the mostly unremarkable events of the past week:

On Monday morning, Frank Weed put on a mask and circled the station at full tilt in an effort to see how quickly a thirty-minute MSA bottle would run out of air. The goal was to simulate a working fire, and he managed to suck it dry in nine minutes.

On Monday afternoon, Claude Pettigrew came into the station after work and threatened to sue anyone who called him an arson suspect. It was well known that Claude had large caches of money he had been awarded from various lawsuits hoarded in four different banks.

On Monday evening, Fontana and Brendan played two hours of Monopoly. During their tournament, Roger Truax, trying to hook up with Aimee Lee, left three messages on Fontana's machine.

Tuesday night, Engine One responded to a vehicle in a ditch. The car was empty and turned out to have been stolen in Seattle.

Wednesday, the medic unit caught seven alarms and the engine company didn't catch any.

Thursday, the engine responded to a baby with her head stuck between the rungs of a hand-me-down crib, to an elderly patient falsely reported to be choking on an egg roll in the Chinese restaurant, and to the odor of natural gas behind the train station. Les and Opal

Morgan came into the station and told Fontana they thought the Lutheran pastor was setting the fires. They had spent quite a long time formulating theories and charting timetables. Fontana had a brief chat with the pastor and learned he'd been out of town on two of the nights they'd had fires. His alibis were readily confirmed.

On Thursday morning when Fontana went into his office, he found Truax waiting for him, dressed in a three-piece suit. "You got supper fixed up with Helen and I and Aimee Lee yet?" he asked.

"I'm working on it."

"What's the holdup?"

"She's a tough nut to crack, Roger."

"This really could mean a lot for the town."

"I think I've finally figured an angle. You got a hobby might interest her?"

"Hobby?"

"Yeah, you know, like running model trains. Stamp collecting. Horseback riding. You know."

"I have some Neil Diamond albums."

"That's it?"

"I have a *lot* of Neil Diamond albums."

"A hobby, Roger. I'm pretty sure she hates Neil Diamond."

"I collect screws."

"What?"

"You know, in a jar. There's a few odd nails and a couple of bolts in there, but it's mostly screws. Tell her I've been collecting them for almost ten years."

"I won't forget that part."

"I'll go home and get the nails out today."

"That would help."

On Thursday afternoon, Mo Costigan came into his office on her way to work, leaving her Porsche to idle on the ramp in front of Engine One. She wore a blue business suit that had power shoulder pads, an effect Mo wasn't going to give up despite their having gone out of style, and carried a cup holder securing a plastic cup of coffee. Currently serving her second term as mayor, Mo was a short, buxom, brown-haired woman who ran a CPA firm in Bellevue and was only just past thirty. She had a bootlegged sticker in her rear window allowing her to park in handicapped zones, and Fontana had once caught her cheating Brendan at checkers.

"Mo. How many times have we told you no one can park on the ramp in front of the rig?"

"I understand your girlfriend is in the movies," Mo said.

"Which girlfriend would that be?"

"You don't have to be coy with me, Mac. We all know you're sleeping with Aimee Lee."

"That's ridiculous."

"Whatever you say."

"Mo, what do you really want?"

"I've been thinking about an Aimee Lee film festival. We could advertise in the California papers. It'll put us on the map."

"Mo, I believe Ms. Culpepper moved here because the town wasn't on the map."

"But this is our big chance. Listen, I gotta go. Just don't get too involved with her, okay? For your own sake."

"What are you talking about?"

"For one thing, she's a lesbian. Or hadn't you heard?"

"Thanks for looking out for me, Mo. By the way, don't rush off. We've gotta discuss manning problems. I'm going to run the full-timers at night."

"In a hurry, hon. Kiss, kiss. I'll come in later and we'll schmooze."

During the week, Fontana had taken fourteen phone calls from the media concerning Aimee Lee, refusing to talk about her to one and all.

Mary's voice brought Fontana abruptly back to the present, as she began clearing the dinner dishes from the table. "Mac, remember, Mother and I and Brendan will be at the Sutterfields' tomorrow. I promised to watch their kids Friday night because her mother's had car trouble and won't get up here from Oregon until probably Saturday morning. She'll be staying with their kids while they go to Mexico for a second honeymoon."

"I'll keep him Friday then."

"Not on your life. With all those children around he'll keep Mother calmed down."

Lorraine still hadn't touched her food, nor had she looked away from the TV. "What do you think?" she said to Brendan who had finished eating and was back in position on his end of the couch.

Mary said, "I've been visiting the QFC a couple of times a day, but so far I haven't gotten lucky. Have you boys seen her?"

Brendan looked up from the television. "Seen who?"

"Audie's mom," Fontana said.

"Sure. They have a neat rope swing."

◆

THIRTEEN

FIVE SMALL COFFINS,
NO ICE, PLEASE

The fire happened shortly after eleven-thirty on Friday evening, right after they'd responded to an accident at the on-ramp where Stooly Road crossed over the freeway. A pumper, a medic unit, and four state troopers were already on the scene of the wreck when Fontana arrived.

Windshield blown out, a battered white van lay on its side in the center of the intersection. On the ramp leading back down to the freeway, a crumpled Camaro sat askew, the radiator steaming, various colored liquids bleeding from beneath.

As Fontana pulled the parking brake on the chief's truck, he watched a young man in a bloody white T-shirt being handcuffed by a state trooper. Pressed into his bloodless face like black screwheads, the boy's eyes locked on to Fontana as if he were responsible for his predicament.

The Camaro's air bag had deployed, and the deflated skin dangled off the steering wheel like a used condom. Two teenaged girls in shorts and halter tops tiptoed around in the broken glass carrying small knapsacks. One of the girls had a cut lip and was crying. Kingsley Pierpont and Heather Minerich were doing their best to get the girls to come out of the glass and sit down.

Fontana had been at the accident almost ten minutes when another alarm came in, a full response to a reported house fire off Cove Road. "Flames visible," said the dispatcher. "Repeat. Flames visible." Cove Road was where Mary and Brendan were baby-sitting the Sutterfield children. The thought made Fontana's stomach roll over.

"We're rockin' and rollin'," said Lindoff, scooping up the backboard and running to the medic unit with it. Though Fontana had always hated that kind of talk, he said nothing. These volunteers could have been home in bed with the rest of the town.

He sped around the zigzagging dry hose line laid down as a precaution, headed across the overpass, and took the freeway west, running only his emergency lights. At highway speeds, the sound of a siren never got far enough in front of an emergency vehicle to do anything but confuse people.

Traffic was surprisingly thick for this time of night and he slipped around other vehicles. When he skidded through the stop sign at the end of the exit ramp, a cloud of smoke came off his tires.

Cove Road was on the opposite side of the valley from the main section of town and ran along the base of the foothill they called Rattlesnake Mountain. There were probably sixty houses off Cove Road, as well as twenty or thirty off a spur that usually had chickens roosting in the potholes. Shadowed in the winter from the low sun, the area was infamous for holding frost on the roads and for the moss-infested roofs that had to be replaced every five or six years.

The odds were a hundred against one that this fire involved the Sutterfield house, but still, the steering wheel was slippery in his fists.

He knew he was going to beat the first engine to the scene, for he had easily outrun Engine One and hadn't yet seen Engine Two responding from the station.

At a few minutes before midnight there were bound to be people home. If it was an actual fire and they hadn't escaped already, they'd be in the bedrooms, most likely asleep or unconscious from smoke. Fontana mentally rehearsed his priorities. Get the people out. Get the hose lines in. Ventilate the structure. If the bedrooms were upstairs they might need ladders.

Fontana headed for the base of the foothill and turned left onto Cove Road, sliding in the gravel at the turn. He saw smoke up ahead. The two-lane road was slightly humped in the center, and the area was spotty with trees and lone houses at the ends of long driveways.

A half mile farther along, he saw Les and Opal Morgan parked alongside a huge laurel hedge.

Beyond the brush bracketing the driveway, slow smoke rose into the night, embers climbing like monstrous fireflies. He couldn't recall where Les and Opal lived, but this was the third instance in a week they'd been the first to a fire scene and it was beginning to make him wonder.

Carrying his portable radio, Fontana parked across the road and jogged onto the property between two sprawling overgrown laurel hedges and a tilting mailbox. Once in the yard, he was confronted by a dark house two and a half stories tall. The right wall, the south wall of the house, was being chewed by a sheet of flame that extended from the ground to the roof. Smoke puffed out from the eaves.

On the north side of the house, the dark side, he spotted a pickup truck. A motor home beyond that. Instinctively he looked for toys, for evidence of children, but the yard was empty. There were no people in bathrobes in the yard and no faces in the windows. No barking dogs. And no open doors.

Fontana stood under a sycamore on the unmown grass in the corner of the yard and keyed his portable microphone. "Staircase One at 8200 Cove Road. Establishing Cove Command. We have a two-and-a-half-story wood-frame residence approximately twenty-five by forty with flame on the south side on both levels. Engine Two, lay a line through the north entrance. Engine One, lay a supply line. I want all unattached volunteers to report to me in the front yard with masks."

Seconds later, as the dispatcher repeated his report, Engine Two shuddered to a halt on the other side of the tall laurel hedge. Fontana heard the bells as his people donned air masks, heard the driver slamming the automatic transmission into fifth, heard him throwing the vehicle into pump mode, metal compartment doors opening and slamming as firefighters procured equipment. He got on the radio again and called for Puget Power to come out and shut off the electricity.

A tall figure in full bunkers galloped into the yard with a pickhead ax in his gloved right hand. Frank Weed stopped in front of Fontana and put his facepiece on, activating his mask. Fontana said,

"Hang on a second. I'll get you a partner," and stepped back around the hedge searching for somebody to pair up with the rookie. These days, people didn't go into fires alone if they could help it. He saw only Les and Opal Morgan, who were still fiddling with their equipment. When he stepped back into the yard, Weed was already on the move, heading for the dark north side of the house, saying, "There's gotta be people in there. I'm going to search."

"Try that door behind you."

"I did. It's locked," said Weed, dashing around the corner.

He didn't like sending Frank in alone. His gut told him he should have gone in himself, but that would have left the site without an incident commander, which would have been a little like an orchestra conductor deciding to sit down with the tubas for a while and leaving the orchestra to tend itself; maybe worse, because when the violin section gets out of sync with the clarinets, nobody ends up dead. After years of rushing into fire buildings as a firefighter, it was still hard to think like a chief. Besides, Frank was wearing a mask and he wasn't. Frank had twenty good minutes due him inside. Fontana had three, maybe four.

Les and Opal Morgan stepped through the laurel into the dark yard, fumbling with the straps and regulators on their MSA masks, staring up at him through their blue facepieces like frogs peeping out of a bowl.

"Try the door here," Fontana said, opting not to send them around the north side behind Weed. He had a feeling this was a more direct way into the house. "I've got one man searching already."

"You got it, chief," Les said calmly, giving Fontana the thumbs-up sign as he and Opal trudged toward the house so slowly he felt like booting them in the rear. The Morgans ran a service station at the outskirts of town and fought fire at almost exactly the same pace they changed oil.

Sandusky and another firefighter dragged a nozzle and line through the dark yard, nearly knocking Les and Opal down. The hose line began filling as they hauled it around the north side of the house, for the pump operator had grown anxious waiting for the call for water that hadn't come, charging it while Sandusky was still running, so that several coils of heavy, charged hose leaped off the second firefighter's shoulders.

Without missing a step, Sandusky manhandled the line and continued to rush the house. His partner, now carrying nothing—a man who was both shorter and wider—could scarcely keep up.

When Fontana turned back to the Morgans, they were using their boots on the door. Finally the door burst inward and a great wash of flame rushed out. Without a hose line nearby, Les reached in and closed the door, shutting off the air once more while Fontana requested a second line from a volunteer who was coming through the gap in the hedge.

Surveying three sides of the building, Fontana walked the width of the building twice. The nearest door, the one with flame behind it, looked little used, as did a wooden staircase on the north side of the house that stretched first to a small deck with a patio slider, then to an upper level.

For some reason Sandusky had sprinted past the staircase, past both doors on the north side of the house.

To his discredit and chagrin, Fontana wasn't sure where Weed had gone.

Sandusky dragged the hose line around the far corner of the house. A third firefighter following in a mask and bunkers bent over laboriously and helped feed the heavy hose while Les and Opal Morgan helped another volunteer stretch a line to the nearby door that appeared to enter an enclosed sunporch. Fontana said, "Just dust it off, folks. I don't want you charging in there and pushing the fire into the uninvolved portion of the house. You're just the exposure line here."

Assisted by Heather Minerich, Lieutenant Kingsley Pierpont dragged a third line through the yard.

Kingsley put his facepiece on at the patio door, Heather Minerich doing the same behind him. Kingsley was a solid, no-nonsense firefighter who stuck to fundamentals, so if Sandusky didn't tap the fire with the first line, Fontana was confident Kingsley would with his.

When Kingsley forced the sliding glass door open, billows of gray smoke flooded out. Fontana heard the air rushing out of a hose line inside the building as somebody opened a nozzle. Then there was the thundering sound of a heavy hose stream reverberating off walls and ceilings inside. Shouting voices. Grayish smoke and a dingy cloud of steam pummeled Pierpont and Minerich as they made their way into the building, crawling below the heaviest concentrations of heat.

Through a narrow fissure in the laurel branches, Fontana glimpsed the white medic van as it pulled up. He was hoping its services wouldn't be needed. Four more firefighters jogged into the yard pulling at the face straps on their MSAs. Fontana directed them inside to help with the search. That made four people inside with lines. Five searching. Nine all told. That was a lot of manpower to be stomping around a blacked-out house, upsetting chairs, knocking over lamps, bumping into each other. He'd seen apartment hallways clogged with so many firefighters nobody could move.

It was a shabby house in need of paint, the gutters sagging on one end. When Fontana ran his battle lantern over the near upper windows, he saw concentrations of heavy smoke inside.

He glimpsed a figure passing in front of the window on the second story and thought for a moment it was a victim, but then an ax crashed through the glass in the window, clanking around the edges of the frame to clear out the broken chunks like a ranch cook beating a dinner triangle. He didn't have any idea who it was.

When two more volunteers charged into the yard slinging masks, Fontana told them to get another line and brush off the south end of the house where fire had come out a window and was climbing the wall. "Do it from an angle so you won't be pushing any heat back inside."

"Right, Chief."

As more volunteers showed, he told them to ladder the building at this end and open the roof over the fire. After they'd gone for the ladder, he realized two women in bathrobes had appeared behind him. "This your house?" he said.

"Goodness, no. They're in Mexico. They won a vacation."

"The Sutterfields?" Fontana's voice broke.

"Do you know them?"

"Did the kids get out?"

"I haven't seen any kids," one of the women said. "Have you, Grace?"

Grace's hand flew to her mouth. "Oh, my God. They must be in there."

FOURTEEN

FIRE IS LIKE A CAT

As Fontana heard windows breaking on the south side of the house, he squeezed the mike button and said there was a report of children trapped inside.

He paced the width of the building and peered down the north wall again. The hose line that wormed around the corner was jiggling, in use. A bulky figure in bunking clothes and helmet appeared at the far corner, stooped clumsily and wrestled with the heavy, water-filled, inch-and-three-quarters hose. Fontana picked up the line where he was standing and helped feed it the forty-odd feet to the struggling firefighter.

It seemed as if hours had passed, but it was only a few minutes since the first firefighters had entered the building. He had to remind himself Weed was wearing a half-hour mask and had already proved just that week that he could suck it dry in nine minutes, so it couldn't have been long at all.

Pointing his battle lantern into the windows as he passed them, Fontana paced the length of the hose lines along the north wall of the house, catching glimpses of smoke, closed blinds, and firefighters.

No children.

No elderly women.

When he reached the patio where Lieutenant Pierpont and Heather Minerich had entered, he saw a firefighter kneeling inside the doorway, smoke mushrooming out the entrance, entombing the figure in a cathedral of gray and black. Farther inside, Fontana heard mask-garbled speech. Could anybody without a mask be alive in there?

Again, he was tempted to climb over the figure in the doorway, but he knew he would have been just one more blind man waving his arms in a house that would bake him like a gingerbread man in an oven.

Fontana held up his radio and said, "Cove Command to Engine One portable. Do you have a report? Cove Command to Engine One portable. Give me a report."

After a few moments, a message adulterated by static came over the air. He recognized Lieutenant Pierpont's voice. "Engine One portable. We're having trouble finding the seat of this fire. It seems to be in the walls on the first level. We've searched the downstairs. So far we can't find the stairs for the second floor."

"We have a report of children inside," Fontana said.

"We haven't seen anybody." Could Mary Gilliam have taken everybody out? He looked around and spotted her empty Buick parked on the other side of the motor home. If she was outside, he would have seen her by now.

They couldn't find the interior stairwell. He'd assign a team to climb the outside wooden steps and enter the second floor from the patio. He was jogging back to the base of the stairs to give the assignment when he heard footsteps on the rickety wooden stairs above.

A woman was descending the staircase, a child on either side of her. The railing creaked under their combined weight. They were all breathing heavily.

The toadlike silhouette he recognized as belonging to Mary Gilliam. The tot on her right was too small to be his son, but he instantly recognized the figure holding her hand on the left. He would have known those bony knees anywhere.

Fontana knew he'd have this portrait imprinted on his brain for the rest of his life—the smoke, the silhouettes through the slats of the wooden stairs, his son's bare legs and knobby knees, the spotlights from the rigs on the street marking everything in a purple fog.

At the top of the stairs, large pills of smoke emerging past his form,

Frank Weed turned around and headed back into the house, the regulator on his mask working rhythmically. A moment later, Weed came clumping out and charged down the stairs, a child under each arm, so that he and Mary and Brendan and two other children reached the deck simultaneously. A burst of brilliant light caused all of them to blink for a moment. At first Fontana was afraid it was an arc from a fallen electrical line, but then a photographer stepped forward.

Weed handed one toddler to Fontana and one to Mary Gilliam, then, breathing as heavily as any man could breathe and still be standing, he went back up the stairs.

"Let me go up," Fontana yelled.

"No way, Chief," Weed gasped, through his facepiece. "I know exactly where to look."

When the photographer, a woman Fontana recognized from the local weekly, tried to take a picture of the infant cradled in his arms, Fontana turned his back to her and waved over one of the medics. After the medic had taken the boy, Fontana stooped and hugged a barefoot Brendan. "You okay, son?"

He nodded. "It sure was smoky."

"I was worried for you. You sure you're all right?"

"Yeah. But it sure was smoky. We couldn't even see the floor. Why are you crying?"

"I'm happy to see you, that's all."

"I'm happy to see you too."

"I've never been so frightened," Mary said, wrapping the halves of her sweater tightly about her pear-shaped torso and enclosing a three-year-old inside the folds. Fontana didn't believe he had ever been quite that scared either. "Lord almighty. I agree to baby-sit these darlings, and the first thing happens is I burn down the dadblasted house."

"What happened?"

"The kids had been watching some Disney videos, but they all fell asleep and I was reading and then I guess I was dozing and then I woke and heard this sound. I still don't know what it was. It was so smoky I couldn't tell where we were. But then I heard the sirens. And then that blessed man came and got us."

"How many more inside?" Fontana asked.

"Let's see. We've the four Sutterfield kids plus Brendan. That makes five kiddies." She coughed. "Oh, my God. There's only four here. The little one!"

Fontana waylaid two masked firefighters and had them go up the outside wooden stairs to assist Weed. A hose stream began drumming the walls inside the house, breaking out a window, throwing broken glass and cold water into the yard near where Mary and Brendan were standing.

Fontana picked up Brendan and herded the others toward the backyard, now filling up with the second and third wave of volunteers. He whispered to his son, "I love you."

"I love you too."

Another radio report filled with static came from inside the house. "Engine One portable. We have a tapped fire. Checking for extension."

"Cove Command. Tapped fire. I'll send some lights in. Be informed there's one more victim inside. Probably on the second floor."

A moment later, Frank Weed carried her down the wooden steps and into the backyard, leaving in his wake the smell of smoke and baby talcum. She was about two, wrapped in a pink and yellow blanket, the youngest of the Sutterfields, still asleep. When Mary Gilliam tried to take the bundle out of Weed's arms, he half turned away and shook his head. Except for Brendan, who had now grabbed the tail of Fontana's bunking coat and was following him around like a puppy, the other children were with the medics.

Fontana sent a pair of masked firefighters inside to perform a secondary search of the first floor, another pair to do one of the second floor and attic spaces. "Give it a good once-over," he said.

A chain saw began screaming away on the roof, the operators engulfed in a wash of dirty smoke. The photographer continued to snap pictures.

"They hide on you," said Weed, his face blackened by a mixture of soot and perspiration. "I had to look all over for that little redhead. I found him, but with my gloves on, he felt like a toy. I don't think he was scared of the fire. I think he was scared of me. Damn. It was just luck I went to the right room. They were all in there. The woman even. I had to keep picking her up off the floor. Her knees kept buckling. Good thing they had the bedroom door shut or the smoke would have killed em."

"I told her to close the door," said Brendan matter-of-factly. "She wanted to keep it open, but I told her my dad said fire is like a cat. Open the door even a crack and it will get in."

"That was a good call, son. And nice work, Frank," said Fontana. "You rescued five people. You were great."

Relinquishing the child to the medic, Weed looked up. "Thanks, Chief. Really?" After a moment, he showed his teeth and said, "You gonna take that one home with you?"

"I probably will." Fontana hugged Brendan again. "He lives with me."

"Brendan?" Coughing, Weed stooped to look at the boy, placed a hand on the ground to keep from tipping over. "How did you get in there?"

"I was staying over," Brendan said, cheerfully.

"Well, hey, kid. I'm sorry," said Weed. "It was just luck we were able to get you out at all. I can't believe the luck. If I'd gone in any other door."

"You did a fine job, Frank," Fontana said. "An excellent job. Thanks." The smoke-cloaked firefighters on the roof shouted a warning as a large section of roof tumbled noisily into the yard thirty feet away and kicked up smoke, dust, and flame. Somebody directed a hose stream onto it.

"So what door did you take my mother out of?" Mary asked. "Where'd you put my mother?"

Fontana and Weed looked at each other with the special recognition of two men entertaining the same appalling thought. "Oh, shit," said Weed.

FIFTEEN

◆

ET CETERA, ET CETERA, ET CETERA, ET CETERA, ET CETERA

Fontana's fire crews had twice scoured the house, upstairs, downstairs, two volunteers with flashlights going so far as to pry open the padlocked crawl space in the back and crab-walk among the spiderwebs, antique lawn mowers, an odd barber pole, and forgotten Christmas tinsel packages from thirty years ago.

In addition, the normal litter of a house fire was everywhere—fallen ceilings, curtains that had been dragged down, pictures and bric-a-brac and debris lying everywhere, a grab bag of odds and ends spilling out of closets that had been searched, pieces of broken wallboard and sooty rubbish with footprints on it marring the floor.

Before Fontana had taken over the department, one out of four structure fires in Staircase found a way to rekindle. In a year with arsons accelerating the number of fires, he'd reduced the ratio to zero out of seventeen and was planning to keep it that way.

While the secondary search dragged on—Mary and Fontana waiting nervously at the patio door—another crew began hacking with axes at the walls in the fire rooms. Any amount of fire hidden in a wall could take off, particularly in an old building such as this one with no fire-stops and plenty of hidden spaces from remodels.

Fontana turned to Mary. "You think she might have wandered out into the woods?"

"It'd be nice to think so, but Mother won't move for heaven or earth. She's right where I left her."

"Where was that?"

"On the sofa downstairs in the sleeping room."

"They've searched it."

"That's where I left her."

"Can't find her, Chief," Mo Costigan said. Her face sooty where her facepiece hadn't covered it, Mo wore a yellow volunteer fire-fighter's helmet that looked huge on her. Mo had recently earned her first-responder's card and seemed more vain about that than of being mayor, if such a thing were possible. "We've looked everywhere. You got your dog? Satan could find her."

"He's still too lame to be working."

Accompanied by Frank Weed, who was devastated over the missing woman, Fontana walked to the patio. He'd left Brendan with the other children at the medics' van.

Volunteers nailed up light strings on heavy, waterproof electrical cords as they stepped past the noisy portable generator on the wooden patio. The kitchen and dining room were pretty much intact, although smoke damage had blurred everything above knee height to a uniform gray. Overeager hose men had puddled water on the floor.

From the look of the walls and ceiling, the living room at the far east end of the house where Sandusky had taken the first line through had been a fireball, the walls still giving off residual heat. If the children and Mary had been on the first floor, or if there'd been an open stairway, nobody would have escaped.

In a back bedroom, several firefighters had taken their masks off and were tearing into a wall with axes. Somebody set up a power fan on the patio, and the house suddenly cleared of smoke.

Although most of the room was already stripped, when Fontana rounded the corner he found eight firefighters elbowing for a chance to tear wallboard off. Moist from water and sweat and breathing, the warm room stank of char and smoke. In places, the rubble on the floor was knee deep. Steam meandered up off the debris, off the bent backs and bare necks of firefighters. From the day the house had been built, there probably had never been this many people in the room.

"This the main fire room?" Weed asked, crowding against Fontana at the doorway.

"This. Two down the hall. And upstairs right above here," said

Sandusky. "But not as bad. It must have started in that enclosed porch on the west end of the building and spread through here."

Fontana thumbed the rubber button on his battle lantern and began a systematic search of the floor, kicking broken lathe out of the way. It was a wonder they hadn't found her earlier. She was facedown, directly below three firefighters, underneath a tarp and a foot of rubble. If she hadn't been dead already, the weight of the firefighters would have killed her.

The room was quiet as they pulled the lathe and plaster pieces and chunks of ceiling away from the body. Fontana told them to leave her in position, facedown, trampled, burned.

"Oh, God," said Sandusky, when they'd removed the last of the tarp and could see her pink nightgown as well as the rose in her hair. "I don't know whether to laugh or cry."

"If it makes you feel any better," Fontana said, "she was dead before you got here. See the ring of soot around her nostrils? This whole lower floor must have been full of smoke long before the fire reached her. The smoke killed her. Nothing you could have done."

"We could have moved her before all eight of us walked on her," said Lieutenant Pierpont.

"God, she must be about a hundred and eight," said Opal Morgan, running her flashlight along the corpse while her husband peered over her shoulder. Neither of them moved for a good while, piling bonus points onto their reputation as the department ghouls.

"We really smoothed her out," said Sandusky. "The undertaker won't have to iron that nightgown or nothin'." Everybody in the room looked somber.

"This is horrible," said Weed, almost in tears. "This is really awful."

It was quiet for five or six seconds before Sandusky, who had seen more dead bodies than anyone in the room but Fontana, guffawed. "We could prop her up in the beanery and she could watch TV with Claude," he said. "Hell, we could set her up on a date with Claude."

"Settle down here," said Fontana. "She was my neighbor and my friend."

Fontana went outside to wait for the county fire investigators and to tell Mary, who said, "Just tonight I told her again, 'Mother, when are you going to die?' With my bad heart, I never thought for one second she wouldn't outlive me."

"You took good care of her," Fontana said. "She couldn't have asked for more."

"No, she couldn't, could she?"

The fire had started just inside the door at the west end of the house, where Fontana had stood initially, the door the Morgans had kicked in. It was an old sunporch, enclosed and walled in, with a second door leading into the main house. The interior door had glass in the top half, and somewhere in the early life of the fire the glass had gotten hot and fallen out, allowing the smoke and heat to creep through the rest of the downstairs. The upstairs had gotten smoky but there'd been no flame.

Lorraine had been sleeping in a small room with an open door in the main portion of the house fifteen feet from the door on the re-modeled sunporch. Flame had extended down the hallway, filled the room, then crept along the ceiling into the living room where San-dusky had entered. Altogether it had gutted three rooms and smoked up the rest of the house before Sandusky and his partner tapped it. It was almost a total loss for the Sutterfields.

Fontana suspected the first firefighters in the death room had over-turned the burning mattress and without realizing it spilled the old woman, who didn't weigh much, onto the floor. The two volunteers who'd sent the burning mattress out the window were big, burly car-penters, and they'd no doubt missed her through a combination of zeal, strength, and adrenaline.

Fontana knew he'd have to organize a meeting to debrief the par-ticipants at the fire, a formal opportunity to talk it over. He'd call a clergyman/psychologist he knew of from Seattle who did that sort of work.

"I don't get what happened," Brendan said. He was sitting in the chief's truck looking cold and small in his shorts and T-shirt. Fontana had secured a blanket and wrapped him in it, and now he tugged a pair of his own spare socks on the boy's feet, pulling them up to his knees. "How did the house catch fire?"

"It started on that old sunporch. There's no electrical out there and Mary says nobody'd been out there all night, so I'm not sure how it started, but we'll find out. Were any of you kids out there?"

"No. We were watching videos. Did somebody try to burn us up?"

"I'm not sure, Brendan. I hope not."

"Why would somebody want to burn up Caroline and Ian and Brett and Brita?"

"I'm not sure they did." It was almost midnight. It was a Friday night. And from what Fontana could see of the burned-out sunporch, the fire had traveled along the path of least resistance, which was directly into the main floor of the home. From what he could see, several sheets of fiberglass roofing material had been piled under the inside door and then lit. "There's one other thing," Fontana said.

"What?"

"Not everybody got out. I'm real sorry, but Mary's mother didn't make it."

"Lorraine?"

"I'm afraid so. Yes."

Brendan stared at his father while his large gray eyes filled with tears. Gritting his jaw, he said, "Did she get burned up?"

"I'm pretty sure she breathed some smoke in her sleep and the smoke killed her. That's how people usually die in house fires."

"I hate him. I hate him. I hate him. I wish his house would burn down. And I wish . . . his dog would burn up. I hate him."

"The man who started the fire?"

"I hate him."

Fontana put his arm around the boy and pulled him close. "I think you're right. I think somebody did start this one. And I hate him too."

A few minutes later, Roger Truax and Mo Costigan walked alongside the overgrown laurel hedge and, cupping their hands to their faces, peered into the chief's truck.

"Got a minute?" Truax shouted through the glass.

"Sure." Not wanting to leave him alone, Fontana carried a weepy-eyed Brendan down the road forty feet to where Mary Gilliam and some of the neighbors stood with the four Sutterfield children at the back of the medic unit.

"What can I do for you?" Fontana said, as he walked along the road with the mayor and the town's safety director. Mo Costigan loved rushing to an alarm and tapping a fire, but as soon as the shoveling and carrying of trash commenced, she was apt to locate urgent mayoral duties nearby.

The three stopped and formed a triangle in the middle of the road. Truax was decked out in pressed slacks, a sport coat, and dress shoes and seemed more pleased with himself than normal. Mo wore her bunking pants, boots, and the heavy bunking jacket, the latter open to relieve body heat. The navy-blue Staircase Fire Department T-shirt she wore was damp with sweat and hung heavily on her breasts, a phenomenon that hadn't escaped Truax. In fact, the mayor's nipples seemed to be Truax's central focus for the evening. He would look at the medic unit and then Mo's chest. The sky and her chest. Et cetera, et cetera, et cetera.

Even though she was just past thirty, it was rumored that Mo had had dozens, if not hundreds, of lovers, which Fontana believed she might have had, and the rough, scratchy voice of someone who'd smoked twenty thousand cigarettes, though he'd never seen her with a single smoke. She was short and thick and naturally chesty, which was accentuated by the aggressive manner in which she stood, thrusting herself up toward whomever she addressed.

"It was a bad fire, Mac," Roger Truax said.

"I'd say so."

"What do you think? Electrical? Maybe a heater?"

"I doubt they were using a heater on a warm June evening, Roger. And there were no outlets out there. You can see where somebody stacked a couple of loose pieces of fiberglass up against the interior door and lit them."

"So what are you saying? It was arson?"

"That or mice with matches."

Truax mulled it over for a few moments. "You think it was our boy?"

"Hard to tell."

"Listen, Mac," said Mo. "I want you to drop everything and investigate. Somebody else can handle the fire department. We've lost one of our townsfolk here, and I want you to give this your full attention."

"I am investigating, Mo. But I'm not going to abandon the department. Somebody could get killed. I mean, somebody else could get killed."

"That's no problem," said Truax. "I could run the department while you were poking around."

"Sorry," said Fontana. "I'll do what I can, but I'm not handing the department over to anybody. Nothing against you, Roger, but it's my baby."

"Mac. We've got a death here," Mo said, stepping toward him like a belligerent dog deciding whether or not to bite.

"I know we do. And the best way for me to make sure we don't have another one is to keep a tight rein on the department."

"Don't be stubborn," said Truax. "I'd love to run things. It'd be fun. I've already got half a dozen new programs lined up."

"Like hell you do." Fontana turned and walked back to the fire building.

♦

THE WICKED TWIN

It wasn't until Fontana had released most of the volunteers, along with Engine Three from the satellite station up in Wilderness Rim, that the other fires began coming in. Five more alarms. If they hadn't known it was arson before, they knew now. A shed fire a mile away near the freeway interchange. A broken-down barn that never really got going several hundred yards beyond that. The same Dumpster behind the Bedouin that had been torched last week. The rear wall of a real estate office in town, which only smoldered. A weathered shack on the old highway. It was as if the arsonist had waited until the excitement at the Sutterfield house abated before moving on, as if he or she or they had been waiting until everyone had regrouped before setting more fires.

At the Sutterfield fire, just before they dug Lorraine's body out, Heather Minerich met Fontana at the doorway and said, "Hold out your hand."

"Excuse me?"

"Hold out your hand."

Almost as tall as Fontana, Heather had brown eyes and short brown hair, a somewhat lanky build with a heavy bottom, and a mild slouching walk with an exaggerated waggling of her hips that had not gone unnoticed or unimitated among the volunteers. She spoke her mind, more than held up her end in the exchange of off-color jokes among the incorrigibles, and most of the time took orders as if they were some sort of personal affront. To date, she had passed all the tests, performed adequately at fires, and was driving a pumper when the need arose. She wasn't imbued with the aggressive mentality Frank Weed carried, but few were.

"Come on, Chief. Hold out your hand." When he had done so, she smiled broadly and dropped a cigarette lighter into his palm. It was clear red plastic and was stamped WASHINGTON STATE FERRIES. It was empty of liquid.

"What's this?"

"I found it."

"Where?"

"Out by the corner of the house here. It's gotta be what he used, Chief. He must have dropped it in the dark and was afraid to go back and look."

"How many people have handled this?"

"Oh, crap. Fingerprints, right? Oh, crap. I was pretty sure it was important evidence and then I brought it in here and now I feel like a dope. Crap. I thought I was going to be the big hero."

"Don't worry about it. It was a nice find."

Fontana dropped it into an evidence bag and passed it to Jenny Underhill when she came out of the house with her partner, a short, black-haired, thick-browed man named Beasley. The wooden deck under their feet vibrated from the rhythmic pummeling of a portable generator. One of the lightbulbs in the string they'd nailed up threw a stern glare across Jenny's face, making her cheeks look plump and lax.

She said, "I understand the deceased was a friend of yours?"

"A neighbor, actually. They were over here baby-sitting. My son was in the house too."

"Christ," said Beasley. "You must be pissed."

"He killed Lorraine. My son was in there, plus four other kids and one of my best friends. It could have been seven instead of one. My people did a bang-up job."

"That's for sure," said Underhill. "That new rookie you have is terrific."

"Guess what?" said Beasley, showing his gapped teeth. "There's an arson spree in north Seattle tonight. Right this minute."

"What are you saying, exactly?"

"Well, whoever did this can't be in two places at once. So we've either got a pretty good copycat in north Seattle or we've got one out here. This is the first time the north Seattle arsonist, who we've always considered to be the original one, and your arsonist were busy at the same time. Until tonight they could have been the same person."

"A wicked twin," Fontana said.

When the three of them walked around the building together, it was obvious there had been only one point of ignition. Somebody had walked into the yard, found three large sheets of fiberglass, part of an old carport roof, somehow gotten into the sunporch with them, and set fire to them, perhaps with the cheap lighter Heather Minerich found.

It was several minutes later when Beasley said, "Hey. We hear you've got a celebrity living in the community. Have you seen her?"

"As a matter of fact, I have."

"What's she like?"

"She shot two dogs," said Underhill. "That's what I heard."

"It's true," said Fontana.

"Sounds like a tough gal," said Beasley.

"You never know," said Fontana.

SEVENTEEN

◆

HANDING OUT CHEWING
GUM TO DEAD MEN

At eleven o'clock on Saturday morning, Fontana convened the participants of the previous night's fatal fire in the classroom upstairs for a post-fire evaluation, the agenda to include equipment malfunctions, if any, a review of tactics, a discussion of the death, and so forth. Several intruders had to be turned away at the door. The only one Fontana recognized was Robinson Jeffers, the reporter who'd been hanging around town for the last week or so.

The last person to arrive was Sandusky, clad in jeans and a torn T-shirt. In the hallway outside the door, he shouted, "Heeeeey, Paco. Let's go pick up some meeeentally ill women."

It was a catchphrase with Sandusky, always shouted with gusto and in a staged Spanish accent, and it was a rare day when he entered the station without hollering it. He was loud and unrestrained, and his puerile sense of humor was sometimes but not always appreciated in the fire station. If he was late for a drill session, he'd say he'd stopped on his way out the door to "service the old lady." Whenever he got a chance to write the Morgans' names on the blackboard downstairs, he spelled Les "Less" and wrote "More" instead of Opal, then acted innocent when the always-sober Morgans made a big production out of it.

Nine months earlier, when Sandusky had rescued a baby from a burning car on Staircase Way, flame had melted his nylon jacket until it clung to him in dirty brown sheets as if he'd been shrink-wrapped by a mad grocer. Seconds after he'd pulled the wailing baby out, the car flamed over with a dull pop. The editor of the local paper casually offered to interview Sandusky, but he declined, saying, "That's what I'm trained for. It was no big deal."

The editor believed him. Fontana did not.

Sandusky had scorched all the hair off one side of his head, burned both ears, a cheek, and a forearm. Despite the fact that he spat out the word "fuck" more often in a day than anyone Fontana had ever encountered, he was hands-down the best volunteer Fontana had.

In the doorway Sandusky stopped, looked around the classroom, and grinned. "Sorry, Chief. I got tangled up with those TV yahoos downstairs."

"Who?"

"The whole station's filling up with clipboards and cameras. Bree McAllister's down there talking to the mayor. We're big time today."

"Shit," said Fontana.

"TV people?" Frank Weed, the only person in the room tall enough to see out, stood on tiptoe at the wall and peered through the high louvered window. "They want to interview me, Chief. Called me this morning at eight. I guess I forgot to tell you. Is it all right?"

"I don't think I can stop them now, Frank."

A standard practice at a post-fire evaluation was to have each unit leader tell what he saw when he arrived, state the assignment he'd been given, and explain what he'd accomplished. By the time everyone had made a contribution, a fairly complete picture would be drawn.

Sandusky's hose partner nervously said he'd tried to back out several times but Sandusky wouldn't let him. "God, it was hot. I can't even imagine how hot it must have been in front of me." Everybody had seen the melted face shield on Sandusky's helmet the night before. Under slightly altered circumstances, he and his partner might have been the heroes.

Weed had made the biggest save in Staircase history, bigger even than Harold Suman leading forty-two cows from a burning barn in 1958. Harold Suman was still around, and people still bought him beers on the strength of that rescue, so it was hard to imagine what sort of legend Frank Weed's exploit might evolve into.

"I don't know what to say, you know," said Weed, when his turn came. "I arrived in my private car directly behind Chief Fontana. The engine wasn't there yet, you know, so I parked down the street. I bunked up, and by the time I had done that, they got there, you know, so I grabbed an ax and a mask and went into the house. You know, the time of night—it was a residence and all—it seemed like there had to be people inside.

"I tried a couple of doors and then found one I liked and went in. I suppose I should have started at the fire and worked my way out, but I went upstairs first. It was smoky as all get-out, so I had to feel my way around. I figured later there were four bedrooms and the bathroom and a little storage room up there. The curtains in the bathroom were burning from the outside-wall fire, but other than that it was mostly smoke and heat. I'm just sorry we didn't get the other lady. Geez, if she'd only been upstairs."

The room grew quiet.

The volunteers in Staircase took pride in their firefighting prowess, and until last night most had considered themselves superior to Weed, who was still a rookie. Sandusky, in the rare position of being a volunteer in Staircase as well as a paid professional in Seattle's department, looked particularly peeved. The truth was, as in all successful firefighting operations, it had been a team effort, and Fontana reminded them of that.

"I just feel bad about walking on a dead woman for fifteen minutes and not knowing it," said Kingsley Pierpont.

"Dead bodies have a habit of getting lost in the debris," said Fontana. "Once back east, after about two hours of chasing fire through a tenement building, we took a break in the dark. Two of us offered a piece of gum to a man sitting against the wall next to us. Somebody even stuck a cup of water between his legs and wondered why he didn't drink. Turned out he was the fire victim we'd been looking for. Man, was he toasted."

"So what finally made you realize he was dead?" Lindoff asked.

"He wouldn't laugh at our jokes."

"Well, hell, by that measure my wife's dead," said Sandusky. Laughter. Applause. Everybody knew Sandusky's wife unfailingly laughed at all his jokes, no matter how lame.

When Sandusky was questioned about why he had taken the first line to the back door, Fontana listened closely to his answer. He said, "When we got to that patio slider, I could see flame in the back of the house. I figured from looking at the traffic patterns in the lawn, there was another door around the corner. I hated to go the long route, but it seemed like the best bet to push the fire straight out the west end of the house."

And Lorraine? How had she ended up on the floor?

Nobody knew.

The last time Mary had seen her mother, she'd been asleep under the partially open window on a daybed the Sutterfields used for the children's naps. By the time Sandusky and his partner reached the death room, it was a fireball, and by the time they'd blacked it out, knocked down all the fire, two other volunteers had folded the burning mattress into a cylinder and shoved it out the window. Then, still without lights, they began pulling walls and ceilings, probably burying the corpse under debris at that time.

As the meeting broke up, Weed ducked into the rest room across the hall and a minute later emerged pulling a comb through his prematurely thinning hair. Fontana had never seen him so exhilarated, not even at last night's fire.

The ground floor of the station was bursting with television crews, on-the-spot radio interviewers taping snippets for their newscasts, photographers, Staircase volunteers, former volunteers, and would-be volunteers. The rescue of the five children had brought instant celebrity to the tiny department. In the hallway, Fontana heard somebody recounting the last fire death in Staircase, which had occurred a hundred and four years earlier when Elsie Hoffstadder, a three-hundred-pound alcoholic, burned her cabin down around herself.

Because it was the first homicide connected to the serial arsons, the fire death had become headline news throughout the Northwest, and all morning the station phone had been ringing off the hook. Most of the callers were members of other fire departments asking for particulars of the fire, but each time Sandusky answered, he told the caller about the nude footrace at Sun Country next month, urging them to bring their wives or girlfriends and participate. Though he knew it wasn't true, he claimed the entire Staircase Fire Department would be there.

When Frank Weed swaggered into the beanery from the apparatus floor in front of a man with a TV camera on his shoulder, the camera-shy volunteers scattered like bottom fish in a tidal pool.

Dressed in a suit and heels, Mo Costigan read a prepared statement to the cameras in front of the station, then next door in her office, then later in front of the fire engines, where Frank Weed was being set up for filming, in full bunkers, gloves, and carrying the same six-pound pick-head ax he'd carried the night before.

Kingsley, Heather, and the others looked on in disbelief as Weed spoke to the cameras with the élan of a man who'd been on stage. Anytime Kingsley spoke to the media, which wasn't often, he hesitated and stuttered and sweated. The only person in the department who felt comfortable in front of cameras, until now, was Fontana. Nobody had expected the recruit they called "the stick" to be so composed.

At one point during a holdup in the proceedings, Weed sidled over to Fontana and said, "I know you guys are looking at me funny, but you gotta realize this might be the best thing that ever happened to me. The rest of my life could be downhill from here."

"Hey. You've got my blessing. Go for it. None of us ever saved five kids."

"You mean that?"

"Go for it."

"But you really never saved five kids?"

"I saved one kid. Once."

"Some of these guys seem to have their noses out of joint."

"I wouldn't worry about it."

"Because, you know, Chief, I don't want any controversy. I'm just out here telling it like it was."

"They're calling you."

Shortly before noon, Frank Weed's incredibly tall girlfriend showed up. It always tickled Fontana to watch Frank and his girl-friend driving together because Weed was almost six feet five inches tall and she was only an inch shorter, so they looked like a couple of side-by-side broomsticks about to go through the roof.

When he grew tired of watching the interviews, Fontana found Sandusky behind the station scrubbing hose with a long-handled brush. Heather Minerich stood beside him with a second brush. Other volunteers were hauling dry hose from the hose tower and packing it into the rear of Engine Two. Everyone seemed strangely silent. "What's the matter?" Fontana asked.

Sandusky looked up. "What do you mean, what's the matter?"

"You guys upset with Weed?"

"Not really."

"He's just getting a little full of himself," said Heather.

"You sure you're not unhappy about something?"

"Me?" said Sandusky, scrubbing more briskly than ever. "I'm happier than a little boy with two peepees."

◆

EIGHTEEN

PEEPSHOW

Minutes later, Roger Truax and Robinson Jeffers ferreted out Fontana as he was giving the boot to a pair of mild-mannered newsmen who'd had their muddy feet propped on his office desk. Truax and Jeffers stepped in and closed the door to the office while Fontana brushed raisins of dried mud off his desk calendar. "Jeffers would like to ask you a few questions," Truax said.

"About the fires?"

"That's what I'm writing about," said Jeffers.

Truax muttered something about going outside to watch the filming and left. Jeffers closed the door with his colorless fingertips. Once again the reporter wore khaki pants and a gray windbreaker zipped to the neck. Fontana wasn't sure he had ever seen anyone wearing a frayed twelve-dollar jacket and carrying a two hundred-dollar ink pen at the same time.

"You mind if I tape this?" Jeffers said, pulling out a recorder the size of a cigarette pack. "I have a poor memory."

"No problem."

Jeffers balanced the miniature recorder on his knee. "Everyone is pretty upset over the fire death. Could you comment on it?"

This was just the sort of public relations chore Fontana hated, even though he knew it was an integral part of his job. "It was a terrible tragedy. The type of thing people working in the fire service hope they never encounter. I don't know what else I can say. It was unfortunate. And regrettable. And the department extends its heartfelt prayers to the relatives and friends of the deceased. Each one of us feels a very personal loss."

Jeffers scribbled. "And how old was she?"

"Ninety-three."

"I understand there were extensive burns over the body. I also understand some of your people may have unintentionally walked on the victim during the course of the fire."

"She was dead when we got there. Her body was under a good deal of debris and not discovered until after the fire was tapped."

"If you were forced to put your finger on a guilty party, who would you finger?"

"Fortunately I'm not being forced to do that. It's much too early in the investigation to make any accusations. We don't even have a suspect."

"Do you think whoever set it will be held accountable for the death?"

"By state law a death resulting from an arson is automatically murder."

"There were five children in the house. One of them was yours. How could . . . ? I mean, how could the son of the fire chief end up in a burning house? Don't you think that was a most extraordinary coincidence?"

"Yes, I do. And as far as anybody knows, it was just that, a coincidence."

"Why didn't you go inside to get him? I mean, if your son was burning to death, it seems like you would want to do something about it."

"To start off with, I didn't realize he was inside until well into the fire. Besides that, a chief has a particular function at a fire, and if he abandons that post, all hell is apt to break loose. The best chance we had to get all of the victims out was for everybody to do their own job in the way they've been trained. And that's what we did. And we got them out."

"All but one."

"Right."

"What if you hadn't? Wouldn't you have felt bad about not going in personally?"

"Of course I would have."

"When can I speak to your son about this?"

"You can't."

"Well, if he's got something going on today, I could talk to him tomorrow. I'm flexible."

"He's eight years old. I don't want him interviewed at all."

"I can talk to an eight-year-old. I won't have any problem with that."

"You don't understand. *I* don't want him interviewed."

"I see. Okay. Sure. Did you know people are blaming the fire death on the disorganization of your fire department?"

Fontana took a deep breath. "What people?"

"Not that you could help that. I mean, you're given what you're given. This is a tiny department."

"Including me, we have four full-timers and thirty-seven volunteers. Six of our volunteers are professional firefighters in other departments. I haven't heard anything about the blame for the fire death. Where did you hear this?"

"Just around. How many people from your department were at the fire, total?"

"I'd have to check the report, but I think around twenty-five fought the fire." Fontana was still bristling from the accusation.

"In Seattle, for instance, how many would have responded?"

"It's hard to say. But no department in the country could have saved that woman. She was dead before we arrived. My people did a good job. Don't forget we rescued five children and one adult and preserved a good portion of the house. It was a good fire stop."

"How many fire deaths have you had in Staircase?"

"This is our first in a hundred years."

"What can you say about the man who made the rescue?"

"Weed's a good firefighter. He's been with the department about seven months. He went in there without a moment's hesitation and brought five people out. What else can you say? He's tremendous. We're lucky to have him."

"I can't help thinking, what if he hadn't been there?"

"Everybody in the department is trained to do what Weed did. He performed exceptionally, but if he had not found them, the next firefighter would have."

Jeffers smiled. "Let me get this right. You're saying what he did was routine and he shouldn't be treated as a hero?"

"I'm not saying that at all. He did an outstanding job and he deserves everything he's getting. But the truth of the matter is, we would have gotten them out one way or another."

"Yet you didn't get the old lady out."

"Unfortunately not."

"Did the coroner confirm the woman was dead before your arrival?"

"King County has a medical examiner, not a coroner, and they won't do the autopsy until Monday."

"How long did it take to get there?"

"Between two and three minutes. We were responding from another alarm. Coming from town, Engine Two arrived shortly behind me. Less than a minute later, I would say."

"I see." Jeffers flipped through his notebook. "Did it occur to you that the man who ran the stop sign on Stooly Road might have been fleeing a crime? If you look at the time frame, the car accident must have happened only minutes after the fire was set."

"It occurred to me, but it doesn't wash. He was arrested at the accident scene. If he had been the arsonist, then who set the five arsons after the fatal?"

"Mr. Truax has expressed the opinion that the tactics last night lacked precision. He tells a pretty convincing tale."

First Truax wanted to take over as chief and now he criticized Fontana's fire operations to the press. "You know anything about fire tactics, Mr. Jeffers?"

The reporter touched his glasses with one finger and said, "Not really. But I think I know a little bit about firefighting. I used to cover the beat for the Sacramento paper. And frankly, Truax's critique of your fire operation makes a lot of sense to me."

"But you've never actually put on fifty pounds of equipment and walked into a burning building?"

Jeffers looked down, paging through his notes. "What about the . . . ventilation?"

"We used vertical rooftop ventilation. Later we used fans."

"And is that a standard order for ventilation? I don't know any of this myself. You're going to have to fill me in."

"It was about normal for the fire we had. We cut the roof open to allow hot gases and smoke to escape the building. In effect, we cut our own chimney."

"But the house was already full of smoke. You were trying to put out the fire, not build it."

"That's right. But the smoke and steam need an exit."

"Interesting. What do you think is going to come of all this? I mean, the town being in an uproar. The megastar, Aimee Lee, living here. Even the probability that her son is involved in the arsons."

"I'm not going to tell you again. We have no suspects, no leads, and it would be criminal of me or anyone else to suggest that her son is a suspect."

"Isn't it true he admitted setting a fire several months ago and that you decided not to prefer charges?"

"Listen, Jeffers. I'm going to have to cut this off."

"How did you feel when you realized your son was inside the house on Cove Road?"

"Good-bye."

"If Lee's son set the fire and you and Lee are lovers—"

"Get out of here."

"Yeah, but if you were lovers and if he did start the fatal fire last night, would you be the best person to investigate?"

Fontana glowered.

It took Jeffers several beats to realize the interview was in fact over, several more to gather his belongings, all the while surveying the room like an off-duty cat burglar. Once outside the office, he turned and said, "So you're not going to comment about your alleged affair with Aimee Lee?"

In the watch office Roger Truax, Mo Costigan, Kingsley Pierpont, and Sandusky had been in a heated conversation near the front door, yet mention of Aimee Lee and an alleged affair froze them in place.

"This town is just a peepshow to you, isn't it, Jeffers?"

"No. Of course not, Chief. I'm only doing my job. Same as you." Jeffers left the station.

♦

NINETEEN

FASTER THAN GRASS
THROUGH A GOOSE

Because it annoyed her that Fontana was so mightily amused by her temper, Mo Costigan did everything possible to avoid displays when he was around. Nose-to-nose with Kingsley, Mo realized Fontana was listening and dropped her voice. Fontana could hear the sound of the priming gears in the rear of the station as volunteers practiced pumping water with the engine. The priming pump sounded like a bellowing calf and matched Mo's voice perfectly.

"Mac, why don't you explain it?" Truax said, drawing Fontana into the conversation. He'd been standing to one side, kibitzing on Mo's behalf.

"Explain what?"

"Tell your lieutenant," said Mo Costigan, "that he cannot be abusing our female firefighter the way he's been abusing her." Kingsley looked profoundly embarrassed.

"What the hell are you talking about?"

"Don't tell me you haven't seen it," Mo exclaimed. "Every time there are dishes to be done, she's doing them. This morning, she was out back on her hands and knees scrubbing dirty hose. Every dirty little chore."

Kingsley wasn't fond of confrontations and generally spoke softly when challenged, as he did now. "She only does what all boots do," he said.

"I was out back scrubbing hose with her," said Sandusky.

"She's always the one cleaning the countertops and mopping the floor. And why is it that every time the phone rings, everybody sits on their duff until she answers it? And I don't see her mixing with the rest of the crew the way I want."

"You don't see Weed mixing with the crew either," said Fontana.

"You're right. I don't. Why is that, Mac?"

"They're recruits, Mo. Boots. They're on probation. They're expected to do the grunt work. To answer the phones. To prove a willingness not only to be part of the team but to show how much work they can handle. Every firefighter goes through probation. One year. What you've done here, Mo, is misinterpret a recruit's work for women's work. Weed does exactly the same chores she does. They have to work together. Their lives are going to depend on one trusting the other."

"Does she have to be doing the dishes while we have newspeople in the building?"

"If Weed wasn't out there handling all those interviews, he'd be helping. He does as many dishes as she does." Pierpont fiddled with a silver bar on his collar.

"I know how to solve this." Sandusky grinned. "Next time there's a rescue, let Minerich make it. Then she can handle the interviews and Weed can handle the dishes. Simple, huh? Make the girl the hero."

Mo gave him a sour look and turned to Fontana. "I'm serious. You cannot lean on her the way you've been leaning."

"Nobody's leaning on her, Mo. She's just a recruit. I'm sure Roger went through the same thing in Tacoma, right, Roger?"

"Well," said Roger, "I wasn't a girl."

"I don't understand this," said Kingsley. "When I was a boot, the mayor never came down and told people to stop leaning on me. People lean on boots. You accept it."

"The press will not accept it," said Mo. "And neither will I. Not in *my* town. Not in *my* fire department. Not with the whole world watching. Do you know all our motels are filled to capacity? That's never happened outside of hunting season. This harassment has got to stop, and it's got to stop now. And Mac? You'd better move faster than grass through a goose seeing that it does."

"Want me to shine her boots too, or just wipe down the rig for her?" Fontana said.

Kingsley said, "She ain't even at work today."

"What?" Mo asked.

"She ain't even officially at work. We had this meeting, and then we're all supposed to go home and come in tonight. She's here on her own time. Anything she does today is strictly voluntary."

"Maybe if I could interject an opinion here," Roger Truax said, dropping his voice into a deeper register the way he often did when he made a pronouncement. "I think Mo's right. I know how you can get set in a routine and not realize what you're doing. For instance, last night at that fire I happened to notice Lieutenant Pierpont took the nozzle inside and left Heather by the door feeding hose to him. Now that could have been construed by the media as putting her in a subservient position." Truax waved a finger. "Not good."

"See?" said Mo. "Even Roger noticed."

"Mo. We'll review our policy with the recruits," said Fontana, trying to cover his bases in the event Mo was planning to build this up into a case against the fire department. Minerich had never complained to him or anybody else that he knew about, and he didn't see an issue. But then, it was just like Mo to turn Minerich into some sort of pawn in a power struggle.

"I have already reviewed your policy. Change it."

"Heather's a good kid," said Truax. "But this doesn't really involve only Heather, either, Mac. You're going to have more women in the department eventually, and guidelines need to be set. For instance, what's your pregnancy policy?"

"Pregnancy?" blurted Sandusky. "Pregnancy? Good God! You mean she's already been knocked up?" Everybody looked at him. "Who's the lucky joe? The proud poppa?"

"Sometimes," said Mo, glaring at Sandusky, "I think we need to review our volunteer ranks."

"You know you love me," said Sandusky.

"At the very least, you're going to have to let her go into the fires with everybody else."

Mo and Roger Truax left by the front door. After the cowbell had stopped clanking, Sandusky muttered, "Somebody doesn't go into a fire it's because they don't want to, not because we're not letting them." Sandusky looked out the window. "Maybe I better tell you something. The other day I was upstairs in the bunk room changing my clothes when Heather walked in. I'm standing in my Jockey shorts and my socks, and she opens her locker not eight feet away and takes off her shirt. It's not even a sports bra. It's one of those lacy things. So I says to her, 'Do you mind?,' and she says back, 'No, I don't mind.' And then she takes off her pants."

"What'd you do?" Kingsley asked.

"I hid in the bathroom until she was gone."

Fontana sat on the edge of the desk in the watch office and looked at his lieutenant. "What happened at the fire?"

"I was gonna talk to you about that."

"And what about this other? The locker situation?"

"I thought you knew," Kingsley said. "I guess I better pull your coat to what's been happening." Together they walked down the hall and went into Fontana's office.

"I thought you gave her a locker in the old aid-car room," Fontana said.

"I tried to, but she wanted to be out with everybody else."

"But the women volunteers all have their lockers in the old aid-car room, right?"

"Right," Kingsley said. "But like she said, all the regulars have theirs in the bunk room. I wasn't going to tell you this, but I went up there about a month ago when somebody was in the shower. I didn't know it was her until she pressed up against that pebbled glass door to tell me I got a phone call from the dentist's office earlier but she'd forgotten to tell me."

"What'd you do?" Fontana asked.

"Are you kidding? I ran," Pierpont said. "There's just one more item. I don't know how to tell you this exactly, but at that house fire last night, all she did was sit in the doorway and pull hose."

"She's had all that house fire training up at the academy," said Fontana. "They told us she tied for number one with that kid who went to Shelton. And she's always done fine in our training. Hell, she should have been on the pipe. Why wasn't she?"

"I dunno. I guess I grab it by instinct."

"Next time we have a fire, you're going to have to forget your instinct and let her be in front. We need to see what she can do."

"Near as I can tell, it won't be much. I covered and then had to wait a good forty seconds for her to finish masking up."

"She does fine masking up on the drill floor. What happened?"

"I don't think you're hearing me, Chief. She was poking along on purpose so I'd go in ahead of her. After the fire was pretty much tapped, she grabbed the nozzle and anybody came in later saw her standing there with it."

"I don't recall this happening at other fires."

"That was the first real ripper she's had. What am I supposed to do on the report?"

"Write it the way you saw it. We'll give her a chance to respond and we'll keep an eye on her. The next time we get a good fire, I want you teamed up with her so you can observe what she does, and I want her on the pipe."

On the drive home, Fontana thought about Sandusky. Sandusky'd been a Seattle firefighter for twelve years, and from that quarter Fontana had heard nothing but praise. He was liked well enough in the Staircase department, although his mouth got him into trouble from time to time. Fontana thought Mo's intensely displayed but infrequent antagonism toward Sandusky could be because they'd possibly had an affair once, but he dismissed that idea. Even though he made jokes about his marriage, Sandusky was fiercely loyal to his wife.

But then, Sandusky had more angles than a runway model. Addicted to practical jokes, he frequently made calls from one station phone to another, asking one of the crew to run an errand for him that entailed passing him as he sat laughing. He often took Moses, the disreputable station cat Mo hated, and placed him on the roof of Mo's Porsche out behind the station, stroking him until he stretched out and fell asleep.

Until today, there had been no evidence of friction between Sandusky and Minerich. His calling her "the girl" and his remarks about her getting "knocked up" may have just been nothing. But Fontana knew Sandusky had thought he was a shoo-in for Minerich's position, and it could be that he was harboring resentment because he didn't get it. As to why Sandusky had come up short when he tried out for the Staircase Fire Department last fall, Fontana knew little, except Sandusky had made himself scarce after the list was published, emerging from semi-retirement only after the arsons began.

♦

TWENTY

IT GETS WEIRDER
AND WEIRDER

Fontana drove to the Mexican restaurant in the 1960 GMC he'd repainted the original colors of palomino white and titty pink— the former chief's truck he'd bought from the town, the one he'd plugged with Bondo after Warren Bounty put twenty-seven bullet holes into it. On the way he decided to drop in on Mo Costigan.

He and Brendan were taking Mary Gilliam to dinner to cheer her up, though now that they had her in the truck she seemed to need little if any cheering, cracking one joke after another.

Brendan had been somber all day. He'd wept twice when Lorraine's name came up. They'd taken naps that afternoon, and when Fontana woke, he found his son on the dike road beside the river with tears in his eyes, an unused slingshot dangling from his fingertips. "Brendan. How are you doing?"

"I miss Lorraine."

"So do I. I know you loved her and I know she loved you, probably more than anyone else in the world."

"Do you think wherever she is she might see Mom?"

"I think she's probably talking to her right now, telling her how you've been, what you've been up to."

"You think so?"

"Yes. I do."

Brendan picked up a pebble and shot it into the river.

When they went next door, they learned Mary had spent the day packing her mother's belongings for the Salvation Army.

"Oh, don't look at me like that, Mac. It's too bad she died the way she did, but I'm not going to squander the rest of my life mourning a woman who lived twenty years longer than she had a right to. I know it sounds hard, but I have my sewing room back and that's what's important. Mother would be the first to agree."

"Lorraine would be watching TV," said Brendan.

Taken aback by Brendan's tone, Mary said, "You're right. Mama would be watching *I Dream of Jeannie*."

"And I'd be watching with her," said Brendan.

That pretty much ended the conversation.

Pondering last night's events, Fontana realized that had the fire progressed further or had the outside stairway not been accessible, they would have lost everyone. Brendan wouldn't be sitting beside him and neither would Mary. He had spent most of the day second-guessing the decision not to go into the house himself, and even though logic was on his side, whenever he tried to sleep, the second-guessing kept him awake. When he did sleep, he found himself stumbling through hideous dreams. He'd known firefighters who'd made split-second decisions that ended up haunting the rest of their lives, yet he'd always been foolishly confident it would never happen to him. And now it had, for in his mind, there was nothing worse than having someone die on his watch when there was anything he might have done about it. It was a rare event in his career, and he knew he would replay it endlessly.

Now as he drove to the mayor's house, he pulled out the note Mo Costigan had left in his office that afternoon, a note that said simply, "A man named Jeffers would like to ask you a few questions. Your friend, M." Only Mo would abbreviate a two-letter name.

Mo lived in a gray house with a cedar shake roof, picture windows facing Mount Gadd, and a string of sickly rhododendrons planted under the eaves. Her red Porsche sat in the drive. Hole number eight on the golf course abutted her backyard. The neighboring lawns and yards were impeccable, as was her own.

While Mary and Brendan sat in the truck playing rock/scissors/paper, Fontana walked across the yard and knocked on the front door. After almost a minute, Mo answered in a silky cobalt-blue robe she held together with her fists. Her makeup had been recently applied and her eyelashes were like spiders. He was surprised to see a gold bracelet on one ankle, hadn't thought she was the type.

"You on your way out?" he said, handing her the note, which she read dutifully.

"Yeah, what? You need me to interpret?"

"I'm not going to talk to the Dugan, Mo."

"For godsakes, quit whining. He's just a little flea-bitten reporter with mustard on his collar. Answer his questions and tell him to scat."

Fontana looked at her.

"Well, crimenently, Mac. You don't have to answer any questions you don't like. I shouldn't have to tell you this. He probably only wants to ask about that actress everybody says you're sleeping with. Just cooperate with him and he'll go away. Jeffers is a genius. Everybody knows that."

A genius. Now Fontana *knew* he was in trouble.

He had been assessing the expensively furnished room behind Mo's shoulder, noticing two anomalies, the first a twisted pair of blue sweatpants on the floor, the second, the discarded top to the same sweat suit farther along the carpet. He might have assumed they belonged to Mo if he hadn't spotted a man's wristwatch, a money clip, some keys, and a sapphire pinkie ring on a coffee table. He knew Mo wasn't living with anybody, nor was she dating regularly, for Mo rarely dated the same man for more than a couple of weeks, long enough to "screw him and get sick of him," she had once confessed. A hat emblazoned with a WASHINGTON STATE FERRIES decal sat on the table next to the money clip.

"Mo, who belongs to the hat?"

"What hat?"

"You know what hat. Right there on the table."

"Nobody."

"There's a man here, isn't there?"

"There's nobody here."

"I really would like to know."

"I'm not going to tell you," she said, slamming the door. "Listen to me," Mo shouted through the tiny peekaboo gate in the door, but he was retreating down the steps and along the concrete sidewalk.

"You don't seem to understand I am the mayor of this town. You take orders from me. Talk to Jeffers."

"Mo."

"What?"

"Those socks on the floor look like they'd fit an elephant."

DURING DINNER, Brendan seemed to be more his carefree self, sharing some of the vital statistics he kept in his eight-year-old head, such as the fact that when a piece of glass broke, the crack traveled three thousand miles an hour.

On the drive home, they saw a boy no older than Brendan piloting a small pickup truck forward and backward in his father's driveway, using the left front wheel to flatten aluminum cans. When they turned onto their street, they encountered a familiar hound named Barney trying to get an empty can of beans off his snout.

While Fontana was dressing for the Bedouin, Mo, who could never let a dispute terminate unless it was on her terms, telephoned. "Mac, I didn't have anybody here."

"Mo, I don't know if you're aware of it, but we found a Washington State Ferries lighter at the Cove Road fire. Whoever you had in your back room might be connected to the arsons. I would appreciate it a whole lot if you'd tell me who it was."

"There wasn't anybody."

"You sure?"

"Nobody at all."

As they spoke, he thought he heard the sound of rushing water on her end of the line, a noise he often heard while on the phone with the mayor. "That noise on your line, Mo? It's the toilet flushing."

"It most certainly is not."

"It's not the first time I've heard it, either. Mo, how would you feel if I called you from the crapper?"

"Well, really, Mac. Now you are being crude."

He hung up on her, not because he was outraged—in fact, he didn't mind in the least either being called crude or getting calls from someone on the toilet—but because he knew it would get her goat.

As he was leaving the house, the phone rang. He stopped in the doorway but only to count the rings. Nineteen before she quit. A new record.

By the time he parked behind the Bedouin, rain was audible on the truck roof. The arsonist had never deliberately visited Staircase in the rain, although a squall had come in unexpectedly once and put out one of his fires, so Fontana felt reasonably sure he wouldn't start tonight. There had been seven arsons in Seattle last night, all within a three-mile radius of each other, all during a forty-minute time span that precluded the Seattle firesetter from being the one who'd torched the Sutterfields' house.

Situated in the geographical center of town, the Bedouin fronted Staircase Way and was known as the slow-dancing capital of the Northwest. It was a barn of a building with a broken-down Alpine motif that made it look like a Swiss chalet gone to seed. Housing a restaurant that was open twenty-four hours a day, it also enclosed two bars, one on either end of the building—the first ritzy by Staircase standards and the other more famous for its "biker chicks," although Fontana had seen almost no "chicks" in the area and precious few bikers.

On Friday and Saturday nights, the Bedouin was crowded with locals, Seattlites, hikers in the spring and summer, bow hunters, black-powder aficionados, skiers in the winter, kayakers, and rock climbers. On the weekends, college students traveling to and from their eastern Washington schools dropped in.

Before his eyes had adjusted to the darkness, Mrs. Kilpatrick grabbed his hand and dragged him onto the dance floor. Steeped in a cloud of gardenia-scented perfume, she plied him with questions about the arsons in her soft Georgia accent and then, before the tune ended, said kiddingly, "I thought you were *my* guy. But now you're runnin' around with movie stars."

"I've been hearing that all over. Where did you pick it up?"

"Myra at the shop. Hank told her, and he heard it from Sid who heard about it in Yakima."

"Yakima?"

"I ain't kiddin' you, honey. Sid heard it at a truck stop. Supposedly come from some Frenchie drivin' down from Calgary. What's the matter, honey?"

"You ever have the feeling your life is sliding out from under you and there's nothing you can do about it?"

"All the time."

Tonight, the Bedouin was full of journalists trying to blend in with their pastel polo shirts and pressed Dockers. Near the jukebox, the leggy Bree McAllister schmoozed with her husband and some of the network news people. Fontana thought she was trying to catch his eye but wasn't sure until she approached. In person, she was prettier by a good bit than on the tube. After the introductions and small talk, she asked if she might have a few words with him. He escorted her onto the dance floor, where they danced like a student with a teacher, each keeping a respectable distance.

"We're here in town to do a show on the Falls and the hiking and, of course, on your local hero. It's a great story and he's a perfect interview. So we were wondering if you would consent to be shot too."

"I'd be more than happy to talk about Weed. It was a hell of a rescue and he's on cloud nine where he deserves to be."

"Actually, we were thinking of doing a story on Aimee Lee and the fact that she's found this quiet little hideaway. Maybe with some speculation on how she managed to stay hidden for so long. We were thinking of doing some computer graphics on the disguise we've been told she wore. I guess—we hear now—she actually was tracked to this area by several reporters from New York, and at least one of them actually met her and didn't realize it was her. A man named Jeffers?"

"I wouldn't know about that."

"Anyway, we didn't want to do the story if we couldn't find some key people willing to be interviewed. So far she hasn't returned our calls."

"I'd be happy to be quoted if you're doing a story about Weed, but I won't cooperate with this other. Culpepper wants her privacy, and I have to respect that. I'm sorry."

"I doubt we'll do the story if you don't want to be involved. Unlike a lot of TV producers, my boss isn't in the business of invading lives."

"I'm glad to hear that."

"Oh, boy. Chad's going to give me a ribbing. I'm usually pretty good at getting people to tell their secrets. Could you tell me something privately? Not for publication?"

"What's that?"

"Does Aimee Lee's living out here have something to do with the kidnapping?"

"What kidnapping?"

"When her son was kidnapped?"

"I don't know anything about that."

After the number, he watched the other couples on the dance floor and found himself foolishly looking for Aimee Lee, perhaps in disguise, though he had no reason to suspect she would ever wear a disguise again. Mo was talking to some women near the main doors. Ken Valenzuela and his wife were nearby. Heather Minerich was dancing with a volunteer. He'd never really seen Heather in a purely social context before, but it didn't surprise him that, after Mrs. Kilpatrick, she was the most obvious flirt in the room. Her short hair had been frizzed by the rain, and she looked as if maybe she'd had a couple of beers before applying her makeup because the colors seemed a little too stark. She wore baggy jeans, a Soundgarden T-shirt cut short to expose her midriff, and large silver hoop earrings.

He was making his way through the crowd when Heather caught him from behind, tugging on the baggy part of his shirt that ballooned out over his hip, then grabbing the thumb on his left hand and pulling him onto the dance floor. "Oh, come on, Chief. You're not going to say no, are you? I've danced with the whole department. I can't let you get away."

Weed bustled past holding his girlfriend's hand and grinning. "Hey, Chief. You going to dance with me too?"

Fontana smiled weakly. "No, you're too damn tall." Heather pressed into him until he smelled soap and shampoo and the clean odor of a woman with rain on her. Her back muscles were hard under his hand. Dancing with Heather was dangerously close to sex on two feet. It occurred to him that she'd found out he and Kingsley had been discussing her firefighting skills and was attempting to influence his judgment.

"You working tonight?" he asked.

"I'm reporting in half an hour and then I got a few days off. That was a good fire last night. I'd sure like a couple more."

Without being conspicuous about it, Fontana had been politely trying to pry Heather off his chest, but she stuck like a piece of newspaper the wind had blown against a post. They were so close he could feel her thighs on his, the heat of her bare belly through his shirt.

He saw a look in her brown eyes that seemed to be a fusion of coquettishness and victory. He thought by now they must have been seen by every volunteer and full-timer in the department except Kingsley Pierpont, who rarely came to the dance hall. "See ya later, alligator," Heather said cheerfully, when the song ended.

"Mac, I'm really mad at you." Mo Costigan was blocking his path as the music for the next number began.

"Good. Let's dance and talk it over."

He'd never told her this and he probably never would, but the mayor was the best dance partner he'd ever had, a trait he couldn't account for because it wasn't as if they were ever on the same wavelength and it certainly wasn't their physical matchup, since she barely came to his shoulders.

"I don't like being conned, Mo."

"Okay. I'm sorry. I *was* on the toilet. That's exactly where I was. I don't know why I lied. I guess I was caught off guard. If you want the truth, I make most of my business calls on the toilet. There. Now I've made a fool of myself. Friends?"

"I wasn't thinking about the phone call. I was thinking about whoever you had at your place this evening."

"I told you there was nobody there."

"Yeah, and I can't very well get a court order to have you reveal who you've been sleeping with. But I would like to know. That hat I saw bothers me. A lot."

"It shouldn't. You can take my word for it." He knew he couldn't take Mo's word for anything. He had always known that. "You're not going to tell people about my toilet calls?"

"Probably not, Mo. Not unless I get mad."

"Are you mad now?"

"Only a little." He wondered if her legs went to sleep making all those phone calls.

TWENTY-ONE

◆

THE BAG LADY TESTIFIES

The phone woke Fontana. "It's seven-thirty on a Sunday morning, Mo. What happened? You eat something last night that didn't agree with you?"

"Don't get cute. You haven't seen the paper?"

"The valet hasn't brought it in yet."

"Just get up and go read it. Then call me back. And Mac?"

"What?"

"I'm behind you one hundred percent."

"What does that mean?"

"Call me back."

When he unfurled the thick *Seattle Times,* he saw the teaser above the headlines next to a tiny color photo of the burning Sutterfield house: FIRE CHIEF ADMITS ERRORS.

He sat on the living-room couch next to Brendan, who'd gotten into the habit lately of returning from Mary's before anybody else was up and conking out facedown on the couch like an unrepentant drunk. Nothing ever made Fontana feel guiltier than the sight of his son on that couch, and he knew sooner or later he was going to have to hire somebody to spend the night at their house so Brendan could sleep in his own bed when he took fire calls. They had an extra room, but he'd been putting it off, wanting to keep their tiny family inviolate. Beside Brendan sat Lorraine's magnifying glass that Mary had given him, a piece she'd used to study the evening paper. It had always fascinated Brendan. Fontana picked up a quilt Linda had made and draped it over the boy, found his stuffed pig on the floor and tucked it under his arm.

He took the paper into the kitchen, laid it on the table, and boiled water for tea. It was cold in the house, and his ankles were still chilled from the outside air.

An article on the front page, penned by a staff reporter and headlined ONE LOST IN ARSON BLAZE, was more or less a recitation of the facts Friday evening. Inside on page A-8 another headline blared: DISTRUSTFUL CHIEF LASHES OUT AT REPORTER. Farther down the page was a caption beneath a color photo of the Cove Road fire: CHIEF STANDS BY WHILE ELDERLY WOMAN DIES IN FIREBALL. All the articles had been written by Robinson Jeffers.

At the bottom of the page were more pictures: the Sutterfield kids, a photograph snapped over Fontana's back of Frank Weed handing him one of the tots—Weed looking almost evangelical in his intensity. The first time through, he read only snippets, but each of them implied Fontana was an out and out incompetent.

"How did an insignificant fire grow into a raging inferno, a fireball that consumed one woman and nearly killed another along with five children? How did the fire get away from firefighters under the eyes of their chief? Why was the chief's own son in the fire building?"

Farther down, the article stated:

Chief Mac Fontana didn't even know how many firefighters were at the fire. Seeming confused and hesitant as he did throughout the interview, he guessed twenty-five when the total was actually thirty-five firefighters and aid personnel, nearly the entire complement of the minuscule Staircase department, a department which has gotten smaller since Chief Fontana was handed the reins. . . .

Chief Fontana admitted that this sort of inattention to proper procedures is "about normal for the fire we had." . . .

Desperately trying to outguess the medical examiner's report, a fidgety Fontana speculated that the fire victim was dead before they got there. . . .

MacKinley Fontana is a shadowy figure who first appeared in the state a year ago to take the dual jobs of fire chief and sheriff in the small town east of Seattle. Our sources have been unable to confirm why he was removed from the sheriff's job, although rumors continue to circulate that he was implicated in the shooting death of a man last summer. As of this writing, charges have not been filed against him in that case, but there has been much speculation suggesting that the killing and his loss of the sheriff's position were linked.

. . . seemed almost vain of having lost a citizen to fire. "It's the first time in a hundred years this town has had a fire death," said the chief, giving this reporter a look that could only be described as self-satisfied. . . .

Chief Fontana, when asked about his department's actions at the fire scene, seemed to acknowledge the miscues when he said, "Unfortunate and regrettable." . . .

The chief asserted it took two minutes to respond, but King County dispatch records reveal it took three minutes and forty-eight seconds, nearly twice the claim. Other units took longer. Where was the chief and what was he doing for those all-important missing minutes? . . .

While other firefighters at the fire regarded Frank Weed's dramatic rescue as nothing short of miraculous, Fontana seemed contemptuous of the acclaim Weed received. The embittered fire chief said, "If he hadn't found them, the next firefighter would have." Early yesterday morning observers wondered what really took place during the secret post-fire meeting from which outsiders were barred. Filing out of the meeting, members of the Staircase Fire Department appeared quiet and despondent, several near tears. . . .

Claiming no knowledge of her personal life, Fontana refused to discuss his long-term relationship with actress Aimee Lee, who, according to friends and neighbors, he's been secretly involved with for much of the past year. Real estate agent Saul Hepfield says Aimee Lee moved to the area two years ago, paying $525,000 cash for a four-bedroom house and four outbuildings on a section of secluded acreage, and that Fontana moved to Washington a *year ago. Speculation in the small town is rife that Fontana followed Lee there. "They probably knew each other back east," said Staircase auto mechanic Hy Kamen. Eva Montgomery, a long-time Staircase resident, said, "I've seen him around town with her. That's what happens when we encourage California types to move on up."*

Fontana had never heard of Hy Kamen. Eva Montgomery was a drunk who walked the area towing a two-wheeled cart filled with old coats and shoes.

Shrouded in secrecy is a mysterious fire that occurred at Aimee Lee's estate over a month before the current string of arsons struck the Northwest. The details surrounding the April fire have been so carefully hushed up by fire officials in Staircase that most citizens of the town know virtually nothing about it, but it was allegedly ignited by Lee's fourteen-year-old son. All charges against the boy were dismissed by Chief Fontana himself. Asked about the incident, the chief became visibly agitated and abruptly ended this reporter's interview. It remains to be seen what connection Aimee Lee's son may have with the current arson string.

Fontana was almost finished with his second reading when the phone rang. "Isn't it awful? I've been on the horn nonstop, Mac. Everybody wants to know what the hell's going on. What am I going to tell them?"

"Tell them Jeffers twisted the facts, Mo."

"But, Mac, did you say any of those things? 'If he hadn't done it the next firefighter would have'?"

"He's good, Mo. He's a regular little purveyor of hate. I did say most of those things. It's the spin he puts on them that makes them lies."

"Listen, Mac. Anybody else asks you any questions, I want you to refer them to me. Savvy?"

"Yesterday you were ordering me to talk to Jeffers."

"I've changed my mind. But tell me something. You've been seeing her all along, haven't you? You followed her out here."

"Who?"

"Aimee Lee. No wonder you were never interested in anything but dancing."

"Mo, a little while ago when you said you were on my side it meant a lot to me. Don't go ruining it."

Her gravelly voice became subdued. "But, Mac? How could you have said our actions Friday night were unfortunate and regrettable? Everybody worked so hard at that fire. I have bruises all over my legs."

"I said it about the fire death."

"Let me read you something here. 'Chief Fontana admitted that this sort of inattention to proper procedure is "about normal for the fire we had." ' Why on earth would you say that?"

"I said the *ventilation* was about normal for the fire we had. And thanks for the support, Mo."

"I don't know if I am supporting you."

"Yeah. Thanks."

Later in the morning Fontana dialed Sally Culpepper's number, but it had been disconnected.

Around eleven the incoming calls began.

By noon, in the middle of a mammoth Monopoly game with Brendan and Mary, he'd received close to two dozen calls from volunteers and townspeople, some commiserating over his mistreatment by the press, most accepting the article at face value and wanting explanations. Few callers were able to purge their voices of judgment. Fontana found himself angrier and angrier. People grunted and said they understood, then wondered aloud why Robinson Jeffers would write something that wasn't the truth. After all, Jeffers was a genius. Everybody knew that.

What stung more than anything was Mary sitting across his kitchen table from him with the Monopoly thimble in her hand. "Lordy, Mac. You were featured in the Sunday *Seattle Times*. How many people can say that? So you people walked on Mother. We're going to bury her in two days and then everybody can walk on her."

Brendan grew quiet and wide-eyed. Fontana said, "We'll miss her, won't we, Brendan?" The boy nodded.

"Oh, I'll miss her, too," said Mary. "But not enough to keep her aboveground."

Brendan said, "Why didn't *you* come get us?"

"What?"

"Mary said you were coming to get us. But it was Frank."

"Brendan, in the fire department we all work as a team. I have my job and Weed has his. If I'd gone inside, nobody else would have known what to do. I wanted to get you. Believe me I did, but I knew you were going to be all right."

"You knew Frank was going to save us?"

"I knew Frank was going to save you." It was hard to tell whether Brendan was buying it, even harder to tell if he was buying it himself. "Do you understand?"

"Sure."

"You know, Brendan, you're a hero too. When you told Mary to keep the door closed, you probably saved all of your lives."

"I did?"

"You betcha." Brendan grinned.

When the phone rang, Fontana picked it up and carried it into the other room. "Mac? This is Sally."

"I tried to call you earlier, but your number's been disconnected."

"We had to change it. I called because Audie brought the article from this morning's paper to me and it pretty much names him as a suspect. He's awfully upset. Can you come over?"

A half hour later, Fontana and Brendan pulled up to the black, wrought-iron gate in front of Sally Culpepper's home. He thought at first she'd invited others, but when he got close he realized the two cars parked in front were tourists snapping pictures. The gate opened, and he drove past the rubberneckers into the circular drive where one of the garage doors was rising.

Looking drawn and tense in the dark garage, Sally waved them in and watched them park, leading them out the rear of the complex into the backyard out of view of sightseers.

Fontana followed her onto the deck while Brendan authored a trail of blurry footprints in the grass, running to greet Audie at the rope swing. When Brendan said, "Did you know there aren't any snakes in Ireland?" Audie replied, "Not even pythons?"

She wore khaki shorts and a blue halter top, the tanned muscu-lature of her midriff standing out when she moved. She had on step-in sandals, and her legs were browned evenly. A pitcher of lemonade sat next to a plate of cookies on a small glass-topped table. When she called them, the boys ran over, scooped up a handful of cookies each, and traipsed back to the swing. She was smaller than she looked in the movies and somewhat prettier; or was he only comparing her to the Sally Culpepper he'd met on the school playground, the woman with the pistol and the buckteeth and the padded pantyhose? Her greenish-brown eyes seemed more alive than the gray eyes she'd had the night of the shooting. Of course, in the movies, she'd changed eye color depending upon the role, icy blue being the one Fontana re-membered most clearly.

"Audie collects newspaper accounts of these serial arsons. When he was mentioned in the paper this morning, he started trembling and I couldn't do anything to get him to stop. It wasn't until I said I'd call you he relaxed a little."

"He seems all right now."

"I know." She crossed her bare legs. She was sitting in a white deck chair with her back to the yard, Fontana across from her facing the boys and the trees. Through a wooden fence on one side of the yard near the garage he could see the pasture but not the horses. "What troubles me is that the article more or less implies that Audie is the number-one suspect. I'm wondering if he didn't get that idea from Truax."

"I wouldn't worry about it. Our suspect is somebody who has a driver's license." Even as he said it, he realized that had been true for the first three nights of arsons but not necessarily for last Fri-day. Somebody on a bicycle could have lit the Sutterfields' house, then the Dumpster behind the Bedouin and the smaller fires on the old highway.

The sky had been overcast all morning, but the sun emerged now and was warming the yard and the deck and his legs.

"I'm sorry about what they did to you in the newspaper." She held her lemonade glass between her knees so casually he thought she was going to drop it. "I've had the same thing happen. All I ever wanted to do was to be an actress. To work in plays and maybe even the movies. Then everything just went blooey, and I had bodyguards and death threats and my photos in the tabloids. A reporter once told me *The National Enquirer* had fifteen people assigned to me full time. Can you imagine?"

"No."

Sally's mouth was full and wide. Her nose was long and had a slight curve at the tip. She looked at him and he could see the tendons in her neck. "I probably shouldn't be telling you these things. I'd tell my friends if I had any."

"I thought I was a friend."

"I guess I don't know what a friend is anymore. I thought I had two of them in L.A. They ended up blabbing all my secrets on a daytime television show. My druggist kept records of every prescription and eventually turned them over to a tabloid. Last night I watched the man who sold me that Bronco out there telling a national TV audience I'd talked to him about sleeping with an unnamed president. Like I would discuss my sex life with a total stranger?"

"Jesus," said Fontana.

"I'm not trying to say you're not my friend. I'm just saying I've been burned."

"Not by me."

"We went into town yesterday to buy groceries and I didn't wear my disguise for the first time. By the time I got to my truck there were so many cars in the lot we couldn't get out. I had to use the cell phone to call Greta and have her pick us up." Across the yard, Audie and Brendan were on their hands and knees huddled over Brendan's magnifying glass, frying twigs, leaves, and—if Fontana knew boys—ants. "You were kind to me before you knew who I was. You were kind to Audie."

He shrugged.

"And thank you for not saying anything to Jeffers about our . . . 'long-term relationship' . . ." She gave him a look, and after a moment they burst into laughter. They laughed so hard the boys looked up from the smoking ants.

TWENTY-TWO

◆

LISTS

The fire death Friday night aroused panic and paranoia in the Northwest, especially in communities that had experienced arsons.

In Lake City, a cab driver who'd walked an elderly woman to her door was jumped and roughed up by three college football players who thought he was the arsonist. While investigating suspicious activities in an alley on a block where two fires had occurred a month earlier, a Seattle policewoman was shot at by an unknown assailant. Seattle's two daily papers penned editorials about vigilance and community spirit. All three major television stations began weeklong specials. Coverage was given to the fire death in Staircase, with a brief bio of Lorraine; to recaps of the arsons—dates, locations, dollar losses; and to statements from various members of the State Arson Task Force, including Jenny Underhill. One enterprising reporter went so far as to solicit observations from incarcerated arsonists.

With the exception of the Sutterfield fire, most of the Staircase arsons had been relatively minor; not so for the rest of the Puget Sound area. The majority of newspaper accounts centered on details of the fires. Maps were printed with keyed legends depicting the fire locations within the three counties involved. Interviews were conducted. Angry survivors vented their rage. Burned-out business people provided lost-job stories. The letters columns in the papers were swamped. Feature stories were written on the Seattle firefighter who'd fallen off a roof and broken her back at a fire. Most of the radio and television stations and all of the newspapers advocated smoke detectors.

By Monday afternoon Fontana had spoken to enough townsfolk that he knew he wanted to avoid the others. Three council members cross-examined him, each with his or her own unpleasant technique for diplomacy, each carrying a copy of Sunday's paper. Did he really think *anybody* could have rescued the victims? Why had he allowed them to trample the old woman? How had the fire gotten out of control? And worst of all, why had Fontana denigrated his own fire department?

Frank Weed and his girlfriend subscribed to a local clipping service to augment the half dozen newspapers they purchased each day. "Never know when you're going to miss something," Weed said, happily. "That piece in the *Bremerton Sun* we found was sheer luck."

"Good you caught it," Fontana said, thinking he heard a note of condescension in his own voice.

"Sheer luck."

During the first four days of the next week, Frank Weed's fire-fighting exploits were chronicled in many of the dailies and weeklies in the state. *People* magazine commissioned a piece on him, flying a photographer up from San Francisco. Oprah contacted him for inclusion in a program to be titled "Reluctant Heroes."

"I don't see nothin' reluctant about it" was Kingsley's comment.

Weed's hometown paper in West Virginia called and conducted a telephone interview. Two radio commentators and a television news show from West Virginia aired interviews by phone. A journalism student from his old high school called and wanted to do an article. Frank had been entertaining an on-again, off-again relationship with his girlfriend during the past few weeks, but now Sheri was firmly by his side and ecstatic.

Sheri began spending time with Frank at the station, scissoring out articles and sealing them into a pair of leather-bound scrapbooks, discussing the most recent interview requests with anybody unable to think of a good excuse to slip out of the beanery.

Bree McAllister's producers decided to reenact the fatal fire on film and, in an astonishingly short time, found an old house not five miles from the station, received official permission to set contained fires in it for the reenactment, and recruited King County Fire District 10 to help out Staircase with manpower and equipment.

Fontana knew a training fire would serve his tiny department well, but he wasn't convinced that exploiting Lorraine's death for television was a decent or even a moral act.

In the end, after the city council began putting on pressure, he went along with it.

Tuesday, at the training fires in an abandoned house near the Mount Gadd trailhead, film crews shot Weed running back and forth with a pick-head ax. Nearly three quarters of the volunteers showed up.

Once again, Weed stunned everyone with the ease with which he slid into the role of television notable. In fact, Weed's readiness to play the hero was beginning to get on the nerves of more people than just Sandusky and Lieutenant Pierpont.

Most of Thursday was spent cleaning equipment used at the training fires and hanging wet hose in the tower. There had been no arsons anywhere in the state all week.

Between Sunday and Thursday, Staircase had only a few alarms. There was another false alarm at Sun Country; a campfire under a bridge that had been mistaken for a hostile fire; an EMS run during which a fifty-four-year-old man with chest pain was taken to Overlake Hospital in the medic unit; a "man down" alarm that turned out to be a tourist from Virginia who had fallen asleep in his car while waiting for a glimpse of Aimee Lee; and a tripped system at the nursing home, where they eventually got blind Jake to admit he'd pulled the alarm box again.

Thursday night a community meeting was scheduled. Mo Costigan, Roger Truax, Jenny Underhill, and Fontana were to address the meeting and field questions. Larry and Rena Sutterfield, who had been on a cruise ship off the Mexican coast the night their house burned, had been, due to a series of untoward complications, unable to fly back until shortly before the meeting. The children were still with their grandmother.

When Fontana and Brendan arrived at the elementary school a half hour prior to the eight o'clock meeting, a thin cloud blanket had blurred into pinks and oranges in the west. It would have been a good evening to spend at the river with his son and his fly rod, Fontana thought.

In a town as small as Staircase, people didn't have to show up early for meetings, yet the elementary school lot was full, as was the auxiliary lot near the gym. They parked two blocks down the street, and as they got out of the truck, two more cars parked behind them. Outside of deer season, Fontana had never seen so many filled gun racks. Despite jacking up their prices, the owner of the sporting goods store in town bragged he'd sold every pistol he could get his hands on. Fontana wondered who these people were planning to shoot. So far, nobody had seen anything.

Girl Scouts in uniform stood in the doorways passing out printed programs. Brendan took one and studied it with his tongue at the corner of his mouth. The credentials of each speaker were itemized behind his or her name and Truax's résumé was longer than the other three put together.

"Dad, can I sit with Audie?"

"Is he here?"

"Gee, Dad," Brendan said, taking his hand and dragging him up the aisle. Audie was sitting in the fifth row back.

"Hey, Audie," Fontana said.

"Dad's gotta talk. But I'll sit with you. Can I, Dad?"

"Sure." Fontana absently scanned the milling men and women over his son's head. "Just be sure and stick around afterward. I don't want to be looking for you."

Since Mo's announcement of the meeting, a general stir of excitement had been coursing through the town, flavored with a liberal portion of machismo, as if they were somehow going to apprehend the arsonist at the meeting—perhaps lynch him from a basketball hoop.

Men were armed with personal video cameras. Women were armed with infants and baby bottles. One aisle over from Fontana, a local CBS affiliate news crew was shooting a clip. More cameras and newspaper photographers were lined up against either wall under the tilted-up basketball backboards.

As Fontana scanned the crowd, a middle-aged woman with bad teeth winked at him from several rows back. He looked over the crowd once more, but his eyes fell on the woman again. Her ears jutted out of a mass of gray, uncombed hair. He moved down the aisle toward the rear of the building.

When he got halfway down the aisle, Fontana heard somebody whispering, "Chief. Chief." It was the gray-haired woman who'd winked.

"Good God," he said. "What the hell are you doing?"

Placing her index finger across her lips, Sally Culpepper looked forward and said, "I didn't need to sit with Audie. A lot of people know who he is."

"You are really good, lady."

"Thanks."

Packed into an ivory-colored suit, Mo Costigan was waving her arms in a heated discussion with a tall newsman. Her high heels compressed her calves into knots.

"Mac?" Mo Costigan barreled through the crowd, pushing men, women, and children out of the way, smiling officially at her victims. "This has been mapped down to the very last detail, and I don't want you throwing any wing nuts into the gears. Are you listening?"

"Mo, why do you always assume I'm going to spoil your events?"

"We had to give CBS the local live exclusive, but we've got three national crews filming as well. It's going to be great."

"I'm happy for you, Mo. Maybe we'll get some national exposure, and it will lead to a flood of newcomers and a new goddamn home every fifty feet all the way up and down Rattlesnake Mountain."

"We can only hope." The gymnasium was more crowded than he had ever seen it, the running children and the occasional laughter only making things noisier. A strand of hair had come loose and was pasted to the perspiration on Mo's forehead. Her neck and breastbone were shiny with sweat. "Mac, I forgot my notes, but I need to organize the rest of these people. Would you be a dear and run back to my office? They're in a file folder on top of my desk. Here." She pulled a set of keys out of her purse.

Clad in his black dress uniform, Lieutenant Pierpont met him in the doorway. "Can you run me over to the mayor's office for a minute?" Fontana asked. "Mo forgot something."

"Sheeeeeiiit," Kingsley said. "Sending the chief on errands. She forgot on purpose."

"Yeah, I think maybe she did."

As they exited together, Frank Weed lumbered up the walkway wearing bunking pants and carrying his coat and helmet, perspiring heavily from the combination of heavy pants, warm air, and exertion. "What's up?" Fontana asked.

"Oh, no," said Weed. "I thought you knew."

"Knew what?"

"The mayor wants me in my bunkers." Weed rolled his eyes as if perturbed by the request, though he clearly was pleased.

"I'm sorry, Chief," said Kingsley. "The mayor said you knew. We can keep him out here on the rig if—"

"No, that's fine. Whatever dingleberry plan she's hatched is fine."

Manned by two volunteers, Engine One was parked in front of the flagpole in the fire lane at the school's main entrance. Fontana and Kingsley rode in the crew cab behind the driver, the breeze chilling them after the muggy gymnasium.

In front of the fire station, Fontana got off the rig and walked around the corner to the permit office, using Mo's key on the door. The stairs to her office were dark, and he didn't bother to switch on the light because there was a haze of amber light filtering through the high windows. It was a spacious room with a large maple desk at one end, windows overlooking the street at the other. He quickly found the folder marked ARSONS SPEECH and then spotted another manila folder on the desk labeled ARSONS: QUESTIONS AND ANSWERS.

He sat down.

There were two pages of handwritten notes. The first page contained lists. The first list was labeled "Suspects." Under that was written, "Seattle firebug? Volunteer? Culpepper brat?" He recognized the small, crabby penmanship as Roger Truax's.

Farther down the page was written, "Audie Willeford Culpepper." And then "Q & A session." Had they brought Audie into the office for questioning without Fontana's knowledge or authorization? Next to several of the questions was the notation "R. Jeffers." Had Jeffers been present? As near as he could tell from the scribbled notes, the questions had been an equal mix revolving around the fires and Sally's personal life, but judging from the sporadic notes in the answer column, Audie had not divulged much of anything. Fontana was willing to wager Audie's mother knew nothing of this, because if she had, he would have heard from her.

Another list on the second page was labeled "Allies." Below that were the names of two city council persons, Mo, Truax, Jeffers, J. Clunk, and a deputy chief in Seattle's department Fontana had antagonized last year. Among the rest of the names, fifteen in all, he noticed Kim and Jesse Rothem, the well-to-do couple who'd had the garage fire over near the golf course. Allies? Allies against whom? And to what purpose? The two council people listed were known to be in Mo's hip pocket, but the others were a cartel of staid citizenry and misfits. The only commonality Fontana could find was that none of them particularly liked him.

TWENTY-THREE

♦

EASY EXITS

In the gymnasium, people were beginning to overflow into the aisles. Fontana sat on the podium on a metal chair beside Jennifer Underhill. "I miss anything?"

"A kid threw up over in the corner."

Thirty feet distant, Mo Costigan was on the gym floor yakking at a camera crew. The other speaker, Truax, was not to be seen.

"By the way," Underhill said, "we found out something interesting about one of your fires."

"Let me guess. The Rothems'?"

"How did you know? In New Hampshire back in 1980, when he was married to his first wife, Jesse Rothem's condo, which he'd been trying to off-load in a down market, was conveniently gutted by fire. He and his wife claimed they'd gone to the opera and left a candle burning. The opera. Some people are so much closer to God. Three years later, in the middle of an ugly divorce, his wife goes to the New Hampshire authorities and tells them Jesse had hired some crazy high school kid to burn the condo down, that their valuables and photo albums had been moved to another location beforehand. Rothem claimed his wife fabricated the story because he was planning to marry his secretary—her former best friend. For lack of any real proof the insurance company ended up allowing the claim. Then in 1984 in Cincinnati, Jesse Rothem's BMW was torched by vandals. Same thing happened to his Mercedes in 1988 in Philadelphia."

"He get paid off on the cars?"

"Yep. The house here was put on the market six months ago. The people we spoke to said they're asking about thirty grand too much."

"I didn't see any real estate sign."

"Took it down a couple of days before the fire. They could have planned this and then sat back and waited for a night when our friend was in town. Used a fire scanner."

"You talk to them?"

"We asked them to come in yesterday. Our answer was a polite call from a law firm in Federal Way."

"We were wondering why our arsonist would hit a home in a cul-de-sac. The rest of his fires had easy exits."

"The only glitch is the other fire a few blocks away."

"Maybe the Rothems set that as a diversion."

"Maybe."

The crowd seemed at times to veer toward becoming a mob. Fontana recognized most of the faces, even if he didn't know all of the names. He saw neighbors, volunteers, volunteers' wives and girlfriends, and in one case a volunteer with his wife on one side and his girlfriend sitting a row over. He saw local merchants, teachers from Brendan's school. He saw the Rothems, Kim and Jesse. One foot dirtying the wall behind him, Joshua Clunk stood against the far wall next to a news crew. Having already seen three guns dangling from pockets, Fontana wondered if Clunk was carrying one.

In the first row, Frank Weed sat in full bunkers, his heavy coat buttoned, his yellow helmet on the floor at his feet. Beside him, the four Sutterfield kids sat kicking their legs contentedly, the youngest in trapdoor pajamas. Their grandmother sat at the end of the row.

Stumping purposefully across the front of the gym, Jenny Underhill's partner, Beasley, operated a video camera. Fontana thought him too short to do an effective job of capturing faces, and as if reading Fontana's mind, he climbed onto the small stage and resumed filming. "I'd be surprised if you don't have him on film already," Fontana said.

"I'm sure we do," said Underhill. "We've recognized a bunch of firebugs in our pictures. Checking them all out is the problem. None of us have ever worked on anything with this much evidence. We've got interviews and physical evidence from almost fifty fires, plus probably fifty tips a day from the public. There's no way we can check it all out.

"We have ten volunteers working seven days a week entering data—every name, every address, every tip—into our computer, and they haven't even scratched the surface. Without another piece of new data, it's going to take two months to enter it all."

At the side entrance at the far right of the podium, H. C. Bailey, in her natty brown King County Police uniform, her hand resting on the butt of her holstered gun, looked over the gathering as if deciding which of them to shoot first.

Another three or four minutes passed before Truax came in, and then Mo Costigan hiked up her skirt and stepped onto the podium, tapping the microphone with a fingernail. As soon as the room quieted, she called for the Pledge of Allegiance. Afterward she said, "I'd like to have everyone remain standing so that we can bow our heads in a moment of silence for the member of our community we've lost. Let us also pray for the gallant brothers and sisters in our little fire department who risk their lives every time they go out on a call."

Except for some restless babies, the entire congregation lapsed into a silence that was noteworthy for its unexpected solemnity. Even the flag salute hadn't stopped the background gibbering the way Mo's prayer had. She held the throng in silence longer than anybody would have guessed possible, her head bowed long after others were surreptitiously checking to see if everyone else had tiptoed out. She had taken total charge of the assembly. One of the reasons Fontana had never written Mo off was just this sort of astonishing moment she seemed instinctively able to conjure up.

"Before we do anything else," Mo said, her words prompting the crowd to sit in unison, "I'd like to reunite four children with their parents, whom we've just now flown in from Mexico."

"Oh, no," groaned Fontana.

Lights blazing, television crews converged on the Sutterfield kids from two directions. It wasn't until Frank Weed stood and put his helmet on that Fontana realized what Mo was planning.

Following some hidden cue, H. C. Bailey opened the outside door, letting in Larry and Rena Sutterfield. Inspired by the cameras and the lights, the crowd began clapping, slowly at first, and then faster and louder, stamping their feet, whistling and cheering, as Frank Weed staggered toward the Sutterfields with their four children, carrying the two little ones under his arms like bed rolls. Even if no one else did, the smaller children realized the ridiculousness of their situation and giggled throughout the long trip across the floor. The wooden gymnasium floor pulsed. Onlookers craned their necks, rushed forward in the aisles, or stood on chairs, some surreptitiously dabbing at the corners of suddenly moist eyes.

Rena Sutterfield broke across the gym floor, sweeping up her two oldest in her arms, while Frank deposited the other two at her feet. When Fontana looked up at Mo, she was watching him, tiny tears dimpling her eyes. She mouthed, "National. National." Fontana gave her a limp smile.

Mr. Sutterfield pumped Weed's hand, but the mother kissed Weed on both cheeks, then hugged him for a good fifteen seconds. She looked tiny clutched in Weed's arms, Weed in his bulky bunking trousers and coat and tall rubber boots. The rookie firefighter took it all with stoic grace, although he hadn't had the sense to remove the liners from his bunkers and consequently was sweating like a banker in a sauna. Sheri stood near the doorway next to H. C. Bailey, looking surprisingly grim. Fontana would have thought she'd be beaming.

The crowd, which had been clapping to some sort of phantom beat, grew louder and shriller, whistling and hooting and rattling the metal fold-up chairs. Kingsley Pierpont caught Fontana's eye from the back of the room and, shaking his head slowly, mouthed his pet expletive, "Sheeeeiiit."

Weed, his girlfriend, the Sutterfields and their children, the grandmother, and one news crew exited out the side door. Last in line, Frank Weed turned and waved slowly to the crowd, moving his arm like a beauty queen on a float. The gesture spurred a tidal wave of noise throughout the building, louder and more deafening than anything before.

Oddly, the crowd settled down quickly. Mo stood at the lectern one more time, notes in hand. "Ladies and gentlemen. Boys and girls.

Victims. We are facing a crisis the like of which we have never before faced. . . ."

It was a poignant speech, but each time Mo made a point, a drunk in the middle section shouted, "Amen, Sister!" prompting stifled giggles here and there. Before she finished, Mo said, "I'm very happy to announce that the head of our fire department, Chief Fontana, will be stepping down from his chief's duties for a few weeks to work exclusively on this string of arsons. In the meantime, Roger Truax will head up the department." In your dreams, Fontana thought.

Truax spoke next, and having Truax give a speech, Fontana decided, was a good way to leach the spirit from any mob. Truax's dreary monotone and self-conscious use of six-dollar words blunted their blood lust the way no amount of common sense could have. Only the drunk in the middle section kept his spirits up. Each new "Amen, Sister!" sparked a wave of laughter and caused Audie and Brendan to burst into paroxysms.

". . . Finally, the constituents of our community have three specific avenues of redress," an undaunted Truax droned. "Firstly: regularly scheduled vigilante patrols from midnight to six A.M. At this point in time I will be organizing and facilitating said patrols. Secondly, Mayor Costigan has previously explicated: having Chief Fontana relinquish his customary duties so as to enable him to serve pro tem on the arson investigation. Thirdly: as your community leaders, we are requesting property owners habituated in the valley to clear their establishments of all unsecured debris or detritus: loose lumber, derelict automobiles with inflammable components, dry vegetation, and such. Every blade of dry grass will be cropped. All outbuildings will be secured. We will be processing informational flyers this weekend, and the fire department will be expediting block-by-block inspections as well as follow-ups. Hopefully, inside of two weeks every homeowner under our umbrella will have been contacted by fire department personnel pursuant to this end."

"Amen, Sister!"

"As you are aware, this serial arsonist we are confronting scrutinizes targets of opportunity. At this point in time we can only downsize the quantity of those targets. It will necessitate some diligence on the part of the populace, but if we all cooperate, we can make this a town you'll be proud to drive through once again." Truax sat down to a smattering of applause and some grumbling and shuffling of feet. Fontana heard someone say under his breath, "I'm proud to drive through this town now."

Jenny Underhill spoke next. Jenny gave a brief overview of the arson situation, listed all the region's suspected arson strikes in the past forty-five days, and spoke favorably of Staircase's firefighting efforts.

She concluded by saying: "I don't know if any of you realize it, but you have one of the most renowned arson experts in the country right here. I'd like to hear Chief Fontana's opinion of our arsonist, if he doesn't mind."

She sat down to applause that grew louder and more enthusiastic as Fontana rose and slowly walked to the podium. It was nice to know he still had some support after the article in Sunday's paper.

"I wasn't going to bring this up," Fontana said into the microphone. The applause died down. "But as long as Ms. Underhill has requested it, I will offer a few thoughts. First, statistics indicate our arsonist is probably male. This individual feeds on the publicity he's been receiving and is probably preoccupied with the news reports on the arsons. The empowerment of causing all this ruckus is what keeps him going. His work and sleep patterns might be, and probably are, out of kilter and have been since the start of the fires. It's possible he's dropped hints to his friends or even bragged about it. If you know anybody who fits this profile, give the task force hot line a call. Or call me, and I'll pass it along. Despite what our mayor said, I will continue to run the fire department during the investigation of this case. I have no intention of abandoning my duties to Mr. Truax or anyone else."

Fontana went on to give an overview of their firefighting efforts, their training, the practice fires they'd set on Tuesday, and the regulars switching over to night shifts.

During the question and answer session only three people left the building, each carrying a fussy infant. When the meeting broke up,

Fontana worked his way through the milling masses to Brendan and Audie.

Without fanfare, Audie's mother appeared beside her son, back hunched, shuffling along in a stoop nobody paid attention to. She looked thirty years older and peppery enough to sidestep.

"I need to talk to you," Fontana said.

"We're catching a plane tonight," she replied. "In fact, we're late. Audie just had to see this. I'll be back Saturday afternoon. Why don't we go to the Bedouin Saturday evening? We can talk on the way over."

"You sure?"

"Pick me up at eight."

A moment later, Mo Costigan gripped Fontana's arm and said, "How dare you contradict me in public! Who the blazes do you think you are?"

"How dare you give away my job without consulting me. You thought I embarrassed you tonight? Mo, I gave you a break. Next time I'll really make you look bad."

"A break? You killed me. I gave probably the most important speech of my political career, and after I got done, you stood up and pissed all over everything."

"Mo, you want me to hand over the reins to Truax, you ask me. You don't announce I've agreed to it in front of seven hundred people."

"When I was writing my speech this afternoon, I didn't have time to look you up. I thought you'd want this. For godsakes, I thought you were going to thank me, not stand up and piss all over the salad."

"That's piss in the soup, Mo. Common courtesy. That's all I want." She glared at him for several long moments and then got vacuumed into a conversation that had been going on behind her and to which she had been half listening.

Roger Truax was nearby answering questions of several obviously irate citizens. His wife, who had a chubby little round face that Fontana had always thought looked as if it might serve as a swell pencil eraser, stood quietly nearby, seeming neither interested in what her husband was saying, nor in any particular hurry for him to finish. Fontana had always sensed something awry with their relationship, but he'd never heard it put into words until Sandusky said once, "The first time I saw them together, I tried to figure out why he married a lesbian." While the remark may not have coined the truth, it was an interesting perspective.

Both Truaxes doted on their three-year-old daughter, whom they had recently enrolled in a mail-order intelligence-building program that had them teaching her the state capitals with flash cards.

Fontana moved behind Truax and said, "I have a word with you?"

Excusing himself, Truax stepped close. Even with the doors open, the gymnasium was hot and muggy and saturated with the stink of armpits, chewing tobacco, perfume, body odor, bad breath, deodorant, hair spray, and just a whiff of dog crap.

"Next time you want to take over my job, you ask me, you don't go sneaking around having secret meetings with the mayor and conniving. Got that?"

"It was as big a surprise to me as it was to you. Honestly. I couldn't believe my ears. Me? Chief? What could she have been thinking of?"

"Bullshit."

"I swear, Mac. On my mother's grave. I didn't put her up to it."

"And what makes you think you can triple the workload of my department without consulting me? *You* go around telling people to pick up their trash and *you* inspect afterward. *You* do that. My people are so busy they don't have time to shit."

"Well, what the heck are they doing?"

"They're drilling, taking care of their equipment, attending classes, and doing the regular building inspections they do every year. They're making sure they're well prepared for the next round of arsons, and they're handling the daily emergencies this town expects them to handle. You ought to know the days of checker tournaments in fire stations are long gone."

"But, Mac, the public needs to have the perception that something is being done."

"You've committed the fire department to hundreds of hours of bullshit. And vigilante patrols? Are you nuts? Who gave you permission to do that?"

"The council. Last meeting. You should have been there."

"You can bet your fat ass I'll be at the next one."

"You should have been at the last one. I'm sorry you don't agree, but as safety director, these inspections were my call and I made it the way I saw it. I'll be bringing the forms and the rest of the paperwork around tomorrow morning."

"And I'll be shoving them up your ass."

They stared at each other for a few moments. Until recently, Fontana had mistakenly believed his foremost political foe in town was Mo Costigan.

As if it were a planned ambush, Roger Truax stepped away and Robinson Jeffers appeared from the crowded aisle from behind a photographer. "Mind if I ask a few questions?"

"Get lost," Fontana said.

Outside, Brendan said, "Are you really going to shove papers up—"

"That was just a figure of speech."

◆

TWENTY-FOUR

SECRET LOVE NEST

Like a doting mother checking up on her children, Mo had been in the habit of dropping in at the fire station at least once a day, but Friday and Saturday passed without any communication between Mo and Fontana.

Truax, who had promised to drop by with the paperwork regarding home inspections, had not shown up either.

On Friday afternoon, Fontana learned why Sandusky probably had not scored high enough to get a job in Staircase. He'd had the flu on the day of the physical abilities test.

"Who wanted to work in a Podunk fire department, anyway?" said Sandusky. "I'm in Seattle. The big time."

"Hell," said Valenzuela, oblivious to the hood of despair that had come over Sandusky when the subject came up, "I've never seen anybody get even close to your record for the obstacle course out back. Man, you looked like death on a stick that day. I could see the glands under your jaw." Valenzuela might have said more, but he looked up and realized Sandusky had left the room.

Sandusky's irreverent, often juvenile, sometimes greasy humor aside, Fontana was sorry he hadn't made the cut last fall when they tested for permanent positions.

Late Friday evening when Lindoff came back from his vacation, Weed rushed to his locker, got the videotapes of his television interviews, and inserted one into the video player. "You seen these yet?" he asked.

"He rescues one more kid and we're going to have to put a contract out on him," Lieutenant Pierpont said in the watch office.

"It's even getting on my nerves," said Fontana. "The trouble is, it's nobody's fault, really. You hit the lotto, people hate you. It's human nature."

"No," said Pierpont, touching his mustache. "You hit the lotto, you turn into a butt. *That*'s human nature."

The fact was, any one of them might have been the individual who'd found the children, and they all knew it and accepted it as part of their job description. That Weed had been the hero had been chance as much as anything else, and because it could have been *any* of them, any microbe of gloating on Weed's part was magnified to the size of a redwood by the others.

By Friday night, it became obvious from Frank's moodiness that something was wrong. The station visits by his girlfriend had ceased, and the phone calls back and forth had dwindled. Eventually they wormed it out of him. The kisses Frank had exchanged with Rena Sutterfield in the auditorium Thursday night had lit Sheri up like "firecrackers in a doghouse," Frank confessed.

"The hug wasn't so bad, but she went off on those kisses," Frank said. "She's really pissed. I told her I didn't do any kissing, but that didn't help. She says I enjoyed it waaaaaay too much."

After a few moments, Sandusky said, "How much did you enjoy it?"

Weed looked around the room and slowly grinned. Everybody laughed.

Saturday afternoon in the checkout line at QFC, Brendan, who had a habit of perusing the tabloid racks, hopped forward and said, "Hey, Mac. Look. That's Audie's house."

Feeling the blood drain from his face, Fontana pulled the tabloid out of the rack. One of the cover shots was of him striding across a yard, an out-of-focus building in the background, Sally Culpepper standing behind him at the corner of the building with a wistful look on her face. The headline said MORNING AFTER—FIRE CHIEF LEAVES AIMEE LEE'S SECRET LOVE NEST.

Morning after? Hell, it had been the middle of the afternoon and they'd visited for an hour, sipped lemonade through straws, and munched sandwich cookies on the patio in full view of their children. He didn't even know what the inside of her house looked like. He realized Brendan had been airbrushed out of the picture.

The QFC checker, a dewy-eyed brunette with braces on her teeth, was shy enough she wasn't going to say anything about the tabloids, though he could see she knew all about them. He hadn't made the cover of the second paper, but Sally Culpepper had. The caption said, AIMEE LEE—THE MYSTERIOUS LIFE. Inside were articles about her squandered talent, her "backward" son, and covert visits from a mid-eastern playboy worth billions. And then, EX-SHERIFF MIFFED: THREATENS HASAD.

After Fontana and Brendan had driven home and put the groceries away, they sat side by side on the sofa in the living room. Fontana found his hands shaking, the newspaper blurring.

The first tabloid contended he was having an affair with Aimee Lee and had been for years, that she'd renounced her acting career and gone underground because of him. In an article that was mostly about a billionaire sheik said to be courting Aimee Lee, the second paper called Fontana a "mankiller," branded him a "broken-down ex-arson investigator" who wore shabby jeans and flannel shirts and skulked around town in a beat-up 1960 GMC Carryall.

"Hey, Dad," Brendan said, reading the first paper while Fontana read the second.

"What is it?"

"Is a mankiller what I think it is?"

"Somebody who's killed another man."

"Did you do that?"

"Last summer. When that Dugan was chasing Bobby Joe Allan's wife and her sister with the gun. I told you about it."

"You killed him?"

"I didn't feel good about it, but yes, I killed him."

"How?"

"With a shotgun."

After a while, Brendan said, "Is Mrs. Culpepper my mother?"

"Of course not. What makes you say that?"

"It says here eight years ago Aimee Lee had an affair with you and you kept the child." Brendan's voice shrank.

"Linda was your mother. I was there. I should know. You're the best thing we ever did together. Not only that, I never had a love affair with Aimee Lee. I didn't even know the woman until this month. I loved your mother very much and she loved us very much. And I love you. These are all lies." He ruffled his son's coarse chestnut hair which looked and felt so much like Linda's, then kissed the top of his head.

"If it's a lie, why did they write it?"

"I don't know."

Brendan read slowly, helped with the more difficult words by his father. " 'A fuming Chief Fontana concedes Aimee Lee's son is the chief suspect in a fatal fire that killed the Chief's own neighbor.' Did Audie set that fire?"

"I don't think so."

"But didn't anybody ever tell them it was wrong to lie?"

"Brendan, when you get older, you'll see that what you think is the right thing to do and what will get you money are often two different critters. A lot of people end up making the wrong decisions." Fontana realized there was nothing as heartbreaking as an eight-year-old's indignation at his first inkling that the world was crooked.

The room was quiet for a few moments. Satan made noises licking his flank on the hearth. Still swollen and green from melting snow in the mountains, the river whispered against its rocky banks. From somewhere high in the sky came the loud, clear whistle of an osprey.

At a quarter past seven that evening the phone rang. It was Audie asking Fontana to bring Brendan when he came over to pick up his mother. They arrived five minutes early, and the front door of the house swung inward to reveal Audie's pale, oval face floating in the blackness. The front gate clicked and swung around on its motor. Fontana drove around the circular lane to the house and watched Sally come down the front steps. Brendan gave him a kiss on the cheek and shot out of the truck like a piece of wadding out of a cannon. His first words to the older boy were, "Did you know no piece of paper can be folded in half more than seven times?"

Her hair was cut bluntly at chin level and swung from side to side across her bloodless cheeks when she climbed into the ancient GMC, slamming the door twice before it was secured. She wore a violet silk blouse that brought out the highlights in her jet-black hair, and snug jeans tucked into cowboy boots with purple floral designs etched into them. He wondered if she was embarrassed to be riding in the truck. A lot of women would have been.

"I thought you wouldn't come," she said.

"I thought you wouldn't want me to."

"I'm sorry about the stories. You *have* seen them?"

"*You* didn't write them."

"No. Jeffers did."

"Did he? They weren't signed."

"Robinson Jeffers. He's been writing about me for years. He must have been on my trail, and then I went and shot those dogs. Why didn't I just send up rockets and wave a flag? I'm worried for Audie, though. You know he was home with me at the time of the fatal fire last Friday night. We were watching Bette Davis in *The Petrified Forest*. Was she really your neighbor? The woman who died?"

"Yes. It's hard on Brendan. He liked her a lot."

Avoiding the freeway, he took the old road past Truck Town and the State Patrol offices, past the isolated Mount Gadd tavern with the usual flock of cars and motorcycles parked outside, over the railroad tracks, past a cedar-shake mill, and then past one of the eleven Christmas tree farms in the valley. A trailer court. Past the side road Joshua Clunk's junkyard was on.

"Clunk ever bother you?"

"Who?"

"The man who owned the dogs."

"Oh, him. Not really. He followed me around the store the other day. Him and everyone else. That person you call the mayor was the worst. She tried to get me to autograph a can of Campbell's tomato soup. Asked me if I'd had my boobs done."

"Did you?"

"Have my boobs done?"

"Autograph the soup."

She laughed. "No."

High broken clouds had bedeviled the region all week. Tonight the streets were wet from a late afternoon shower, steam rising off the pavement and evaporating in the headlights. They drove past fields guarded by motionless horses. Beyond the pig farm, the eight-hundred-foot peak called Little Gadd rose in the darkness, the summit spotty with moss-covered boulders. A month earlier, Fontana and Brendan had lunched on those rocks.

"You asked me out when you thought I was overweight and unattractive," she said. "I wouldn't think a big, dog-killing woman would be your type."

"You were intriguing."

"And romance isn't part of your agenda anyway, is it?"

"Not really. Not anymore."

"It isn't part of mine either. But I'm glad to be finally getting out."

"I'm glad too."

♦

TWENTY-FIVE

GOING CRAZY IN PUBLIC

"You mind telling me something?" she asked.

"Not at all."

"How have you managed to escape all the divorced women out here?"

"It's going to sound dumb."

"I've heard dumb before."

"I'm still in love with my wife."

"That sounds sweet. And a little sad."

"It's pathetic, is what I think. I thought I was over it, but I guess not."

For reasons he'd never really figured out, he had been cheating on Linda for about a month right before a drunk crossed the center line and killed her. It wasn't something he'd done before, cheating, and he continued to feel guilty over it. She found out about it and then was killed before they had a chance to work it out together. Now it would never be resolved.

"I'm sorry."

"Everybody's got their crosses. At least I don't have Robinson Jeffers hounding me."

"You do *now*." She laughed. It trickled down from a high place somewhere and continued until it fused with laughter he recognized as his own.

He told her about the notes he'd found in the mayor's office, about Jeffers and Mo and Roger Truax and the conspiracy he thought they'd entered into to railroad her son. "You didn't know they questioned Audie, did you?"

"If I had, I would have left him in Carmel with my mother. I wish you hadn't told me. I am so upset."

"I wish it hadn't happened."

"Yeah. Me too. Well, let's go inside and try to forget it for a while." Fontana parked the truck in the angle-in parking behind the Bedouin. Twenty feet away, a group of college-age youths got out of a van and headed for the rear entrance. "The hurdle is my mother believes almost everything," she said. "If there's no truth to it, she says, 'Where did they get the story, then?' She reads I'm making it with Tom Cruise, even though I've only met Tom once, and she calls me up and chews me out for being promiscuous. She wrote a letter to the First Lady apologizing for an affair I supposedly had with the president. The Secret Service came out and interviewed her, if you can believe that. I've never even met the president."

"So you went down to prepare her for all this?"

"I had to. She's already had two heart attacks."

Making the best of the fact that nobody recognized her immediately, they went to the dance floor in the crush of couples, the jukebox and the monster speakers precluding any possibility of normal conversation. Culpepper's anonymity didn't last long. Hawkins noticed them from the bar at the far wall, elbowing a pair of his friends, Tolmi and Chavarria, volunteers all three, before heading onto the floor in an enormous cowboy hat and cowboy boots and tapping Fontana on the shoulder to cut in. Fontana said, "Not tonight, pal."

Tolmi and Chavarria guffawed during Hawkins's long walk back to the bar.

Fontana couldn't help noticing the news of her presence was now spreading through the crowd as if by osmosis. Newcomers would arrive, even newcomers in hiking shorts and boots, people who clearly did not have ties to the valley, and before they'd ordered their first slice of pizza or quaffed their first brew, a local would sidle over and clue them in.

"I guess you're used to this," Fontana said.

"Once I was. It's not a good thing to get used to. You know what's strange about it? You get famous and everybody changes but you. At least that's the way it seems. It's like going crazy in public."

"Most of these people would give almost anything to be as famous as you."

"They're idiots."

"Maybe it's television. There's a man in our station who's getting a whole lot of press because he rescued five people at the fire Friday night. Says this is going to be the highlight of his life. Says he's not rich but at least he's famous."

They were sitting at a table off in a corner under the gaze of a stuffed deer head, she sipping wine, he pulling on a beer, when Roger Truax deserted his wife and waded through the dancing couples toward them. Roger wore dress shoes, loose-fitting jeans, a fringed western shirt bursting at the seams, and a belt buckle that might have made a swell hubcap.

"Hello there. Hello there," Truax said, in his dulcet tones, never once taking his eyes off Sally. "Miss Lee. We've met before. The night you eliminated those dogs. I'm sure you recall me." His words were soft, and the volume of his voice seemed to go up and down so that if you weren't listening closely, you were bound to miss some words— as if he were purposefully probing the patience of his listener. "I testified on your behalf."

"Was that before you threatened me with the penitentiary or after you took my son into a room and tried to trick him into confessing to arson?"

Truax gave Fontana a look that was simultaneously stern and bruised and, like a trouper, pressed on. "I feel like we almost have a working relationship, the two of us. You know, after testifying on your behalf." He tried on a laugh, but it was too tight and came out in a short, high-pitched burst. "So, how do you like our little dance palace?"

"Mr. Truax, there's nothing I detest more than an obsequious social climber, and you, sir, are just that."

She stood, took Fontana's hand, and walked him out onto the dance floor to the accompaniment of Dinah Washington singing

"Stormy Weather." Truax's wife had joined them too late to catch anything but their backsides.

"I'm sorry if I embarrassed you," Sally said.

"Are you kidding? I loved it."

When the song ended, Sally asked directions to the powder room. After she'd left, Sandusky sauntered over and said, "Holy shit, I think I'll buy my wife a pair of Wranglers like those. Just exactly like those. Hot damn."

"You working tonight?" Fontana asked, noticing the club soda in his fist, as well as the absence of his wife. A moment later he remembered Sandusky didn't drink.

"Doing a sleep-over in an hour. Acting lieutenant."

"Good. I'd like to see you in the officer's seat more."

"I don't know what you said to old True-Ass over there, Chief, but you got him into some sort of catfight with his old lady," Sandusky's teeth flashed in the darkness. "So, what's going on with the investigation? Anything new?"

"Not that I know of."

"Come on. You can tell me, Chief. They gotta be getting something. Is it a local?"

"I'm telling you, I don't know."

When Fontana spotted Mo Costigan talking to Kim and Jesse Rothem near the front doors, he excused himself and invited her onto the dance arena. They danced through "Lavender Blue" by Sammy Turner and then partway through Gene Pitney's "Only Love Can Break a Heart" before either of them spoke. "I haven't been getting any phone calls from you," Fontana said. "I was thinking of sending over a can of prunes."

"Ha, ha."

"I wanted to ask you a couple of questions."

"Like what?"

"Like why are you grooming Truax to take over my job?"

"Don't be silly. Besides, he's not in the least interested in being fire chief in a small town. If you haven't noticed, Roger has ambition."

"If he's not interested in my job, why did he apply for it?"

"When was that?"

"When I applied for it. I went through the records the other day."

"But we gave it to *you*."

"Mo, I don't know what this arson problem has done to your brain, but it bothers me when local politicians get in bed together."

"What? Who told you that?"

"I didn't mean it literally, Mo . . ."

"We're doing no such thing. I hate rumors. Like last fall when everybody down at the beauty parlor said I was sleeping with those . . ."

"High school quarterbacks?"

"You don't know how ugly gossip can get, Mac."

"I think I do, Mo."

They were well into "I Only Have Eyes for You" when Sally approached and looked questioningly at Mo, who said, "Sure." Mo walked away, twice glancing back over her shoulder.

"I forgot what it was like," Sally whispered.

"What what was like?"

"Eight women followed me into the rest room."

They danced and then shared a table, then danced some more. Oddly, only a few people approached. The conversations were short and polite, and almost nobody mentioned Sally's celebrity, although one and all addressed her as Aimee. Fontana had expected by the end of the evening that a lot of the staring would have ceased, but it didn't, Roger Truax being among the worst.

They chitchatted with various volunteers and their spouses, mostly about the fires and the growing community panic, and spoke briefly to an off-duty H. C. Bailey, who had been dancing with a petite blond woman ten years her junior. Shortly after eleven-thirty, Sally asked Fontana to take her home.

Outside the Bedouin in the alley, two women huddled together in identical tan raincoats. Both cold, sullen, and pale, one wore horn-rimmed glasses, ankle-length white socks, and deck shoes, and the other had a beehive hairdo.

Fontana noticed they avoided his eyes. Before he knew what was happening, the one in the glasses stepped forward and spit on Sally Culpepper's blouse. When the second woman moved forward, Fontana stepped in front of her and said, "What the hell do you think you're doing?"

The second woman's spittle lacked the momentum of the first woman's and struck Fontana on his knee. "She's a fake," said the first woman.

"A Hollywood whore living in our town," said the second.

"She's sleeping with an Arab."

"Trash. Nothing but trash."

"The only trash around here is you two," Fontana said. "Now get out of here before I get mad."

"All she thinks about is herself. She could easily do a benefit and make us all enough money to pay for these fires. We lost our garage. But she doesn't do it. She only thinks of herself."

"Move!"

The women loitered nearby as Fontana and Sally climbed into his truck. Fontana fumbled under the seat for a rag, the best he had to offer.

Fifteen minutes later as he drove his son home, Brendan said, "Are you going to marry Mrs. Culpepper?"

"What makes you ask?"

"Audie and me saw you guys kissing."

"Just a friendly kiss." Fontana smiled.

"You sure you're not going to marry Mrs. Culpepper?"

"Pretty sure."

"Because . . . if you did, Audie would be my brother. Wouldn't he? My stepbrother."

"Who told you that?"

"Audie."

"Yeah, he would. If we got married. But we're not going to. You like him, don't you?"

"I like Audie a whole bunch."

"He doesn't play with matches or anything when you're around, does he?"

"Of course not, Dad. Don't be silly."

♦

TWENTY-SIX

SPELL IT T-R-U-A-X

Sunday afternoon, Fontana dropped Brendan off at a friend's house and drove to the station where he found Robinson Jeffers at the desk in the watch office. The reporter, who was a master at sideslipping eye contact, shut his notebook and sat without acknowledging or looking at Fontana.

"Library closed?" Fontana asked.

Les and Opal Morgan were sitting on the bed in his office waiting for him. Opal Morgan stood. "Chief? We was thinking about that fatal fire."

"Yeah."

"We just keep thinking Sandusky was awful quick to find the way inside. He took the exact path without hesitation. Now what are the odds of that?"

"It could happen," Fontana said. "After all, Weed went to the right door too."

"No. Weed tried that west door first. Then he looked in the patio door before he went up them stairs. He went in the third door he looked at. Sandusky hauled hose straight to the door. You make a mistake hauling hose, you've made a mess. How did he know just where to go?"

"He claims he just saw—"

"We know what he claims. You realize he's tweaked 'cause Weed and Heather got the jobs. He wanted to work out here real bad."

"I know."

"Well, it's just that after that fire, he seemed real jolly," said Opal Morgan. "He was laughing about the dead lady. Nobody else was laughing."

"He's a pretty hard character in some respects," said Fontana. He didn't know why he was defending Sandusky. They were right. "He's seen his share of fire victims and it doesn't affect him much. Besides, you know most veteran firefighters use black humor to offset things like that."

"Have you questioned him?"

"No more than anybody else."

"Well, we think you should question him."

"I will."

"By the way. Whatever happened with the pastor?"

"He was out of town on the night in question. Do you folks live near him?"

"Heck, no," said Les. "We live way the hell out and back on the North Fork road." The Morgans lived almost four miles from the three fires where they'd been first in.

"It was lucky you got to the Cove Road fire so fast then."

"Sure was. Yeah." The pair exchanged a look. Opal said, "We were over at the new McDonald's stuffing our faces, weren't we, Les?"

"Sure was," said Les.

The Morgans were like salt and pepper shakers, both the same height, both with round faces and pale chins that rode over their collars as if they were wearing turtlenecks that were too tight, and neither one of them had any sign of a neck whatsoever.

After the Morgans left, Fontana checked his office for messages, signed off the most recent probation reports on Frank Weed and Heather Minerich, then walked into the beanery where Sandusky and five volunteers sat in front of the television set. Fontana said, "What'd they have last night?"

"Some drunk fell asleep in his car out on the freeway," Sandusky said. "He was in the slow lane, sawing the Zs, just waiting for a trucker on bennies to take him out. We grabbed his keys and called the State Patrol. When he came to, he claimed Hawkins stole his wallet. He

wanted Hawkins's name. Hawkins spelled it for him. T-r-u-a-x."
Everybody laughed nervously. They'd been on edge since Fontana
had come into the room.

"Funny," Fontana said, looking at the television screen where a
woman was walking along a sandy beach. Except for the barest bikini
bottom, she was completely naked. "What's this?"

"Nothing," Sandusky said. Fontana studied the channel number
on the television and realized it was a video.

"Somebody brought in a movie?"

"Not really." Jim Hawkins's face turned red.

An older volunteer got up and walked into the apparatus bay as if
he suddenly had something very important to do there. The others
left at intervals until only Fontana, Sandusky, and Hawkins remained.
Sandusky slid the remote control out from under the Sunday paper
and switched the VCR off. Fontana picked the remote up and started
the tape again.

"Oh, boy," said Hawkins under his breath.

After the tape had run a few more seconds, Fontana recognized
Sally Culpepper—this the infamous bootleg Aimee Lee tape shot
years earlier from a secret blind during a vacation she'd taken in Tahiti
shortly after a series of episodes the press had characterized as a nervous breakdown.

Fontana stopped the tape and removed the cassette. "Who owns
this?"

Hawkins glanced furtively at Sandusky, who tipped his head
toward the watch office, where they heard a piece of paper rustling
in the tomblike station. Fontana carefully set the tape cassette on the
floor and crushed it with his shoe. When he walked down the long
hallway into the watch office, Jeffers did not look up from his notebook.

"Get out."

Wordlessly, Jeffers shut his notebook, stood up with cracking
knees, and exited through the front door.

In the beanery, Fontana said, "I really would appreciate it if we
tried to respect the rights of others. How would you feel if that was
your sister or your friend or somebody?"

"I had a sister with a body like hers," Hawkins said, "I wouldn't care who saw it."

"Shut up," said Sandusky, softly.

"Well, I wouldn't."

"I should have stopped them, Chief," said Sandusky, who sat in Lycra cycling shorts and cleated cycling shoes. His bike was in the apparatus bay.

"That's right. You should have."

"Hey, Chief," Frank Weed said, bursting into the station. "What's going on? Hey, did I tell you I've just been short-listed for the state humanitarian award from the Daughters of the American Revolution? Pretty cool, huh? You seen my KOMO interview? Here. Let me show it to you. Hey? Did you ever see the KING one? I got that here too."

He keyed open his food locker, pulled out a stack of videotapes held together by rubber bands, and walked to the television stand. Shards of black plastic shot across the floor from under his feet. "Hey, what's this? This better not be one of my tapes."

TWENTY-SEVEN

♦

A ROUNDED AND TAN MIDRIFF

Fat raindrops that had the chill of a late spring storm began falling. It was five o'clock on Sunday afternoon. Brendan and Fontana had been at a small park near where the paper shack had been lit. The park had a creek bisecting a couple of acres of grass and tall alders, swings, tennis courts, basketball hoops, and teeter-totters.

As the rain began, they headed home, Fontana carrying Brendan piggyback. Black clouds inked out most of Mount Washington to the south, and Satan trotted ahead, turning back from time to time to make sure they were coming. They could smell raindrops spattering in the dust alongside the road and feel a vague electric tang in the air. Brendan kept up a commentary on the incoming storm, and as soon as they closed the front door, thunderbolts rattled the house, courting them for another twenty minutes.

Fontana and his son toweled off their wet hair and changed into dry sweatshirts, draped themselves across either end of the davenport, and dropped into one of those lethargic Sunday afternoon stupors when all the chores were caught up and the remains of the weekend slowly ebbed. They grew too indolent to do anything except lie on the furniture and gab.

"Did you know humans are the only animals that sleep on their backs?" Brendan said.

"I didn't know that. That's interesting."

"Did you know that when flies take off they jump backward?"

"Now, that I did know. But it is astonishing."

They talked about the arsons and about Lorraine, and after about half an hour, Fontana went to the video recorder at the far end of the living room and examined the stack of Aimee Lee movies Mary Gilliam had left with him. "We gonna watch movies?" Brendan asked.

"I think the first two of these are all right for you, but the others I'll have to preview."

"Awwww, Mac."

"Besides, I think by the time we watch a double-header here, you'll be pretty tired."

"I don't get tired. I can watch four movies in a row. I can watch *ten* movies in a row."

"We'll see."

They popped a huge bowl of popcorn, and sitting on the counter in the kitchen, Brendan mixed up a pitcher of Kool-Aid and poured himself a glass of it. Even though it was June, the house was cold, so they tugged comforters over themselves. The first film was called *Weird People,* and it was interesting to watch the credits roll and to see, despite the fact that she'd played three parts, how low Aimee Lee's billing had been.

While not a huge moneymaker, *Weird People* quickly established itself with a cult following and remained a moneymaker over the years, played over and over again at parties and midnight showings. As far as Fontana could see, aside from the raucous good humor and Aimee Lee's performance, it was largely unremarkable.

Her second film, *The Jungles of New York,* was a romantic suspense about a hooker falling for a social worker, Harrison Ford, who at first thought he was too good for her. They ended up running from the mob after accidentally witnessing the mass murder of some local politicians. Fontana fast-forwarded through the gruesome assassination sequence. "Awww, Mac. I've seen this stuff before. I've seen worse."

"Not when I was around."

In the past, he'd been less than impressed with the Aimee Lee phenomenon, but tonight, trying to experience it in a strictly visceral sense, he began to get a sense of what her hold over the world had been. Besides being an unparalleled actress, there was something about her that made her seem ordinary and aristocratic and sexy all at the same time.

As predicted, Brendan grew restless before the climax of the second movie, so they fixed a late dinner together: sloppy joes, coleslaw, and canned corn, Brendan's favorites. Tapioca pudding from the refrigerator shelf for dessert.

It wasn't until Brendan had gone to bed that Fontana sat down in front of the recorder and popped in *The Vampire Movie*. In the first half of the movie, the viewer's fear for Lee was almost palpable as Lee played a virginal schoolteacher stalked by vampires. In the second half, as a rapacious vampire herself, she was devastatingly ruthless. *The Vampire Movie* had not yet been released by the time Aimee Lee disappeared, and Fontana recalled vaguely the furor the combination of the two news items created, the movie and her disappearance. It was her third role but her first to call for nude scenes, and the resulting stills had shown up in every men's magazine in the world.

Plaything, her last movie, came out almost a year after her disappearance. The biography of the mistress of the richest man on earth, it was a story in which she aged from fourteen to eighty-two and back again. Theaters in San Francisco, New York, and Seattle had been playing it continuously since its release.

It was almost midnight when he put the last movie on rewind. He let Satan out and checked Brendan, covering his feet with the quilt he slept under. He would only kick them out again. In the summer, Linda had slept with her feet sticking out of the covers too.

Lying in bed, he mulled over Aimee Lee, Sally Culpepper, and all the people she'd been in between. He thought about last night when he'd danced with her. He thought about the women waiting outside the Bedouin in the dark. People were going nuts.

Allowing himself the vice of making sweeping generalizations, Fontana considered that in the year he'd lived here he had found the residents of Staircase to be unusually naive and impressionable. Where else would people drive out into the country to tack up thigh-cream flyers under the stump-removal signs with the full expectation that drivers would stop their cars to read the posters? And where else would people actually stop to do just that? In what other town did serious young men actually think of chewing tobacco as a "babe magnet"? Where else did clerks at the video store fielding inquiries about foreign films reply, "Don't have any. No foreigners living here in the valley." He doubted there was a young girl in the area who hadn't filled her diary with notes on Aimee Lee.

Staircase hadn't had an arson fire since Friday a week earlier, and Fontana was beginning to think the worst was over. Neither north Seattle, Everett, nor Tacoma had had any more arsons, although Puyallup and Fife had had a rash of Dumpster and car fires easily attributable to copycats.

It was possible the fire death had frightened the arsonist off.

Monday morning, Fontana fixed breakfast for Brendan and took him to Mary's.

When he arrived at the station, Kingsley was mopping the downstairs living areas, the rooms smelling of wet wax and of bleach.

"Heather around?" Fontana asked.

"Upstairs doing the bunk rooms."

The upstairs had a classroom, a large tiled bathroom with two shower stalls, a small unused office, and a huge bunk room with windows along one wall that ran the length of the station. Fold-down beds were left in the up position when not in use. Next to the beds, narrow lockers had been built into the walls.

He found Heather Minerich standing with her back to him at her open locker. In a corner of the room, a portable radio was tuned to a classical music station. Heather was nearly as tall as his five-ten, with wide shoulders and a narrow, muscular back that flared into broad hips.

"Can we talk a minute?"

"Sure, Chief."

As he approached, he caught a glimpse of her in the small mirror affixed to the locker door and realized her shirt was unbuttoned. Her face had been tan since winter, but he was surprised to see the rest of her body was just as brown. He turned away quickly.

"Don't have to hide your eyes, Chief. I don't mind."

"That's one of the items I want to discuss with you. I *do* have to turn around."

"I want to be just one of the guys. Really."

"You want this shirt?" Fontana said. A fresh shirt and towel were laid out on the bare mattress of a bunk in front of him.

"Sure." Without turning, he handed her the shirt and the towel both.

When she was dressed, he spoke, "It's come to my attention that the living arrangements up here aren't what they could be. I wouldn't think you would feel comfortable thrown in with all the men here. You don't have any privacy."

"I'm fine."

"It's a gallant attitude, Heather, but you don't have to be dressing or undressing with the men. There's no reason for that. I want you to be comfortable, and I want the men to be comfortable. We'll have to figure something else out."

"I am comfortable. This is just fine."

"It isn't fine, Heather. And it's not a condition of your employment that you dress in the same room with men."

"I'm not planning to make a pass at them or—"

"Heather, there are still courtrooms in this country where a rapist can get off because a woman was wearing provocative clothing. I know it's not right, and I'm not saying anything like that would happen around here, but we have to use some common sense. Everyone will be more comfortable if we can find some other arrangement. Besides, even if you think the living arrangements are great, the next female recruit might not. My guess is we'll have you bunking in that back room we used for the aid car."

"That's not fair. You're punishing me because I'm a woman."

"This isn't a punishment, and it isn't a permanent solution. Maybe we can try partitions in here. And we can install a second bathroom on this floor. We'll think of something. But until then, I don't want people walking in on you and I don't want you walking in on them."

"Because they might rape me?"

"Of course not. I'm sorry I even used that word. Because it's bad policy. Heather, I'm trying to help you here."

"Chief, I eat with the men. I fight fires with the men. I can dress with the men. I don't need any special treatment."

"Heather, I admire your spirit, but I can't let this no-privacy issue continue. It isn't exactly practical to move all the men to the old aid-car room. You want to appeal, go through the union. The second issue I wanted to talk to you about was the Cove Road fire. I'd like you to tell me what you did there."

"What's going on? Didn't I do okay?"

"There was some concern that you weren't on the pipe and that you weren't real close to the Dugan who was."

"But you said I did good at the fire."

"When did I say that?"

"At the meeting Saturday. You told us all we did a great job."

"Generally speaking, that's true. I only want you to explain what you did."

"Everything?"

"Please."

TWENTY-EIGHT

◆

HEATHER PLAYS *JEOPARDY!*
AND DOES PUSH-UPS

"This is Sandusky, isn't it? He put you up to this."

"Heather, this shouldn't be such a hard question. You're a new firefighter. I'm the chief. I need to know."

"Did you ask Weed all these questions?"

"As a matter of fact, I did." Actually, he hadn't. Weed had volunteered every minute of his actions at the fire, and he'd been doing so several times a day.

Heather Minerich faced him squarely, her dark hair in a pixie bob, her bangs ragged, her dark eyes fixed on his. She'd always had the look of a tomboy who'd too quickly grown into a big-hipped woman and perhaps resented it. Her chest heaved. She stuffed her hands into her pockets.

"Heather, this is not supposed to be confrontational."

"I know Sandusky is after me. He said some really dirty things at the fire. He said, 'Nice shiny helmet. Can you polish mine too?' "

"And?"

"Oh, come on, Chief. He asked me to clean his helmet. You know. Like polish his knob? He was asking for a . . ." She whispered, "Blow job."

Fontana crossed his arms. "Heather, I think you've misinterpreted a sarcastic remark. Remember Sandusky's helmet after the fire, the face shield melted down around the main part of the helmet like a slab of cheese? Old-time firefighters look at helmets after a fire to see who got the most fire. I believe he was referring to the fact that Pierpont's helmet was sooty and yours was still bright yellow. It must have looked like you hadn't gotten anywhere near the fire rooms."

"Lieutenant Pierpont told me not to."

"What?"

"He told me to pull more hose. We had coils right there in front of the door, but he kept turning around telling me to pull more."

"He wasn't urging you to get up there with him?"

"No. He was telling me to pull hose."

"And that's the reason you didn't go in?"

"Absolutely. I wanted to go in. He made me stay there the whole time."

"Okay. Fine. We'll talk about that later. Tell me how you think things are going. In general."

Heather sat heavily on the edge of her open bunk and pushed at her cheeks with the heels of her hands, leaning elbows onto knees and crying for almost a minute. Not knowing what else to do, Fontana waited, watching the top of her head, her bobbing shoulders, her knees in the dark trousers, and her black steel-toed brogans. For the first time, he noted three tabloid newspapers under a low stack of magazines on her mattress. He believed two were issues he'd appeared in.

"First of all, I don't feel very good about that old lady who died," she said, her eyes a hodgepodge of water and smeared mascara. For some reason it occurred to Fontana that Sandusky would have said they looked like two piss holes in the snow. "I know we had that post-fire stress debriefing with the counselor from Seattle and all, but I still don't feel good."

"Nobody does, Heather," Fontana said softly. "We can get you more counseling. We'll do that."

"I'm not sure more counseling is going to help."

"It can't hurt."

"And people ride me."

"What do you mean?"

"Somebody called the station a couple of months ago to report a grass fire. When I asked if it was bad, Sandusky said the flames were two hundred feet high. I'm just a rookie. It wasn't until after we got there and I saw a little black spot in the field that I realized he was full of shit. A lot of these men, the older volunteers, won't even look me in the eye. That old man, Valenzuela? He never has spoken to me." Old man? Valenzuela was maybe five years older than Fontana.

"To make matters worse, if Frank does something and it goes right, everybody pats him on the back. I do the same job and people get all quiet. I know they're thinking it was luck. I feel all this pressure that Frank never does."

"I'm sure Frank feels his share."

"And when I do something wrong, people give each other looks, like it's some sort of proof I shouldn't be here. Frank does something wrong, they explain to him what it was he did and how to avoid it in the future. And then Lieutenant Pierpont walked in on me in the shower."

"He made a mistake. We're going to make sure that doesn't happen again. Believe me, Lieutenant Pierpont felt bad about it."

"Sandusky's the one who really bugs me. Remember when we were watching *Jeopardy!* every week? Sandusky would sit there with his big feet up on the table on drill nights telling everybody all the answers. I majored in European history and my mom was always big on old movies and show tunes, so I used to get suckered into betting with him. Ice cream for the house. Twenty-five push-ups. I *never* won. And when I paid off on the push-ups he would kneel down and pretend he was counting and look up my shirt." Fontana believed he was the only person in the department who knew Sandusky's satellite television played *Jeopardy!* one night early. "You know what else he said?"

"What?"

"He said if he had set the fatal he wouldn't turn himself in. Turning yourself in wouldn't do any good. He said he would volunteer for the rest of his life. Don't you get it, Chief? Nobody puts in more hours than him. And he talks about the fires as if somebody around here is setting them. *He* is."

"That's a serious accusation."

"He worked off Engine Two, right? At the Cove Road fire? If you look in the watch book for that night, you'll see he never had time to sign in. Whoever set the fire would have just barely had time to drive back to the station and then go out and fight it—just like him. The timing was perfect. And when you sent Engine Two back to the station, he had to drive his car back. How long would it have taken for him to swing around on the old highway and light those other fires? There was plenty of time. And he's always asking for fires."

"So are you, Heather."

Before either of them could say anything else, the gong in the bunk room clanged. Heather raced across the room and slid down the brass pole, her forearms making a high-pitched whine against the polished brass. At least she didn't use her palms on the pole anymore. Palms left a patina of grease, and using them was the mark of the uninitiated. Fontana had told her about it two months after she'd come to the station, mildly annoyed that nobody else had clued her in. Maybe she was right. Maybe they were treating her differently.

After the engine left, Fontana went downstairs and walked next door. As he climbed the stairs to Mo's office, he thought about Heather Minerich. She had a master's degree in European history. She'd scored well on the entrance tests and done well at the state fire academy, yet she seemed to be unraveling before his eyes.

She was correct about Sandusky having had time to set the fires. She too had had time to set the fatal, since she too had reported late to the station that night, arriving just in time to take the run to Stooly Road on Engine One. For that matter, Weed had missed most of the arsons himself. Maybe he'd been out setting them. And if you singled out people who craved fires, there were half a dozen volunteers who wanted them entirely too much. Hawkins was one. Claiming it was a joke, Valenzuela had at one time put up a fire totem.

A sheaf of folders under her arm, scratched sunglasses perched on top of her head, a steaming cup of half-spilled coffee and a leather jacket in her hands, Mo met him in the dark doorway at the top of the stairs. "I was just leaving, Mac. I have to be at my office in Bellevue in five minutes."

"It's a twenty-minute drive, Mo."

"That's why I can't stop and talk."

"We're going to have to do something about the station. It needs some remodeling."

"Remodeling? That's asinine. It was just redone five years ago. What are you looking for exactly? A spa with built-in headphones?"

"A women's rest room and a separate locker room on the second floor."

"No problem."

"We've got the money for that?"

"No problem—we're not going to build it. I spoke to Minerich about it when she hired on. She said she wouldn't have any trouble sharing the present facilities with a bunch of men."

"Mo, we're headed for a lawsuit here."

"I don't have time now, Mac. Really. I'll talk to you later."

She got as far as the stop sign before she rolled down her window and began feeling around on the roof, dragging her purse in by the strap.

After the engine returned to quarters, Fontana said, "Kingsley. You got a second?"

"What is it, boss?"

When he'd closed the door of his office behind them, Fontana related his conversation with Heather. Kingsley, who had been growing more and more irate as Fontana spoke, said, "I wasn't telling her to pull more hose. I was telling her to catch up with me. How could she have mistaken pulling more hose for coming inside? I was waving to her. 'Come on. Come on.' No, Chief. She's lying. Damn! That really makes my blood boil."

"Maybe she thought that was what you were saying."

"Who are you going to believe, Chief? Her or me?"

"I believe you said for her to come in. What I can't believe is she didn't misinterpret it. How can you even be sure yourself, Kingsley? Isn't there any possibility that she thought you were telling her to pull more hose?"

"Not for a New York minute. Dammit. I hate it when people lie."

"Okay, suppose she is lying. You're never going to be able to prove it. It's all going to be a wash. So let's make it easy on ourselves and assume she's telling the truth."

"Are you kidding me? She was hanging in the doorway. She was scared. I know *scared* when I see it. We wanted a woman so bad, why couldn't we have hired someone like the mayor? You ever see the mayor in a fire?"

"She's a bulldog all right."

"She'd rip a bulldog apart with her teeth." They laughed.

Fontana said, "Well, here's what we'll do for now. I want you to assign Minerich a locker in the old aid-car room with the women volunteers. And make an 'occupied' sign for both rest rooms. I don't know how I let this mess happen. I guess all these arsons have got me off my feed."

Kingsley took a deep breath and walked over to the window in the corner. "I don't trust her at fires, and she's weak on most of her drills. She passes everything but only by the skin of her teeth. She's stronger than some of the men who volunteer—I'll give her that—but you ask her to throw a ladder up against that wall, about one out of four tries she'll get tangled up in her own bootstraps."

"How are you going to write the fire up?"

"I'm still thinking about it."

"Show it to her when you're done. Then show it to me."

"You want me to put in this business about her lying?"

"You talk to her and figure it out."

"I *figured* it out."

"Put it in if you want, but I'm telling you it's a can of worms."

"I know I'm right, Chief."

TWENTY-NINE

♦

THE FIREBUG

Tuesday morning at nine-thirty, Fontana received a phone call from Jennifer Underhill. "We got him. He's in there confessing to Beasley right now."

"The arsonist?"

"We picked him up early this morning. We think he's the primary guy. The original. And he seems to have visited Staircase pretty regularly."

"Anybody I know?"

"I'll let you meet him when you get here. Last time I was in the room he gave up fourteen fires including that door company in Puyallup that went down for one point three mil. We've got gas station receipts that confirm he was in Staircase on three of the nights you had fires. And his father tells us his ex-girlfriend dumped him at the Bedouin years ago. It's beginning to look good. Beasley's in there praying with him."

"You're kidding."

"On their knees on the floor. If you knew what a pagan Beasley is you'd laugh. We'd like you to help interview him."

"I'm on my way."

From the time he pulled into the Public Safety Building parking lot in Seattle and let Satan out to relieve himself, it was only a few minutes until Fontana found himself in a small room with institutional green walls. There was a table in front of a large one-way window that looked into a similar room. The hallway outside was a snake pit of reporters and film crews.

Through the window, he and Jennifer Underhill and two ATF agents watched Beasley talking to a nondescript young man in an unbuttoned dress shirt and rumpled slacks. Beasley was standing. The young man sat at a table, his chin cradled in one hand. Fontana didn't recognize him.

"Doesn't he look like a cross between a fry cook at Burger King and the kid the teacher always put out in the hall?" Jennifer Underhill said. She wore a pink pantsuit and a bouncy hair style, her eyelashes daubed heavily with mascara, ready to be photographed.

"He's pretty unremarkable."

"We're giving you first crack because you're the one with the murder rap. His father turned him in. From all we could tell it was a good family, four older sisters, all married and doing well. Private schools for Peter."

"What's his name?"

"Peter Mark."

"He serve any time?"

"Never."

"What's he do?"

"Real estate. But he hasn't had a sale in over six months."

"No criminal record at all?"

"Lots of traffic tickets. We know he usually goes to sleep around six in the morning, so we got the warrant yesterday but didn't arrest him until six-forty this morning. He's tired and wired."

"Good."

"Brought him in without saying a word to him. A big convoy. Fourteen cars. Made a real production out of it. He seemed impressed. He's been a firefighting groupie for years. Applied to a bunch of departments, but he's never had the strength to pass the physicals. His apartment was filled with models of fire engines and pictures of fires. He even had a technical manual for an LTI aerial he must have stolen somewhere. He had a scanner in his car. You know what he said on the way out the door of his apartment? 'Will I be back in time to feed my fish?' He thinks he's going back. You ready to go in?"

"I've been ready for weeks."

"Our problem is, with all the receipts we've got, we can't put him in Staircase on the night of the death. We'd sure as hell like to. You want the truth, I think he didn't do that one, but he kind of wants us to think he did."

"He set fires in Staircase but he didn't set the one that killed my neighbor?"

"We think that's the situation."

When Jennifer Underhill and Fontana walked into the interrogation room, Peter Mark stood, blushing. Fontana couldn't tell if it was because he was embarrassed to be under arrest or because he was indulging some sort of fantasy dialed in on Jennifer.

"Go ahead. Sit down, Peter. This is Chief Fontana from the Staircase Fire Department. Do you know why we've asked him to come, Peter?"

"No." Mark's voice was delicate. He was slim and had the look of a man who had always been advised to avoid contact sports. Jennifer had told Fontana he was twenty-seven, but he looked older, had bags under his eyes, a pasty look to his skin, and the mildly hunched back of an old man working in a garden. There was a button missing from one sleeve of his dress shirt. He was not in handcuffs, and rather than looking terrified, he displayed the mild upset of a man who'd just been served the wrong dinner at a restaurant.

"You don't know why we've asked Chief Fontana here?"

"No."

"Can you guess?"

"Because of the fires in Staircase?"

"Did you start any fires in Staircase, Peter?" Fontana asked.

"Yes, sir."

"I would very much appreciate it if you could give me the details."

"I'm not sure . . ." Mark said. "Things are jumbled."

The room was quiet for a few moments. Beasley, who'd remained standing and whose thick black eyebrows were woven into a frown, said, "You've been very cooperative so far, Peter."

Looking at the floor, Peter Mark nodded.

"What about Staircase?" Fontana said. "Can you tell us what you did in Staircase?"

Mark looked at the three interrogators. "What?"

Beasley scratched his scalp with a single finger. "Could you tell us what you remember about Staircase?"

"Let me think. I went up and drove past Sheila's house. I think that was in April. Or May. Her mom saw me, so I stopped in. And then I lit some stuff. I lit a garage across the road."

Fontana said, "Where does Sheila live?"

Mark looked up. His dark brown hair was tousled and thinning on top. A flap of it stuck out over his left ear like a louver. "New Mexico."

"Where's her mom's house?"

"Out on the main road by the pig farm. After I saw you guys tapping the garage, I found a Corvette somebody left unlocked. You have to be pretty stupid to leave a Corvette unlocked." Fontana remembered the fires. They were all small that first night except for the Corvette which had never been reported in the papers.

"How did you start the fires?"

"My lighter."

"Why a lighter?"

"You get caught, it's just a lighter. Everybody's got one."

"What's it look like?"

"Silver. All silver. They got it."

"You ever use any other kind of lighter?"

"Maybe. I can't remember."

"Go on."

"Then I went out there, uh, I don't know, first of June maybe. I visited my aunt in Lakewood, and then on my way back to north Seattle I swung by Staircase."

"That's not exactly on the way," Fontana said.

"For some reason I found myself on Highway Eighteen. I was thinking about Sheila. When we broke up. I don't know. It just made me so . . . She didn't break off with me. I know my father probably told you she did, but I dumped her."

"And you didn't try to kill yourself afterward?" Underhill asked.

"I got mixed up on a prescription. It didn't have anything to do with our breakup. *I* broke it off. You know what she said?"

"What?" Fontana asked.

"She said, 'You're not very interesting.' " He looked around the group for comfort.

"Is that why you set these fires?" Beasley asked. "To be more interesting?"

"No."

"You didn't light the ones in Staircase to get even with Sheila?" Underhill asked.

"I still like Sheila."

"What we'd like to know about is June fifteenth. That was the fourth night of fires in Staircase."

"The night of the church fire?" Peter Mark asked.

"There've been a lot of church fires," Underhill said.

"My church in Alderwood? The Christian Science church?"

"You set that?" Beasley asked. The investigators looked at each other. The alarm for the Christian Science church in Alderwood had been received twenty minutes after they'd gotten the alarm for the Cove Road fire in Staircase, and everybody in the room knew the driving time between the two locations was forty minutes.

"I feel bad because they gave me a loan about a month ago. They're good people."

"Where did you start it, Peter?" Beasley asked.

"At the wall in the back by the parking. Over by that tall window. I didn't mean for the whole thing to burn down."

"What did you think was going to happen?" Underhill said.

"I don't know."

Peter Mark stared at the floor.

"You remember anything else about that church fire?" Beasley asked.

"What do you want to know? The upper windows blew out right before the fire department got there. The flames went right up to the power lines so there were blue sparks everywhere. It was pretty strange. One fireman almost got electrocuted."

"So, Peter," Fontana said. "You didn't set that house fire in Staircase. The one on June fifteenth?"

"I told you. I was in north Seattle."

"You set anything else that night that might help prove you were in north Seattle?" Beasley propped one foot up on the table and clasped his hands behind his head.

"Let me think. Some tires. There were some tires next to this guy's house. I don't remember the street. I put some newspaper in the tires and lit it."

Beasley gave Fontana a look and left the room. Fontana followed while Underhill made small talk with the suspect. "Pretty tiring, isn't it?" she said. "All these interviews?"

"It's gotta be done," Mark said, resignedly. "I'm really sorry for causing you people all this trouble."

"We don't mind."

Outside the room, Beasley moved close to Fontana. "He knows too much about that church fire, Mac. And we never told anybody about those tires. Plus it was his own church. That makes a certain kind of nutso sense if you've been listening to this guy."

"I've got my own arsonist, at least for the night of the fatality," Fontana said.

"Looks that way."

"Shit. Mark set fires in Staircase on three nights, and then somebody waits until my kid is away from home and torches the house he's staying at, trying to make it look like part of Mark's string? If Mark had been home watching TV that night, we would have blamed Mark. No matter what he said, we'd have tried to pin the fatal on him."

"Your killer would have gotten away with it if Mark hadn't been so busy himself. So you've got your own firebug. You kind of knew that anyway, didn't you?"

"I kind of didn't want to know it. I was hoping you would catch him and my troubles would be over."

"We got something just recently out your way, a description of a big man wearing a black or dark blue running suit. A woman saw a figure running around that night and described the running suit. She's been out of town on vacation and just called us today. Couldn't identify the face."

"Could it have been a woman in a running suit?"

"Might be. Could be. She didn't get all that close. Not much to go on, is it?"

When they went back into the interrogation room, Peter Mark was sitting with his back hunched and his knees together. "I took your test, you know."

It took Fontana a couple of beats to figure out what he was talking about. "Last winter?"

"Yes, sir. I missed passing the written by one question. I was thinking of taking it again. You going to have any more openings this year?"

"Not likely."

"Hmmmm."

"Could I ask you one last question, Peter? Why did you set fire to your own church?"

Peter Mark gazed at him blankly and then put the fingers of one hand in his mouth, picking at one of his molars. "I guess, uh, I guess I was trying to show everybody I wasn't playing favorites. You know?"

THIRTY

◆

ONLY COUPLES NEED APPLY

So they had a murderer on the loose, a copycat, probably some local, and maybe someone with a grudge against Fontana.

Jennifer Underhill and Beasley had promised to concentrate on the fatal fire in Staircase as soon as they had their own case organized, but Fontana knew, confession or not, assembling a bulletproof case against Peter Mark was going to take time.

Mark's pattern had been to set a fire, watch the engines respond, then when most of the commotion had died down, drive a couple of blocks and set another one, and another, until both he and the fire department were pooped. The copycat in Staircase had mimicked the pattern, though imperfectly.

The person who'd set the Sutterfield fire had most likely been on the scene watching their efforts. Watching him. Fontana may even have spoken to him. Or her. Or them. Beasley had taken photographs of the bystanders, but Beasley and Underhill hadn't arrived until late, and when Fontana studied the photos he'd found nothing.

It was clear now that he had been targeted personally, his son's life deliberately put at risk. The Sutterfield house hadn't been hit coincidentally as part of a string of arsons. Fontana tried to recall everyone who could have known Brendan would be staying with the Sutterfields, but he'd only mentioned it once, at the fire station the night before the fire. He'd been in the beanery. The room had been full of people. The odds were minimal that the arsonist had not come from that group. A stranger had not set the Cove Road fire.

Who had been there? Damn. Audie Culpepper. He'd been hanging around the station quite a bit lately. And although the first three nights of arsons would have required a vehicle, that last night could have all been done from a bicycle. He could have done them.

Who else had been in the beanery? Truax had been there because Mo had come in to get him for a meeting, but whether or not Truax left before he mentioned where Brendan would be spending the next night, he could not recall. Les and Opal Morgan had been there. Sandusky. Valenzuela. Both rookies, Heather Minerich and Frank Weed. Jim Hawkins had been there.

Mention of where his son would be sleeping the next night was so insignificant, nobody would bother to repeat it or even remember it. Yet one person had taken that information and killed with it.

Depressed and angry, he drove back toward Staircase and was almost to Highway 18 when the alarm for 10010 Hays Road came across the radio. The nudist colony. Was he the only firefighter in the valley who wanted them to get their system fixed? He'd be the first arriving unit.

Fontana took the Highway 18 exit off Interstate 90 and went up Hays Road through the trees. Before he reached the top, he caught a blur in his rearview mirror, then heard a whooshing sound as Roger Truax's maroon Buick wailed up the hill past his GMC, black smoke jetting from the Buick's tailpipes. Truax didn't look at Fontana, nor did he seem nervous about being on the illegal side of one blind curve after another.

Moments later, when Fontana pulled up at the guardhouse gate at Sun Country, Truax was trying to talk his way past the uniformed guard, a young man with long sideburns.

Ignoring Truax, the guard strode to Fontana's window and held up a walkie-talkie. "False alarm, Chief. We just now got a confirmation from our head janitor. The system's been going off all day. The alarm company's in there right now."

"No problem," Fontana said, picking up his mike and giving a code green to the other units.

Roger said, "You gotta let us in. We have to confirm any false."

"Who *are* you?"

"The safety director for Staircase."

"You got any ID?"

"ID?"

"Like a badge."

"No, I don't have a badge. The safety director doesn't need a badge. Now open that gate and let me into your facility."

Fontana scratched Satan. Watching Truax attempting to bluff his way into a nudist colony had cheered him up immeasurably.

"Can't let you in unless we have an alarm," the guard said. "And we don't have an alarm."

"But you just had one."

"It wasn't real. We just forgot to call the alarm company."

"That's an alarm. And technically you can't reset a system without us being there."

"We didn't reset it. The alarm company repairman reset it."

"It would help if we could go in and see what he's doing. After all, the next time it goes off, you might not have any personnel from the alarm company standing around."

"Let's go home, Roger." Fontana put his truck into reverse. "And you'd better check your Buick. It was burning oil pretty good on the way up that hill."

"You're not going inside?"

"I sure do appreciate you trying to help, but I have to pee. So does my dog."

"I don't understand it. In Tacoma we would have caught hell if we'd let the residents tell us the emergency was over."

"You want to go in there that bad, get your wife and sign up. It's just a bunch of people playing table tennis without any clothes on."

When Fontana backed the truck up, Truax ran after him and grasped the windowsill. "You don't think that's why I want to go in, do you? There's protocol involved here. We can't let a man making six dollars an hour intimidate us."

"Badges? We don't need no steeenking badges," Fontana said in a heavy accent.

"Now you're making fun of me."

"Look, Roger. They won't take single men, but if you talk your wife into it, they'll accept a couple's application. With all your schooling and whatnot, they'd be tickled to have you."

Engine One from Staircase chugged over the crest of the hill, labored past, turned around in a cul-de-sac farther up the road and went back down the hill, air horn tooting. A moment later, Fall City's new engine came over the crest and repeated the procedure. Then came the engine from Preston, followed by five or six volunteers in private vehicles. All performed the same ritual and all eyeballed Sun Country's gate with the same wistful look.

"I heard something on the news about them catching the arsonist?" Truax said.

Fontana explained the situation.

"You mean this real estate salesman they arrested didn't do the Cove Road fire?"

"It's beginning to look that way."

"Are there any leads?"

"Sure are, Roger. A big Dugan. In a blue sweat suit."

After a moment, Roger peered down at his own dark blue sweat suit and gave Fontana a sickly grin. "You're joking, right?"

"No joke."

"That's quite a coincidence."

On the drive down the hill, Fontana began formulating a mental list of possible suspects: Roger Truax, Les and Opal Morgan, Frank Weed, Heather Minerich, Mo Costigan, Sandusky, Valenzuela, Jim Hawkins, Audie Culpepper. Sally had offered an alibi for her son, but a mother would be expected to do no less.

Now the question was, who of these people could be holding enough of a grudge against Fontana that they would want to endanger his son? An obvious choice would have been Joshua Clunk if he had been on the list. Clunk not only held a grudge against the town, he nursed two separate grudges against Fontana: one for booting him out of the volunteers for theft and one for testifying on behalf of Sally Culpepper after she shot his dogs. Clunk also knew enough about arson to ape the Seattle arsonist. But he hadn't been in the station when Fontana mentioned where Brendan would be Saturday night, and Fontana had to wonder how likely it could be that he would have heard it from someone who was there.

It was easy to think of a motive for Roger Truax. From the moment he'd hit town, he'd coveted Fontana's job as fire chief. What better way to discredit a former arson investigator and take over his job than to riddle his town with hostile fires?

As for Heather Minerich, he'd find out where she had been prior to the fatal. She'd ridden to Cove Road on Engine One—he knew that much. She'd been at the car accident on Stooly Road too, but she'd shown up late for work and had just barely made the Stooly Road alarm. She might have had time to light the fire and then race to the station and catch the alarm to Stooly Road. It had been Heather who'd found the cigarette lighter, Heather who'd smudged the fingerprints on it. But why would Heather start fires? Was the situation in the station worse than he realized?

Another possibility was one he hated to think about: Sandusky.

After contracting the flu and flubbing the entrance test, Sandusky'd fallen into a funk that had lasted all winter and most of the spring. Shunning the station and eschewing the Thursday night drills, he'd returned only after the arsons flared up. The night of the Cove Road fire, Sandusky had arrived in a private vehicle; afterward driven it back to the station. Alone.

Between the time Fontana'd sent Sandusky and the others back to the station and the time they arrived, somebody drove out to the old highway and set four more fires. Fontana made a mental note to draw up a list of all the firefighters who went back to the station either on the tanker or on Engine Two, for they all had alibis for the later fires.

♦

THIRTY-ONE

BUMPING STOMACHS
WITH A FIRE GROUPIE

Thursday night, Fontana was lying in bed trying to sleep, thinking about how bad he would feel if Audie Culpepper turned out to be their copycat arsonist and wondering how he was going to ask Sally if he could question the boy. When his fire department beeper went off, he phoned Mary next door and quickly dressed. Mary was at the front door before he was. "You'll be right back, won't you, dearie?" she asked.

"This is an aid alarm with the police. I don't know why they want me."

When he arrived at the location in the center of town on Staircase Way, Fontana was greeted by two King County police officers and the crew of Engine One: Kingsley Pierpont, Jim Hawkins, and Ken Valenzuela. The engine was parked in the street, beacon lights rotating.

The group's attention was on a stocky male in his twenties on his back on the sidewalk. Pinned to the ground in the position of a crucified man, the patient had a blue disposable blanket draped across his body. H. C. Bailey stood on one of his outstretched hands while a second female cop stood on the other. Kingsley, Valenzuela, and Hawkins formed a half-moon around the patient.

"What's going on?" Fontana asked.

H. C. Bailey said, "He's having a seizure."

The patient's eyes, while appearing slightly manic, were focused and alert, maybe too alert, as he cycled his gaze with amazing rapidity from person to person.

"Doesn't look like any seizure I've ever seen."

H. C. Bailey looked angrily at the patient. "Well, he is. He's having a seizure."

Although she was doing her best to mask it, the other cop clearly thought the incident amusing.

"Get off his hands."

Neither policewoman moved. "We tried that before."

"Let's try it again."

As they stepped away, the patient rubbed his wrists and quickly reached under the disposable blanket where he began masturbating vigorously. H. C. Bailey compressed her face and turned away while her co-worker tried to keep from laughing. The patient's exertions soon knocked the blue disposable blanket off. Everybody stepped back a pace.

"How long's this been going on?" Fontana asked.

"About ten minutes," said H. C. Bailey. "The people across the street in the Sure Shot called us."

"One red ambulance," Fontana said to Pierpont as he headed back to his truck.

"He'll just seize again," Bailey said.

"He's already *seized* twice," said the second cop. "He seized on her shoe the first time."

"Twice?" said Hawkins.

"They wouldn't let us call an ambulance," said Lieutenant Pierpont, nodding toward the cops. "That's why we called you."

"One red ambulance," said Fontana, wondering whether Bailey's plan had been to arrest the mad masturbator or shoot him.

It was eleven-thirty when the engine pulled up in front of the station. While Valenzuela backed the rig in, Pierpont and Hawkins came into the beanery laughing. "Did you see that thing?" Hawkins said. "It was like a Coke bottle."

Kingsley's smile was so broad and tight his words were almost indistinguishable. "Even in the back of the ambulance when they tied his hands down, he didn't want to stop. Maybe we should have let him finish. A couple more times and we probably could have let him go home."

"We could have sold tickets," said Hawkins.

Five minutes later, the engine received an alarm, and Fontana followed them to a small complex of buildings on Staircase Way where dark smoke spilled from the rear of a barber shop. The complex of single-story wooden buildings included a mini-mart service station, a real estate office, a tax preparer's office, and Brendan's favorite pizza parlor.

As Fontana pulled to a stop, Hawkins ran around the back of the engine in full bunkers, jumped onto the tailboard, and jerked the preconnect hose load out of its rear slot compartment, packing the first bundle on his shoulder, dragging the second with his other hand. Helmet askew, he ran for the rear of the barbershop. Fontana heard the hollow metallic sounds as Valenzuela slid the aluminum wheel chocks under the rear duals.

Kingsley jogged back around the building and yelled, "Water! Water!"

The hose extending from the back of Engine One stiffened with water pressure as Valenzuela opened the valve and ran up the revolutions on the pump. The smoke behind the barbershop had grown into a thick, oily cloud that smelled vaguely of burning hair.

Two volunteers showed up in separate pickup trucks and donned their equipment. A third volunteer parked his Maxima across the street and opened the trunk.

Fontana walked around the back of the Last Cut East barbershop and found Hawkins hosing down a small fenced area. A half-melted garbage can stood next to a pile of smoldering tin cans, wet cardboard, and swatches of scorched hair. Fontana used a stick to knock some smoldering debris aside, uncovering the circular base of a second garbage receptacle.

Five minutes later, Lieutenant Pierpont came jogging around the corner. "Chief. The lady over there at the mini-mart says she saw something."

She'd seen a figure running down the alley. At first she thought it was a teenager, but as she told him about it she changed her mind. She hadn't seen enough to tell even what race or sex the individual had been. It might have been a man or a tall woman. The only thing she knew for certain was that the individual had not been short. Fontana was still interviewing her when another alarm came in, this at the shopping center at the opposite end of town. "Smoke showing."

"I thought they caught the bastard," one of the volunteers said.

The second fire was in a parked Ford behind the Thriftway. By the time they arrived, it was a ball of hot, orange flame, black smoke racing skyward.

Moments after Hawkins and Lieutenant Pierpont tapped the fire, Sandusky showed up in his black RX-7. Sandusky wore running shoes, sloppy navy-blue sweatpants, and a Crash Test Dummies T-shirt. His hair was tousled and there was a note of triumph in his voice. "I had a feeling that clown in Seattle didn't do our fires."

Sandusky and Fontana stood side by side watching as two volunteers jimmied the hood with a bar and somebody else pulled the seats out. Using the Wooster nozzle, Hawkins flooded the interior until water seeped out under the doors. Watching the others work, Sandusky folded his arms. "Remember when you were sixteen and your biggest problem was figuring out whether or not you'd really go insane from too much masturbation?"

Fontana turned to Sandusky, who appeared to be in a trance. "Curious you should say that. We had a patient a few minutes ago who did go insane from it."

Sandusky laughed while Hawkins, who'd already told the story once at the first fire and once here, told it again. It was going to be one of those alarms that lived on and on.

The group had dwindled when another alarm came in.

It was a shed fire. Engine Two, manned by Lindoff and some of the others who had gone to the station, was sent on a single.

Fontana got in his truck and headed for the location—out a long country road that ran along the valley floor under the sheer face of the mountain to a spot where tourists drove out with binoculars to watch mountain goats. Just across the north fork bridge was a small farmhouse, the front yard obscured by a battalion of blueberry bushes. The shed was beyond an uneven field on the other side of the farmhouse. Light smoke drifted from one wall. Thirty head of cattle stood watching from the field.

As Fontana pulled up, a small spurt of flame erupted from the back of the shed. In the darkness he glimpsed a figure working with what looked to be a piece of wet burlap, beating at the fire. Thirty yards from Fontana's truck, Sandusky's black Mazda RX-7 was parked on the shoulder.

The crew of Engine Two, Lindoff, Tolmi, and Chavarria, laid the hose through the pasture and spattered the tiny ramshackle hut with water.

"You see anything?" Fontana asked as Sandusky walked back across the uneven ground to the road.

"Not a damn thing."

"North Fork Command," said the dispatcher. "North Fork Command? Is your unit free?"

"North Fork Command," Fontana said. "That's affirmative."

"We have a report of smoke in the area near Northeast Sixth and Baltic Avenue."

The smoke turned out to be from a wooden fence. When Sandusky arrived, he said, "There must be six cars full of volunteers out here looking for that bastard."

"Yeah," said Tolmi. "And every one of those suckers has a deer rifle."

"Not me," said Chavarria. "I'd carry my dad's coach gun. Nothing like a little double aught to convince the motherfucker to leave us alone."

"I'd want my thirty-thirty," said Tolmi.

"I wouldn't get so het up over it," said Sandusky. "It's probably the chief here settin' em because he knows you clowns need the practice."

"That's not funny," Valenzuela said.

They had two more fires in quick succession, the first a mile up the road in a pile of litter that had been pulled up against the side of a residence, the second in the same vacant house that had been torched two weeks earlier across the street from Claude Pettigrew's.

When they arrived, Claude was outside with a garden hose trying to douse a sheet of flame that had climbed the wall of the house and crept into the eaves.

For the next hour and forty-five minutes they fought the fire, using three engine companies from Staircase and two mutual-aid companies from Fall City. When it was knocked down and they'd pulled most of the inside walls and had cut off the east side of the roof, they gave Hawkins and Heather Minerich, who'd arrived late, a hose line, and the others took a break. Everyone was wet and grimy, and most of the bunking coats and all of the helmets were in the grass. Gatorade and donuts were dispensed from the rear of a station wagon.

As the exhausted firefighters reclined on the grass in front of Claude's house, talk turned to Sun Country and the footrace in August. Walking past a cluster of Fall City and Staircase volunteers, Fontana overheard somebody say, "I never had a sister myself so I don't know how perverted that is, but it sounds pretty sick to me." Fontana might have stopped to hear the rest of the conversation, but he wasn't sure he wanted details.

Roger Truax had pulled up in his Buick and was chatting in the road with Mo Costigan. Mo wore her rubber boots, bulky yellow bunking trousers, and red suspenders over a soaking wet Staircase Fire Department T-shirt. Her hair was matted.

Fontana smiled. "You take the test, Mo, I'll hire you."

Dental silver crowded the margins of her smile. "If I got on with the department, you'd be my boss, but I'd still be the mayor so I'd be your boss. We'd both legally be able to yell at each other."

He smiled harder. "Same as now, Mo."

Truax wore slacks and a starched shirt. "It's curious we've had two fires in this particular structure," he said. "Do you think there's any significance to that?"

"You tell me."

His face relaxed and slack, Truax gave him the blankest of looks. Mo fidgeted and played with her suspenders while Truax pretended not to watch. The queer thing was that Peter Mark, who was now under lock and key, had set the first fire here—had admitted as much. So what game was this second arsonist playing? The papers had been filled with news of Mark's incarceration. Tonight's arsonist had torched the barbershop, the Ford behind the Thriftway, this house, the second house that never got going, the fence, and the shack—

probably in that order. Tonight's arsonist had to be the killer, the same person who'd set the Cove Road fire.

Loud voices disturbed Fontana's deliberations. In Pettigrew's driveway forty feet away, Pettigrew and Sandusky stood toe to toe. "Last summer you accuse me of trying to poison half the department, including my own sweetheart," Pettigrew shouted. "And this summer you think I'm burning the town down?"

"Whatever happened to Wanda, Claude?" Sandusky said. "I heard she ran off with a meter reader."

Clenching his fists at his sides, Claude stepped forward and bumped Sandusky backward with his stomach. Since he weighed over three hundred pounds and stood nearly as tall as Sandusky, Claude's move was almost a first blow.

"They going to fight?" Truax asked.

"Sandusky'd kill him," Fontana said.

"Claude's carrying a lot of bulk. It's hard to tell how much of that is muscle."

"You want them to fight?" Mo asked. "Are you crazy? Go over there and break it up, Mac. Hurry."

Fontana walked over and inserted himself between the two men. As he did so, Claude said, "For your information, smarty-pants, Wanda drowned fishing off the coast six months ago."

"Oh, shit," said Sandusky. "I'm sorry. Me and my big mouth. How about the meter reader and all the other guys who were banging her? They drown too?"

"You're an asshole, you know that?" Claude said.

Sandusky looked at Fontana. "I been doing a little poking around, Chief. Know what I found?"

"What?"

"The engine block on Claude's little Pinto here was hot."

"Was not," Claude said. "Feel it."

"Course it's not now," Sandusky said. "That was a coupl'a hours ago when we first got here. You were out catting around, weren't you, Claude? Got a lighter on you?"

"I ain't going to dignify that with an answer." Claude folded his massive arms across his chest.

It wasn't until the county fire investigators showed up and began poking around that Fontana began mentally checking off names of people who'd been incapable of setting tonight's fires.

He could eliminate Hawkins who had been at the station with Fontana when the first fire was set. He was left with Sandusky, Truax, Weed, Heather, Mo, Les and Opal Morgan, and Audie Culpepper. Of those, only the first four would fit the description of a tall person that he got from the eyewitness earlier in the evening. And Heather had been with him at the Sutterfields' when the other fires were set that night. Fontana noted that for the first time since the arsons began, Audie had not come to watch their extinguishment.

By the time the next alarm came in, most of the volunteers had been sent home. The call was two miles east of town.

"Staircase Way and Stooly Road," said the dispatcher. "In the junkyard. This is a trailer fire. Flames visible."

Fontana's heart thumped so hard he could feel it in his chest. The last trailer fire he'd been to had been almost eighteen years earlier. They'd caught an alarm in the middle of the night at a construction site where they found two trailers burning. One fire might be accidental. Two separated by a hundred yards of dirt road couldn't be anything but arson. Young, naive, and eager, Fontana hadn't been at the location five minutes when he spotted a man in the shadows and gave chase. It was because he gave chase that he was far enough down the road when the trailers exploded that he did not die with the six other firefighters. The trailers had been used as storage sheds for ammonium nitrate, a substance often used as an explosive.

Shaking himself free of the memory, Fontana looked at Pierpont and gave him a rented smile. The dispatcher was finishing up her third round of address and information.

"Damn," said Kingsley. "It's three-thirty in the morning. We ever going to get any sleep?"

THIRTY-TWO

♦

THE TURKEY KILLER

Peering down the long channel of firs from half a mile away, Fontana could see flame shooting surgically into the night, throwing tall shadows and snaky orange flashes high into the trees. It seemed as if he were driving along the bottom of a dark trough on this two-lane highway where a new crop of small, dead animals appeared weekly along the dew line.

Joshua Clunk owned the junkyard and the burning mobile home too.

The car accident they'd gone to the night of the Cove Road fire had been three eighths of a mile to the south, and it was not inconceivable that Clunk had driven past it or even that he'd heard the sirens and gone over to watch. Clunk would have realized the accident would produce a window of time in which to set a fire. And, unlikely as it seemed, for most people in the department had abandoned him, there was still the remote possibility that Clunk had heard from a friend in the volunteers that Fontana's son would be spending the night at the Sutterfields'.

"Stooly Command at Staircase Way and Stooly Road," Fontana said on the radio as he arrived, rolling past the fire building in order to view three sides. "We have a trailer fire approximately twenty by sixty, flames showing. Engine One, lay a preconnect. Engine Two, lay a manifold to the hydrant due east of the property. I want the tanker too."

Even for a junkyard it looked threadbare, only a dozen or so rusting car hulks on the premises, most too stripped to be of use for anything but scrap metal. Cast-off car parts and rubble were strewn here and there.

Clunk hobbled back and forth in front of an eight-foot cyclone fence topped with barbed wire. He wore only jeans, his bare stomach rippling from thousands of sit-ups. He was scrawny and hunch-shouldered and hirsute, and tonight he underlined his poor posture by gimping around barefoot in the gravel. Fontana hadn't seen him since the night Sally Culpepper shot his dogs.

"Those raisin-head fuckers!" Clunk said.

Fontana parked the truck and threw on his bunking coat and helmet, grabbing the bolt cutters from the back of the truck. He could feel the heat from the fire. Engine One was still half a mile away.

"You ain't going to bust my lock, are you?" Clunk said. "I paid Mort Halloran eight dollars for that sonofabitch."

Fontana fastened the bolt cutters on the chain and squeezed the long handles until a link snapped. "How much you pay for the trailer?" Walking it as if it were an old man, Fontana swung the gate open.

"I seen him sneaking around. It was that kid."

"What kid?"

"His old lady shot Ron and Nancy."

"Ron and who?"

"My rottweilers. They're over there under those tires."

Engine One pulled up, men and women climbing off, Lieutenant Pierpont's voice vying with the low cutting sound of the flames and the roar of the engine. Heather was driving, so she would remain outside running the pump.

Talking nonstop, Joshua Clunk hobbled around in the dirt and gravel behind Fontana. "I almost had it out. Almost had it out twice. That little fucker. I know his mother put him up to it."

Followed by a trail of smoke, an animal sped from a shadow near the gate, crossed the open drive, and dashed into a portion of the junkyard stacked with detached fenders.

"What the hell was that?" Fontana asked.

"Hector," Joshua Clunk said. "He'd eat you alive."

"What is he, a warthog?"

"Hell, no. That's my new Dobey. His teeth'll go through a quarter-inch steel plate."

"Looks like his teeth are looking for a place to hide."

"He's just shamed 'cause I got a turkey on him. Hector! Here, boy." The dog remained in hiding.

It turned out to be a pretty good fire.

After they'd laid the lines and gotten the pump going, Sandusky and Hawkins stood in the doorway of the burning trailer and threw two hundred fifty gallons a minute into the open doorway while flame and black smoke boiled out of three sides of the trailer.

Followed closely by a throng of cautious volunteers, all of them crawling to stay under the heat, Sandusky and Hawkins bulled their way in with the hose line, a succession of yellow rumps disappearing through the black doorway.

It began as a series of light popping noises, ammunition exploding, .22 ammo probably. The noise accelerated until the trailer sounded like a commercial popcorn machine. When the rifle went off, it shook the walls. Firefighters poured out the front door so quickly they ended up in a heap on an old pink towel Clunk used for a welcome mat.

Except for Sandusky and Hawkins, who could be heard at about the midpoint in the trailer, everybody had bailed out. Then, a few moments later, Hawkins came out a window like a high jumper over a low bar, landing on his back in a stack of old truck tires.

Six or eight firefighters now stood at the entrance listening to shells going off inside, to Sandusky working the hose line alone. When Hawkins looked around and realized Sandusky hadn't defected with the others, he rushed back through the doorway. After a few minutes, clouds of white steam began replacing the smoke.

Fontana was standing next to the bole of a tree when a shivering Joshua Clunk approached. "You getting ready for the next world war, or what?" Fontana asked.

"Them's my guns."

"Them *was* your guns."

"Yeah."

When the bells on Sandusky's and Hawkins's air masks began ringing, the signal that they had five minutes of air left, Fontana sent in a second crew to continue the overhaul, giving instructions to re-move only what was necessary. In one back room, they took the wall panels off. Debris, some of it smoking, some of it wet or aflame, was lobbed out the windows. Clunk seemed to have collected every Na-tional Rifle Association bulletin and publication ever printed, along with dozens of pornographic magazines. On top of a sooty velvet Elvis painting in the yard was a videotape titled *Indonesian Beauties Take a Bath*.

Forty minutes later, while the crews were resting among the junked cars talking about doe tags, bear hunts, and snowmobiling, a pair of King County fire investigators showed up and combed through the wreckage. One of them took Joshua Clunk back to their car for ques-tioning.

Fontana was in front of the burned-out trailer when Mo Costigan and Roger Truax approached. Mo had changed out of her wet bun-kers and was wearing dry clothes.

"Roger's been talking to Clunk," Mo said. "We want you to take those investigators over to Aimee Lee's house and arrest the kid."

"You might want to document it with a film crew," Truax added.

Mo tucked her T-shirt into her jeans. "Clunk is willing to testify he saw the kid hanging around before the fire."

"And that proves . . . what?"

"The kid set it," said Truax dispassionately. "He doesn't live half a mile from here. Just beyond that big cedar by the river where the road bends. It's a white house. I'm sure he set the other ones too."

"Clunk has a vendetta against those two, and you know it," said Fontana. "Not only that, but take a walk around the trailer and tell me where he started the fire."

Mo Costigan and Truax glanced at the hulk. "What do you mean?"

"Show me the point of ignition."

"I don't see what you're getting at," Mo said.

"The only char you'll see on the outside is around the windows and doors where the flame came out."

"You're saying the kid was inside when he set it?"

"He's saying Clunk is a fucking liar," said Sandusky, joining the group. "And you're damn fools to believe him. The fire started inside, and no way Clunk let that kid inside. No fucking way."

"Don't you talk to me like that," said Mo. Truax had not taken his eyes off the trailer.

"Talk to you like what? Oh. You mean my fucking language?"

Jennifer Underhill showed up in civilian clothes, conferred with the first investigators, spoke for five minutes to Joshua Clunk, who was huddled under a blanket in the front seat of the first investigator's car, then walked over to Fontana's group. As she approached, an animal scuttled from one nearby car hulk to another.

"What was that?" Mo asked, startled by the noise. "A rat? I didn't get a good look."

"If it was a rat, it was a *big* rat," said Truax.

"It was smoking," said Sandusky.

"Damn, that's the second time I seen it," said Hawkins, joining the group. "What was it?"

Fontana said, "I think it's a warthog."

"Whatever it is," said Hawkins, moving in the direction of the car hulk, "the damn thing's on fire."

Jenny Underhill spoke to Fontana. "We've got a little problem of veracity here. I'd like to know exactly what you saw when you arrived. Who was first in?"

"I was." Fontana told her what he'd seen.

"Are you telling me Clunk was out here in his bare feet with the gate locked behind him?"

"Yup."

"Well, I guess I've seen people do dumber things," said Underhill. "But some of the rest of this is starting to add up. He claims he had thirteen hundred dollars' worth of money orders in the trailer. Yet we ask where his insurance papers were and he pulls them out of his hip pocket."

"God," said Sandusky. "He's standing in his yard with his insurance papers in his pocket? What a dumb shit."

"We noticed something," said Lieutenant Pierpont. "He's got ammunition for about six different calibers of guns, but there's only one old rifle in the trailer. The TV's missing too. Most of the big stuff is missing."

"Why don't we go over and question the kid?" Roger Truax said.

"Get off it," said Mo. "He set his own fire."

"But if the kid was prowling around, he might've seen something."

"The kid wasn't prowling around."

Before the group disbanded, Hawkins, his red hair compressed from wearing the helmet, dragged Clunk's Doberman pincher across the yard. The dog's head was down, ears lowered in humiliation.

"What the hell is that?" Mo Costigan asked.

"Looks to me like a dog with a dead turkey tied around its neck," said Fontana.

"Teachin' him a lesson is all," Clunk said, approaching the group with a blanket over his narrow shoulders. "He won't kill another one of my turkeys. No siree."

"That looks like a pretty raggedy fryer," Sandusky said. "You sure that's not a pigeon?"

"How long's it been on him?" Fontana asked.

"Four days," replied Clunk. At the sound of his master's voice, the dog broke loose and fled into the shadows, moving in a low scoot. Hawkins, also in a low scoot, gave chase.

"Shouldn't somebody go help with that poor dog?" said Mo.

"Hell," said Sandusky. "The turkey's the one needs help. The dog chewed both his damn legs off."

"That's what I should'a done to that woman," said Clunk.

"What?" Sandusky looked around the group. "Chewed her legs off?"

"Tied a turkey around her fool neck."

◆

THIRTY-THREE

ANOTHER SCREWY
CONVERSATION

At noon the next day, Fontana went to the station and found that even though she'd been up most of the night fighting fire, Heather Minerich had reported to work. So had Kingsley Pierpont. Weed, who had missed all the fires last night, was scheduled to work tonight.

Lieutenant Pierpont stopped in the doorway to Fontana's office and said, "I got something I need to talk to you about."

Before either of them could say anything else, the bell hit. A medic run to the nursing home. Ongoing CPR, said the dispatcher. Kingsley, Heather, and two volunteers scrambled onto Engine One and sped off. The medic unit, which had been out of quarters, could be heard responding from another part of town, probably the doughnut shop, Fontana thought.

An hour later, the engine and medic unit were still out of quarters when Mo dropped in and sat on the edge of Fontana's desk.

"Mo. You're looking refreshed. And that was a nice job you did at the fire—"

"Mac. Did you tell Heather she might get raped?"

"What?"

"Did you tell her she might get raped?"

"Mo, what—?"

"Did you walk in on her while she was dressing?"

"Okay, Mo. Spit it out. What's going on?"

"I had a heart-to-heart talk with Kingsley this morning. About Heather. She's come to me with some problems in the past, girl-type problems, and we've been working together on them. So when she told me she thought she was going to get fired, I had a chat with Kingsley and he confirmed it."

"What exactly did he confirm?"

"That she was not performing to the standards he would like her to perform to."

"I'm surprised he spoke to you. He knows what I think about following the chain of command. You should have come to me with this, Mo, instead of going to my subordinates."

"I'm afraid I told him I'd already spoken to you and you'd told me to talk to him."

"Mo. That was an outright lie."

"No, no, no, no. I'm talking to you *now*. I just did it in reverse. First him and now you. There was no lying involved."

"Well, I'm not giving you permission to talk to him, so now it's a lie. What did he say?"

"He's writing a bad report on her this month over the Cove Road fire. You know as well as I do that if a recruit receives two monthly reports in a row that are below average, they can be fired in the third month. That's a lot of pressure to put somebody under. A hell of a lot of pressure. It would make *anybody* screw up."

"You don't get it, Mo. We put somebody in this job who can't handle it, and the pressure they'll be feeling next is six feet of dirt in their face. Probation is where we sort these things out."

"Are you thinking about firing her?"

"Until now, she's passed everything required of her. We go step by step here. You know that. And to be frank, I don't think Heather had any business going to you with this."

"Did you tell her she did a good job at the Cove Road fire and then amend it by telling her she did poorly? Who influenced your thinking?"

"I told the group they'd done a good job, and she interpreted that to mean *she* had done a good job."

"And then you told her she did a lousy job?"

"No. Then I asked her what she'd done. She told me and we went on to other things."

"Okay, Mac. And this is where your own ass is hanging out a country mile. Did you tell her she might get raped in the station?"

"No."

"Are you sure?"

"I am positive."

"Think back on everything you said."

"I've been thinking real hard ever since you came through that door."

"Did you walk in on her while she was dressing?"

"Inadvertently, I did. I turned around and asked her to finish."

"Did you stare at her breasts in a mirror?"

"Damn it, Mo. She had her back to me. When I saw that she had her shirt unbuttoned, I turned around. That's all there was to it."

"And you danced with her suggestively at the Bedouin, didn't you? Did you tell her it was all right for Kingsley to take a shower with her?"

"You think I'm nuts?"

"Did you tell her you wanted her to sleep and dress in a closet?"

"It's the old aid-car room. Your locker's in there too, Mo."

"Oh."

"Yeah. Oh. Let's just run this whole thing by the rules, Mo. You don't lie to my people. In return, we'll write our reports as honestly as we can. And you don't try to second-guess the reports before they're written."

"Mac, you don't get it. You can't let a woman wash out of the department. I've already bragged about our female firefighter all up and down the coast. What am I going to do? Go back and say we had to throw her out?"

"Mo, nobody has mentioned firing her except you."

"Let me leave you with this thought, Mac." Mo Costigan slid off the desk with a rustle of fabric, leaned over, and straightened her skirt. "Heather successfully sued Burlington Northern for sexual discrimination."

"She did what?"

"She collected almost a quarter of a million dollars. Since the day she was hired here, she's been keeping a journal. Everything anybody has said is written down."

"Good grief. That must take hours every night."

"You don't get it, Mac. She's been recording all of this."

"No, Mo. You don't get it. We haven't done anything wrong. And I really doubt she's going to wash out. She did swell up at the academy, and she was doing swell down here until the other night."

"I hope so. But what if she *were* a little bit afraid of fire?"

"Mo, do you have information I don't?"

"I'm just thinking aloud."

"Tell me what's going on, Mo."

"What if she were just the teeniest bit afraid of it?"

"Mo, if she told you she's afraid of fire, I don't want to hear about it. That's hearsay. I don't want to know."

"But if she were, we could work around that, couldn't we?"

"From what you've told me, I'm not so sure she even wants the job. It sounds like she'd rather sue us."

"And Mac?" Mo had the office door open, was leaning against the jamb. "Don't make any more sexual advances toward your female recruit, okay?"

"Mo, sometimes talking to you is like trying to climb up the inside of a greased pipe." But the cowbell on the front door was clanging. Mo was gone.

♦

THIRTY-FOUR

ROBINSON JEFFERS IS
ASLEEP IN MY CLOSET

Fontana and Brendan were building tuna sandwiches with a layer of tortilla chips under the bread when his pager went off. It was another house fire near Stooly Road. Fontana sent Brendan to Mary's house and, because it was a daylight fire, let Satan ride in the truck.

"Dispatcher from Engine One," Lieutenant Pierpont said over the radio. "We're up on Stooly Road at last night's trailer fire. Give us an address."

While driving into town, Fontana listened to Kingsley's initial radio report. "Engine One, fourteen-forty River Road. Assuming River Command. Nothing visible. Investigating. Code yellow all units."

Even though he'd been given a code yellow, Fontana raced through town and out Staircase Way. He'd recognized the address. As he passed the junkyard and the burned-out trailer, a second radio report said, "River Command. Tapped food on the stove. Ongoing CPR. Code green all units except Engine One, the chief, and the medic unit code red." Cardiopulmonary resuscitation? Who was not breathing? There were only three people in that house.

When he pulled into the circular driveway, Fontana commanded Satan to stay next to the truck while he ran up the steps ahead of the medics. Even in the yard he could smell the acrid odor of burning food on the stove.

It was a spacious kitchen at the rear of the house, a haze of white smoke and Purple K dust lingering in the air. The wall behind the stove was scorched almost to the ceiling. A burned pan and contents sat outside on the deck railing. Fontana placed his bare palm on the wall to see how much heat it had retained.

Lieutenant Pierpont stood at the open patio door giving Fontana a lugubrious look. He held a clipboard with an aid form affixed. An expended extinguisher from the engine stood beside his feet. Another used extinguisher, a small red one commonly purchased in a drugstore or hardware outlet, sat on a cabinet top. Lindoff was on his knees on the floor doing CPR. So was Heather Minerich. Between them on her back lay a woman, her dress cut open to the waist, her flaccid breasts falling down either side of her rib cage.

Heather was bag-masking her while Lindoff knelt at her side, pressing the heel of his palm against her sternum and counting the compressions aloud in cycles of five. Every fifth compression, he paused while Heather Minerich squeezed the bulb on the Laerdal, forcing air into the woman's lungs.

Banging the sides of the doorways with their heavy cases, the medics trudged through the house and into the crowded kitchen, followed closely by Robinson Jeffers.

Clasping a Nikon in both hands, Robinson Jeffers walked with the camera held to his face, straining to angle a shot over the back of a stooping paramedic. Everybody was talking at once, all attention focused on the patient, so nobody noticed when Fontana reached around and whacked the camera lens with the heel of his hand.

"Ouch! God!" said Jeffers, cupping his eye and hunching into a protective stance. "Darn it!"

Gripping the collar of Jeffers's windbreaker, Fontana walked him quickly through the house, propelling him out the front door and onto the stoop. When the reporter came to his senses, he said, "This is a public event. I have every right to—"

"I'm legally in charge of this scene, and I'm ordering you off the premises. Any more lip, and I'll charge you with hindering a fire department operation."

Jeffers stumbled down the steps. "What happened in there? Somebody hit me. My camera. You took my camera."

"This? Let me give it back to you. Oh, wait a minute. Dang. I'm sorry. Does that wreck the pictures when you open it like that?" As he handed the camera to Jeffers, Fontana held the 35-millimeter film strip so that when Jeffers moved, it unspooled.

"She's dead, isn't she?" Jeffers said.

"Do me a favor," Fontana said to a pair of King County police officers walking up the drive. "Escort this Dugan to the gate, and make sure he doesn't come back."

"This is a conspiracy against the American people. She's dead. You can't keep this out of the news. It's my scoop." H. C. Bailey and another officer chaperoned Jeffers out of the yard. Sitting on his haunches beside the chief's truck, his good ear up, Satan watched them pass. "What did she think it was going to be like?" Jeffers yelled. "She worked all her life to be famous. What did she think it was going to be like? I know she's dead."

As the trio passed, Satan growled and launched up off his haunches as if to give chase, then glanced back over his shoulder at Fontana, who said, "That's right. You come back here and he'll be having your family jewels for breakfast."

When he returned to the kitchen, the CPR had ceased. All the firefighters and medics were standing around with grim looks on their faces. The shorter of the two medics explained to Sally Culpepper, who had just come into the room, that her housekeeper was dead, that she probably had suffered a massive heart attack, that there wasn't anything anybody could have done. Sally wept without mopping the tears from her face.

When Fontana asked Sally if there was anything he could do, she grasped his forearm with a surprisingly tenacious grip and said, "Mac. I have to speak to you."

She led him upstairs and down a long hallway, into a bedroom with a cathedral ceiling and an enormous white bed, photos along one wall of Sally in various movie roles. "Audie found Greta. I heard him yelling for me, and I went down to the kitchen and found the stove on fire, Greta unconscious. At first I thought she'd been struck with something because of the blood. But then I realized she must have fallen and hit her head. I used the extinguisher out of the cupboard and then called the fire department. I didn't even realize she was dead until they started doing resuscitation. I'm so useless. And then Audie was gone."

"He's missing?"

"Can you stay and help me find him?"

"Sure, Sally."

Thirty minutes later, the medical examiner's people trundled Greta down the drive on a gurney in a long, zippered, black bag. When the officials were gone, Sally Culpepper pushed a button on the wall near the front door and the wrought-iron gate closed. "I'm really worried."

"You might have told the cops," Fontana said. "We might have started looking when they were still here."

"And see it in the tabloids? Housekeeper dies. Lee's son flees? Not on your life."

Fontana opened the front door and said, "Satan! *Fuss!* Come here, boy." The dog trotted up to the house, hesitated on the stoop, and then entered. "You got any of his clothing? A shirt would be good."

She disappeared and came back a few moments later with a gray T-shirt which Fontana held out for the dog to sniff. "Satan! *Suche! Suche!*"

In a matter of minutes, Satan had cleared the house and was nosing the patio slider in the kitchen. Fontana opened it.

"Mac, thank you for getting that reporter out of my house."

"The funny thing is he thought that was you on the floor. He thinks you're dead."

"You know, Robinson Jeffers has been writing about me for years. I actually found him in my closet once. He'd been hiding in there so long he fell asleep and began snoring. My bodyguard roughed him up and then got charged for assault. It was in all the papers. That stuff made me crazy. Even now I come home and go through the house checking the closets. You should have seen Greta the first time she caught me at it. Poor Greta."

Clouds had moved in, and the sky was a dark gray. When Fontana followed Satan into the backyard, a raindrop kissed his brow. Several more raindrops plopped into the grass around him. The branches of a maple rubbed together in the wind.

The dog had been sniffing near the garage, but then he loped over to the six-foot fence at the back of the property near the rope swing and leaped it in one bound.

Fontana said, "You better wait here in case he comes back." He jogged across the yard, climbed the fence, and followed the sound of the dog ahead of him. Raindrops spattered leaves in the trees above him.

The dog followed a path near the river, doubled back twice, and ended up in a clearing near the fence, at a point from which someone would have been able to view activity in the kitchen across the broad back lawn with relatively little chance of being observed. Satan circled the clearing twice and headed back along a sketchy path near the river.

They skirted the rear of a Christmas tree farm, went through a tilting barbed-wire fence that bisected an open pasture, then turned up a steep hillside into a stand of evergreens. The river was almost out of earshot here, and he hadn't seen a house in five minutes.

Near the top of the slope the dog stopped, glanced back at Fontana, then looked up. When Fontana followed the dog's gaze, he spotted the boy in a tree maybe thirty feet above their heads. The boy blinked, stared at Fontana.

"Hey, Audie. You all right?"

"I guess."

"What are you doing up there?"

"Thinking."

"Would you like to come down and think?"

"I guess."

When he got near the bottom of the tree, Fontana saw a pistol tucked into his waistband. "What you got there, Audie?"

"My mom's gun."

"Can you aim it at the ground and hand it to me?"

"I didn't do it," Audie said, speaking so softly Fontana could barely hear.

"Didn't do what?"

"I didn't set the fire."

"I know you didn't, Audie. It was accidental. It was food burning on the stove. Now hand me the gun." Audie hesitated, then passed the pistol across. "It was just a good thing you were there."

"It was?"

"The whole house might have gone up." Fontana opened the cylinder on the revolver and let six bullets slide into his palm. "In fact, you might have saved your mother's life."

"No foolin'?"

"That's right."

"What about Greta?"

"She had a heart attack. She's dead. I'm sorry, Audie."

"I thought she was. I never saw a dead person before. I got scared 'cause she was all gray. I didn't know what to do."

"Why did you have the gun?"

"I was thinking about shooting myself in the head."

Fontana looked at the boy. "Don't ever do that, Audie. Promise me, if you ever think things are that bad, talk to your mother first. Or me. Okay?"

"Sure."

"Promise?"

"Yes, sir."

Putting his arm across Audie's shoulders, which were cold and wet from the rain, Fontana walked him back to the house. When she saw them, Sally Culpepper ran across the grass and folded her son into her arms. "No, Mom. I got pitch on me. Look at all this pitch. And I'm wet."

"You go take a hot shower. Don't get out until you're pink. And thank Chief Fontana for finding you."

"Why? I wasn't lost."

"Just thank him."

"Thank you, Chief Fontana."

After they heard the shower in a far part of the house, Sally kissed Fontana's cheek and patted the dog. "He would have stayed out all night," she said. "When he gets frightened, he can stay away forever."

"He had your gun, Sally."

She sat on a straight-backed chair against the wall near the hallway. It wasn't a chair that had been positioned for anybody to actually use, but she sat in it as if it were her most cherished refuge.

"Six years ago, Audie was kidnapped in Northern California up near Eureka. It was a long, complicated exchange, but it ended up that they buried him in a park and gave him a little air tube to the surface. He was eight years old."

"Oh, God," said Fontana.

"We were to drop the money in a suitcase in a parking lot, and in return they would leave a map showing where they'd hidden Audie. We didn't know he was buried. Even though the press had been told to stay away, Robinson Jeffers followed the FBI to the drop point. The kidnappers didn't spot the FBI, but they spotted Jeffers. He actually had a man with a television camera in his car. The long and the short of it was, the kidnappers ran, the FBI chased—eventually they caught them—but while all this was going on, Audie was buried alive. When they dug him up six hours later, he was in a light coma. He'd been in there pounding against the walls of the box."

"So Robinson Jeffers nearly got your boy killed?"

"No. I did. If I'd been more concerned with Audie and less with my career, none of it would have happened."

"I'm sure that's not true."

Sally Culpepper's eyes filled with tears. He pulled her to her feet and gave her a hug. "I hate those vultures," she said. "I hate them."

When Fontana left, he noticed Jeffers's car parked a hundred yards away on the road out of sight of the main gate. He stopped, and Jeffers slowly lifted his head from below the window level in the car, a wet rag pressed against his swollen eye.

The reporter rolled his window down. "The kid set the fire. I know the kid set that fire."

"You don't know anything."

"The way I figure it, he was in there playing with matches and Lee came in and tried to subdue him. While they were struggling, the fire got out of hand. He killed her, probably by accident, and ran from the scene. Then the housekeeper called nine-one-one." A gleam of triumph rising off his short teeth and wet gums, he smiled for the first time. "Right?"

"You're never right," Fontana said, as he drove away.

◆

THIRTY-FIVE

I'M NO GOOD.

I'M NO GOOD.

Saturday morning, Sally Culpepper called Fontana at the station. "You going to the Bedouin tonight?"

"I was thinking about it."

"I know this sounds awful with Greta just gone, but I need to get out. I've been cooped up in this house it seems like half my life. I remember reading about a pioneer woman in Kansas who was so crazy from living alone on the prairie she would walk ten miles just to see the faces in the windows of a passing train. I feel like that. I've always been a people person, and I really need to be around a crowd. Would you mind company tonight?"

"Seven-thirty?"

"Seven-thirty would be terrific. I'll be here."

An hour before he was to pick up Sally, he drove to Cove Road and parked in front of the Sutterfield house. They'd begun the remodel, though progress was slow and all the debris from the fire had not yet been cleared out. Rena Sutterfield heard his truck and met him in the yard.

"Mind if I look around?" Fontana said.

Wrapped in a sloppy blue sweater, Rena, a small, dark-eyed woman, said, "Of course not. We haven't got a whole lot done."

Walking around the house, Fontana traced the path Sandusky had taken that night with the hose line, spotting the telltale traffic patterns in the grass that Sandusky had claimed were the reason he went in the east door. Taking a penlight from his pocket, he went back to the road side of the house and approached the west door, went inside.

He examined the burned flooring and charred wall. Most of the ceiling had been pulled down the night of the fire.

He turned to the door he'd been standing beside that night. It was still in the frame, splintered along the edge where Les and Opal Morgan had kicked it in. He pushed it open with his fingertips and knelt with the penlight. He threw the lock in and out, noting that the discoloration on the bolt was at the tip. If it had been locked during the fire, the discoloration would have been toward the center.

"Just kicking over old traces?" Rena Sutterfield asked.

He showed her what he'd found.

"Are you trying to say our door was unlocked that night?"

"It was unlocked during the fire. There's not much doubt about that."

"But your people kicked it in. It was all broken."

"Yeah. There could be a couple of possible explanations for that. They could have done that automatically. After all, it was the middle of the night. It should have been locked."

"And the other possibility?"

"That the people who kicked it in also set the fire, that they didn't want anybody to know they knew the door was unlocked."

"Who kicked it in?"

"I'd rather not say at this time."

"So the implication is that somebody had a key to our door?"

"Not necessarily. Mary was out here baby-sitting. All those kids running around. It could be she lost track and didn't get one of the doors locked, or locked it and one of the kids unlocked it later. What we know for sure is that the arsonist sneaked into your old sunporch there and started a fire. Listen. I want to give you a list of people and I want you to tell me if, to your knowledge, they've ever visited you. I'm interested in people who knew where you lived."

"Sure."

He fed her the names one by one, the people who'd been in the beanery the night he'd mentioned Brendan would be here. Of the nine people who had been in the beanery, Les and Opal Morgan had visited a year earlier, returning a car they'd done some clutch work on at their station. Audie Culpepper had visited during a Scouting project last July. Sandusky had been there once when they'd advertised a riding lawn mower for sale. Truax had visited Larry, her husband, about three months before, though Rena didn't know what the purpose of that visit was.

"And as far as you know, Heather Minerich and Frank Weed and Jim Hawkins had never been out here before?"

"Never. As far as I know. We didn't even know them before the fire."

"What about Joshua Clunk?"

"Sure. He's been out here several times. He's picked up a couple of old car bodies from Larry."

"And Mo Costigan?"

"The mayor? We wouldn't have her. She's in favor of all that growth. She needs to be impeached."

"My sentiments exactly," said Fontana, his grin feeling as tight as a bad suture.

When he picked her up, Sally wore a red blouse, dressy jeans, cowboy boots, and a white leather jacket. The Bedouin was rocking, and a sliver of moon was just rising over the back side of Mount Gadd. They parked a block away behind the train station. Spotting license plates in the alley from British Columbia, Idaho, Oregon, and California, Fontana had a feeling the Bedouin was full of celebrity hunters.

Frank Weed had apparently patched things up with Sheri because they were together. Lindoff, Valenzuela, Hawkins, Sandusky, Les and Opal Morgan were all there too.

No doubt, word of the housekeeper's death had leaked to the press, for they were queued along one wall.

Followed closely by a man with a TV camera on his shoulder, Bree McAllister approached during their first dance and, without asking permission, jabbed a microphone at Sally. "We've heard rumors that you've been reading scripts, looking for a movie to do."

Without losing the beat, Fontana and Sally sideslipped through the dancers, moving near one of the raucous jukebox loudspeakers. Unimpeded by the other couples, who, when they saw the camera, parted like park ducks before a pram, Bree McAllister pursued.

Fontana stopped dancing, turned around, placed Sally squarely behind him, and said, "Listen, Bree. You know she's not going to answer. All you're doing is trashing our evening. Now why don't you go dance with your husband or interview the mayor before you force us to leave?"

"I hope you realize I don't normally do this, Chief," Bree said, staring at him with a glazed look. "I really don't do this, but I was ordered to."

"You really *do* do this," Fontana said. "Because here you are."

"But I don't. I argued with them. I'm sorry." She turned to the man standing behind her with the camera and said, "Joe, let's pick up." Most of the dancing had stopped, and a circle of people were watching, although over the sound of the jukebox, few could hear what was being said.

"Everybody's in an uproar," Bree shouted over the music. "Every news service in the country. Could I just ask one question? She doesn't have to answer. I just want to ask it so I can tell my boss I did. And then I'll go."

Sally, who had been standing directly behind Fontana, cautiously looked around his back. "What is it?"

"Mark Twain said, 'The reports of my death have been greatly exaggerated,' or something to that effect. How do you feel about the reports of your death, Aimee?"

"What reports?" Sally asked.

"Haven't you seen the early edition of tomorrow's paper?" Bree reached into a bag slung over one shoulder, pulled out the first section of the Sunday *Seattle Times/P.I.* and passed it to Fontana, who held it to one side so Sally could read over his shoulder.

AIMEE LEE DIES IN STAIRCASE FIRE was the headline over a large color photograph taken with a telephoto lens through what appeared to be Sally's kitchen window.

The photo had been taken from somewhere in the trees in back of the house, probably from the clearing Satan had found. The picture showed Kingsley Pierpont's back, part of a medic's white shirt, and the feet of a prone woman on the floor, one slipper askew.

The sub-headline said: MYSTERY DEATH CONCEALED BY FIRE CHIEF.

"I'm surprised you haven't heard. It's been all over the television. We all thought Jeffers scooped us until a couple of hours ago when a rumor went around that it was the *housekeeper* who died. And then you showed up here. It's already been on the wire services. This is national news. World news. And it's all wrong. What does it feel like to be dead, Aimee?"

Sally clutched Fontana's arm tightly. "Good-bye," said Fontana.

"What?"

"You had your question. Good-bye."

Face coloring, Bree McAllister turned and walked through the crowd. The song ended. When Fontana turned around, Sally stood close.

"What is it?"

"I've got to get to a phone. If Audie catches wind of this . . ."

The two pay phones near the front entrance were in use by men who stopped talking when they recognized Sally. The phone in the office in back of the building was also being used.

They jogged across Staircase Way in the middle of the block and hand in hand walked to the fire station on the next street, where Fontana led her into his office. "Maybe I should call my mother, too," she said.

"Call anybody you think needs calling. It's on the city."

When she'd closed the door behind herself, Fontana went into the beanery where two volunteers, a pair of Bellevue medics, and Jennifer Underhill were sitting at the table in front of the TV.

"I'm glad you came in, Mac." Jennifer Underhill got up. "We need to talk." He took her down the corridor to the empty lieutenant's office, where she closed the door behind them.

"Mac. There's a volunteer up here named Sandusky. What do you think of him?"

"As a pure firefighter, he's about the best we've got. His attitude isn't always what a chief would love to see, but I was like that too. Maybe that's why I like him."

"The way I understand it, he took a hose line directly to the seat of that fire on Cove Road."

"That's right."

"I don't know that in the dark, with smoke pouring out of every crevice, I would have known the best way to get to the fire. Or anybody would. But he didn't hesitate. You think he might have had prior knowledge of the house? Like maybe he'd been reconnoitering twenty minutes earlier?"

"I was out at the Sutterfield place just today wondering that very thing."

"I heard he went in a door nobody else even knew existed."

"He said he spotted traffic patterns in the grass and guessed there was a door around in back. But I found out tonight he'd been to the house before."

"Did you know he calls me at the office every day? Even at home? He goes through this ritual of speculation. He's listed everyone from co-workers to his boss. A million theories."

"His boss? Was he talking about me?"

"Yes."

"He thinks I set a fire in a house where my own son was sleeping?"

"It was only one of a dozen theories he tossed around. If I had to describe it to an outsider, I'd say Sandusky has an unnatural interest in the arsons. A real unnatural interest."

"It's not like he hasn't been fighting the fires. It's not like he hasn't risked his life. Also, there will be a certain amount of prestige for whoever solves this. Maybe that's what he's after."

"There are a lot of people risking their lives at these fires, but none of the others has called me like he has. Twelve times yesterday. I've been letting him ramble and ask questions, but if I had to name suspects, he'd be at the top of my list."

"Maybe he likes you, Jenny. Ever think of that?"

"Thought about it and dismissed it."

Fontana outlined the theory he'd been working on and gave her the list of names of people who'd heard him say Brendan would be at the Sutterfields'.

"You got any enemies on that list?"

"That I know of? Not really." He told her what he'd found that evening at the Sutterfields' and what Rena Sutterfield had said.

Underhill took a deep breath and sat down on the edge of the engine officer's bed in the corner of the room, leaned back, and crossed her legs in a pose that might have passed, under different circumstances, for provocative. "You're right. It's probably somebody who knew where your son would be that night, somebody connected to the department. We thought about the Rothems, but they have an ironclad alibi for the night of the Cove Road fire. Who do you think it is?"

"My group of initial suspects, only because they were the people who heard me say Brendan would be at the Sutterfields', are the Morgans, Heather Minerich, Jim Hawkins, Sandusky, Mo Costigan, Roger Truax, Audie Culpepper, Frank Weed, and Valenzuela. That excludes Joshua Clunk and Claude Pettigrew. They weren't here. They didn't hear. But of those people, Heather Minerich is out because I know where she was after the Sutterfield fire. She was with us there at the house when the other fires were being set. And Hawkins is out because he was here in the station when the fires were set the other night."

"So if your theory is right, that leaves as viable suspects—"

"The Morgans. Sandusky. Valenzuela. Weed. Roger Truax. Mo. Audie Culpepper."

"So let's discuss these people."

"The Morgans? I don't know. I don't see a motive. The same for Valenzuela and my rookie, Frank Weed. Sandusky we've discussed. Mo? She's crazy, but I don't think she's a firesetter. Audie Culpepper? He's had problems in the past. But his mother says he was with her the night of the Cove Road fire. Truax I can almost see. He wants my job, and if I can look unprofessional with all these fires, he might get it."

"I did some research on Truax. A few years ago, he took the chief's test in Tacoma. It was very competitive, and he didn't fare so hot. He didn't take it well. The rumor was that afterward his best friend caught him running down the middle of the street at midnight stark naked waving a forty-five and shouting, 'I'm no good. I'm no good.'"

"You're shittin' me?"

"I've heard it from several sources." Underhill stood up, yawned, stretched her arms wide and high above her head, then opened the door.

"You checking these people for records?" Fontana asked.

"Clunk has a hell of a history but no arson. He used to be a pickpocket in New York City, if you can believe that. I told you about the Rothems' insurance scams. The others are clean."

"Except one of them's probably burning down my town a building at a time."

"Except for that."

◆

THIRTY-SIX

ORDINARILY I DON'T DANCE
WITH CADAVERS

"I called Audie," Sally said, after they'd crossed the street. "I told him I'd be home around eleven. But when I called California, one of Mother's neighbors answered. She told me Mother had a heart attack late this afternoon."

Fontana stopped. "Oh, Sally. Is she all right?"

"She didn't make it."

"I'm so sorry."

"They'd been trying to reach me for a couple of hours, but at the old number. I've been thinking about it, and I bet Mother heard I was dead and tried to get through on my old number. First Greta and now Mother. To make matters worse, I lied to you. It's possible Audie is starting the fires. I lied about his alibi the other night. I don't know where he was when that lady died. I'm sorry. I don't even know why I'm telling you. It's like I've lost everything but him and I want to make it a clean sweep."

"It's more like you trust me."

He drove her home, saw her to the door, gave her a hug and a kiss on the brow, and, not knowing where else to go, returned to the Bedouin. Fontana couldn't help mulling over Sandusky's obsession with the arsonist. It nagged him, too, that Audie no longer had a valid alibi for the Cove Road fire. He had been counting heavily on that alibi even though he'd suspected it was false. Sally had apologized again and again on the drive home for lying to him.

Shortly before ten o'clock, Frank Weed sat down at Fontana's table while Sheri slipped into the chair across from them. Running his palm across his thinning black hair, Weed fixed his dark eyes on Fontana and lowered his roadkill eyebrows.

"Chief? I just thought I should warn you. There are people talking behind your back. Some of the last ones you might expect." He spoke so softly that over the jukebox Fontana missed close to every fourth word, piecing it together like an incomplete jigsaw puzzle somebody'd left in a vacation cabin.

"What are you trying to say, Frank?"

"Just that everybody who seems to be your friend is not. I'm not going to name anyone. I shouldn't even be telling you this. I realize a person doesn't know what's being said while they aren't in the room, and I just couldn't sit around and keep my mouth shut any longer. There are people out here who blame you for some of this stuff that's been going on."

"The arsons?"

"And other stuff."

"Hell, if you don't have any enemies, it means you're not doing anything."

"I really don't want to say anything more. I just thought I'd warn you. By the way, did you know Bree McAllister's piece on my rescue might get picked up by a syndicate?"

"I hadn't heard."

Weed looked over at Sheri, the room so boisterous she couldn't hear a word they were saying. "She left me two days ago. We're trying to reconcile."

"I hope it's going all right."

"Terrific."

During the week after the rescue, it had taken a while before Fontana realized Weed had been waiting for something that wasn't going to come. It appeared in a half-joking remark Frank made one day. "So when are the groupies supposed to show up?" As far as Fontana could tell, they never arrived.

Dancing with a succession of men younger than herself, Mo eventually paired up with Roger Truax while Truax's wife stood along the wall and steamed. Mo was drinking tonight, and Fontana had already considered driving her home. When they moved closer, Fontana noticed a sapphire ring on Truax's little finger. It made him angry that he hadn't spotted it before.

Toward the end of the next tune, Fontana approached Mo and held out his arms. Mo stepped into them. Nat King Cole's "Unforgettable" was playing. "I'll tell you what I am, Mac. I'm regretful. I'm regretful and a little bit heartbroken. That woman was only about the best hope this town ever had."

"What woman?"

"Aimee Lee. Gawd, I wish she wasn't dead."

"Mo, I just took her home a few minutes ago."

"But it was in the early edition of tomorrow morning's paper. She's dead."

"Mo, you don't believe everything you read, do you?"

"And I heard it on the radio driving over here. She's dead, Mac."

"Sober up, Mo. I was dancing with her, and I ordinarily don't dance with cadavers. By the way, I figured out who you had at your place when I visited last week. It was Truax, wasn't it?"

"I didn't have anybody there."

"I just now saw that sapphire ring of his. I should have known by the size of those socks. He had a Washington State Ferries hat, didn't he?"

"It's an emerald ring, not a sapphire. Can't you tell the difference? His brother works for the ferry system. Big deal. He had a hat."

"You think he might also have a Washington State Ferries lighter?"

"What do you mean by that?"

"We think the Cove Road fire was started with a Washington State Ferries lighter."

Before Mo could reply, several nearby beepers went off and six or seven couples broke up as volunteers exited by the front door. Fontana's pager announced a car fire on the freeway overpass at Exit 35, five miles up the highway in the mountains. The volunteers marching out the doors would man the station while Engine One handled the alarm. Mo went with them.

Sandusky left. Hawkins, Frank Weed, and several others went out at the same time and didn't come back, but Sandusky returned ten minutes later, strode over to the bar, and ordered a club soda, chatting with a couple of middle-aged women Fontana didn't know by name.

Eighteen minutes later, somebody unplugged the jukebox in the middle of "Who's Sorry Now." The houselights came on, and the front doors of the Bedouin were opened wide just as the remaining fire department pagers in the building went off. Before he got out the front door, Fontana smelled smoke. A block away the siren on top of the station wailed.

Outside everything had a gray haze to it. Judging by the smell, Fontana figured it was the lumberyard at the west edge of town.

THIRTY-SEVEN

♦

INFERNO IN G MINOR

As he fought through the dawdling pedestrians and travelers and headed up the sidewalk toward his truck, Fontana listened to the response on his pager. It was a very windy night for a fire.

When he reached Staircase Way in the chief's truck, automobiles and pickup trucks were jamming the avenue, drivers standing alongside their open vehicle doors, staring at a column of smoke riddled with embers that rose like slow, wobbly tracer bullets. The smoke column was on the far side of the Sunset Motel. Wanamaker Brothers Lumberyard.

Behind Wanamaker's there was only wetland, sparse trees, and the south fork of the river; no roads and no fire department access. Staircase Way was blocked, so he took Alice Street, passing the empty firehouse.

At the service station across the highway from the lumberyard, he parked beside the LPG tank, surprised to find no units on the scene. Where were Engine Two and the medic unit?

The fire was in the rear of the lumberyard warehouse, and most of the flame was hidden by the offices and the tall warehouse along the street. He requested a second and third alarm, the police to block off the streets, and Puget Power to cut juice to the power lines he knew would soon be frying.

When the medic unit got stuck momentarily behind a sudden onslaught of local rubberneckers next to the service station, one of the medics leaned out the window and gave a shrug. Then Sandusky barreled around the corner driving the ancient ten-thousand-gallon tanker, air horn pulsing.

Fontana threw on his bunking coat and helmet, grabbed his portable radio and the bolt cutters, and shouted at the medics, "Where's Engine Two?"

"At a carport fire back on Main."

"A carport fire," Fontana said, walking across the highway. "Shit." He turned and yelled at the service station attendant, a boy of about eighteen. "Turn off your pumps and close those bay doors!"

"Yes, sir," said the attendant.

On the highway to the west, a long line of cars heading toward town waited, their headlights casting shadows on the far side of Fontana. Behind him, the medics and two out-of-uniform volunteers began taking the caps off the nearest hydrants so they'd be ready for the pumpers.

The Wanamaker Brothers Lumberyard was the last business on the south side of the street before the city limits. West of the lumberyard were thinning woods, railroad tracks, and near the city limits sign, a small bridge with low concrete side rails under which ran the south fork of the Snoqualmie River. On the town side of the lumberyard stood a small, vacant storefront that had recently housed a fly-by-night real estate outfit. On the other side of the storefront, the Sunset Motel.

Strong winds blowing from the west and southwest tonight did not augur well for their firefighting. The lumberyard Fontana wasn't concerned about. He could smell the heat, could hear the crackling, feel the winds whipping the flames. The fire had a good head start. They were going to lose the lumberyard.

What worried him was the rest of the block, and maybe the next block—the Bedouin and the auto-parts store and bakery. Hell. He could lose the whole town. Already the breezes had fanned what must have started out as a relatively small fire into a minor conflagration.

Still wearing cowboy boots and a silk shirt, Roger Truax fell out of the gang on the corner and accompanied Fontana across the street, walking slightly behind and to Fontana's left like a wing man in a fighter formation. The fire was behind the offices in the storage yard, and Fontana could already see flames eight or ten feet tall through the office windows.

A cigarette stuck to her lopsided lip with spittle, the assistant manager of the Sunset Motel, a bandy-legged woman with a pot belly and dark pouches under her eyes, stood at the edge of the road with hands like clubs in the back pockets of her baggy shorts.

"I want you to evacuate the motel. Get everybody out of there," Fontana said.

"I'm sure a lot of my customers are already in the sack."

"Get them out or we'll start breaking down doors. Your choice."

Flicking her cigarette stub into the gravel, she shambled toward the motel. Because the motel was over a hundred feet from the lumberyard fence, it was hard to fault her for thinking it was safe, and while the fire was larger than it had been a few minutes earlier, Fontana knew it wasn't nearly as impressive as it would be later when the glow would be visible from Seattle.

The outside storage at the lumberyard was in back. In front were four low buildings—the offices, the store and warehouse, and a tidy little slope-roofed hut that had been a saw-sharpening shack when the Wanamakers' father and uncle had operated the business back in the sixties.

To the right of the offices, joined by an enclosed passage, stood a warehouse easily twice the size of the fire station and municipal building, thousands of board feet of lumber stored inside: two-by-fours, six-by-tens, plywood sheets, five-by-nine siding sheets, stacks of roofing material, rolls of tar paper, tiers of doors, molding, and other materials. Except for the hose tower at the station, the three-story warehouse was the highest point in town.

Fontana walked down the slight slope to the wire fence and cut the chain on the gate, kicked the gate wide, and walked onto the Wanamaker property.

From the side, he glimpsed a figure running toward him. Hoping it was a volunteer he could detail to the motel to ensure the manager evacuated the building, he stopped. It was Robinson Jeffers, his lumpy, blackened eye swollen into a tiny slit.

"H'lo there, Robinson," Roger Truax said, as casually as if they were at a picnic.

Fontana pointed his index finger at Jeffers. "I don't have time for you. Out'a here."

"I'm not hurting anything. I have a right to be here. I'm not—"

"Out!"

Jeffers and Truax exchanged looks before Truax raised his eyebrows and shrugged, as if to say, "What're ya gonna do with a crazy man?"

Fontana was already walking down the steep dirt and gravel lane to see whether the fire was impinging on the south walls of the warehouse. He could hear the growl of Engine Two's mechanical siren in front of the building.

"Park on the hydrant," Fontana said on the radio. "Engine Two. Park on the hydrant and bring three hundred feet of hand lines to the east end of the building for exposures."

"Engine Two, okay."

Before a cloud of smoke rolled into his face and blinded him, he counted six stacks of burning lumber, each taller than he was. For a split second, he thought he was not going to be able to fight his way out of the smoke, but then the wind lifted and he could see the edge of the warehouse roof three stories above where it had ignited.

As he headed back up the slope, he glimpsed something galloping low to the ground in the dark at the back side of the yard. Probably a panicked raccoon or an opossum.

Kicking in the front door of Wanamaker's offices, Fontana walked through the sales area to a twenty-foot-tall sliding door. He pushed the door open a few inches and directed his flashlight beam into the dark warehouse, smelling fresh lumber and sawdust. The outside wall and the roof were burning, but it hadn't penetrated the building yet. To keep the oxygen flow to a minimum, he closed the doors behind him.

When he got to the street, Frank Weed ran past him toward the store portion of the building he'd just left. "Frank, it's a closed business. Don't go in. There's nobody in there."

Ignoring Fontana, Weed charged into the building. Moments later, he came out and said, "All clear." He didn't bother to look sheepish about disobeying an order.

Sandusky walked past and muttered bitterly, "Once a fucking hero, always a fucking hero."

Outside, the crew members from Engine Two were working hurriedly, eyes big with fire. Across the street, Mo Costigan squirmed into her bunking pants and boots, her dress hiked up around her thighs and hips. For just a moment, he caught a glimpse of black garters and panties. Drunk as she was, at least Mo was trying to help, unlike Truax who stood on the corner with his hands in his pockets.

Snoqualmie's new engine came howling down the windswept highway from the west, followed closely by two units from Fall City. When he got out of his car, Fall City's chief said, "I thought you folks caught the son of a bitch."

Fontana winked. "We'll catch him tonight."

Backpacks and MSA masks slung over their shoulders, Mo and two other volunteers strode over to Fontana for instructions. "Okay, Mac. Where do you want us?" A Saturday night fire in a town full of beer-drinking volunteers could turn into a tragedy of undreamed proportions. Fontana had always known that.

"You three on a monitor right there," he said, pointing at a traffic turtle in the road.

The three looked at each other and then at Fontana. Mo said, "You sure? It's not that big yet."

"Do it."

Two teams of firefighters from Fall City laid a manifold in the street at the west end of the complex and then hand lines from the manifold through the gated west exit to the lumberyard.

As they worked, a dog with a dead turkey tied around its neck ran up the slope from the rear of the lumberyard and into the street, then, stricken by the sight of so many spectators, dodged into the motel's parking lot.

After Hawkins and the crew of Engine Two had gotten the engine successfully hooked to the hydrant with the four-inch suction and were in the process of stretching two-and-a-half-inch lines from the engine across the street and down the slight incline toward the rear wing of the Sunset Motel, Fontana took Hawkins aside for a moment. "What'd you have?"

"It was nothing, Chief. A carport fire. I thought that's where we got dispatched to. They didn't say nothing about a lumberyard. Flames showing, she said. I saw flames in the carport. I got on the horn and gave them a corrected address, but nobody said anything back, so we tapped it. What was I supposed to do? If I was at the wrong address, they should have told me." Hawkins's face had gone pink.

"Don't worry about it. You made a decision. That's what the officer does. Besides, there's no life hazard here. We were going to lose it from the get-go."

When Engine One rolled down Staircase Way, Fontana ordered them to drop a manifold and drive back to the intersection, a seven-hundred-foot lay. Already Hawkins's cohorts who'd hauled lines down the slope at the east end of the lumberyard were retreating back up as flame and heat curled around the building and blew out windows in the back of the Wanamaker offices. The hollow was layered in heavy black smoke and laced with wind-whipped flames.

Robinson Jeffers chased the crew as they pulled their line back, windbreaker collar up as if to hide from scrutiny.

Conferring with the Fall City chief, an ex-logger, Fontana decided to send a crew inside the warehouse with instructions not to make a heroic stand. They wouldn't open up the outside lines on the building until the interior firefighters had fallen back.

Walking from one end of the fire building to the other, Jennifer Underhill began snapping pictures of the various knots of spectators. Stopping next to Fontana, she said, "One of your residents just reported a fire in his backyard. He put it out himself with a garden hose. You count the carport and this, that's three fires."

"I know."

"He's baaaaaaack."

"Yeah."

"Mac," said Roger Truax, who had taken more interest in the proceedings now that Jennifer Underhill was involved. "Mac, I don't think it presents a proper picture to your troops, you walking around with a pair of bolt cutters in your hands. Even as a captain in Tacoma, I rarely took out any tools."

Ignoring Truax, Fontana walked to the chief's truck and stood next to the passenger window beside Audie, who had arrived sometime in the melee. He was straddling his bicycle, sweating and panting. "Hey, Chief!" Audie said. "That's a great fire!"

"Audie. Does your mother know you're here?"

"Sure. This is the greatest. I can't believe it. This is so neat."

In his jeans and shirt, Sandusky had been hauling hose with the Fall City firefighters, but now he approached Fontana in full bunkers. "This is a set fire, Chief. There was another one over on Main Street. The engine tapped it on the way here."

"I know."

"Damn, he's here." Sandusky glanced around at the growing crowd, mostly men and women in T-shirts and baseball caps from the nearby taverns, children and families and old folks from the neighborhood behind the service station. "He's watching us, isn't he?"

"Maybe we're watching him." Sandusky gave him a look and left.

A few minutes later, the team inside the warehouse stumbled out, followed closely by bales of heavy black smoke. Fontana gave orders over the radio to open every hose stream and monitor they had. From now on, it would be an exterior attack. Surround and drown.

"What's a monitor?" Audie asked, after Fontana had given a crew instructions to set one up in the street. Audie had followed him to the center of the road, where Fontana was watching the motel evacuees in nightclothes as they coughed and stumbled. A huge patch of black smoke smothered Fontana and the boy for a few moments before drifting away.

"A monitor?" Fontana motioned for Mo and her group to check out the Sunset Motel. "Do a quick search!" he shouted. "A monitor is that thing over there on the ground. See how it looks like a cannon? Sometimes they're called water cannons. It's got three lines going into it from the rear and one long pipe with a nozzle directed toward the fire. A big hose line with three men handling it can put maybe three hundred gallons a minute on a fire. One of those monitors can put eight hundred gallons a minute onto a fire, or more."

"Wow."

"Yeah. You sure your mother knows where you are?"

"Sure." It was clear from his tone she didn't.

"Go back and watch from across the street now." As he turned to leave, the dog with a dead turkey around its neck ran from the east end of the complex into the street, weaving in and out of the firefighters and equipment, splashing in puddles. Ducking behind two dumbfounded state troopers who had blocked off the highway with their vehicles and were watching the fire, the dog raced around the back of the service station.

"That dog was on fire," said Audie.

"Just the turkey was singed a little," said Fontana.

THIRTY-EIGHT

◆

SURROUND AND DROWN

The fire formed a rough oblong a hundred twenty feet long and forty feet wide, flame shooting sixty feet into the air at the back side of the warehouse as huge stacks of kiln-dried lumber were consumed.

They had already set up six monitors in the street and one in the woods in the blackberries at the west end of the lumberyard when Fontana noticed a figure skulking around inside the lumberyard gate at the east end.

Climbing onto Engine One, he bumped the built-in monitor mounted above the pump instrument panel until the hose stream pointed in the general direction of the figure.

Sopping wet from various loose fittings around the rig, Valenzuela had taken over the driver's position and was working the pump panel in a T-shirt and bunking pants and boots. He stepped up next to Fontana on the catwalk behind the crew cab. Fontana swept the monitor stream across the driveway and the slope that ran down to the back of the lumberyard.

"I'm sure I seen somebody down there," said Valenzuela. Racing toward the street, a figure tried to claw his way up the slope, digging toeholds in the muddy grade. "You know," shouted Valenzuela, across the sound of the roaring pump, "I think I *do* see somebody down there." Valenzuela directed one of the engine's spotlights into the chaos, but the beam glared off the mist and produced mostly a fractured rainbow. "Damn, there *is* a guy down there."

"Really?" Fontana said, shutting down the monitor. "Down there?"

"Damn, Chief. See him?" Valenzuela pushed the valve handle Fontana had already closed. "There's a guy down there. I hope you didn't hurt him."

"Yeah, gee, I sure hope not."

Blinded by the spotlight, a bedraggled figure in a gray windbreaker zipped to the neck stumbled up the slope minus both shoes. Valenzuela said, "Isn't that the genius writer? How did that little twerp get down there? Gawd, lookit that."

"Valenzuela . . ."

"I didn't see shit, Chief. I didn't see a thing."

"Thanks."

By the time all the hose lines and appliances were in place, water from leaking hydrants, loose fittings, dripping nozzles, and overspray had flooded the street so that the two men from the Public Works Department attempting to clear a storm drain in front of the Moose Lodge didn't make a dent in the puddles. Water coursing through the gutters had run as far as the fire station almost four blocks away and was still traveling. In some spots there was already a foot of standing water.

After flame and heat forced the Fall City contingent out from behind the west end of Wanamaker's, Fontana stationed a team on the roof of the Sunset Motel to hose down falling embers and two more teams downwind to ladder buildings in the next block and keep a watch on the roofs of the Bedouin, the auto parts store, the restaurant, and the bakery.

Surround and drown was the maxim with a fire this large, and that's what he tried to do, first with Jeffers, and now with the lumberyard.

As the flames danced across the roof of the warehouse, the heat grew intense, and in front of the warehouse, firefighters with their collars turned up and their face shields lowered began using the overspray to wet themselves down, tendrils of steam snaking off their backs and shoulders and gloves like an eerie effect in a sci-fi movie.

After all the firefighters and equipment were parked in positions that looked as if they might hold up for the next few hours, while three fire departments pumped thousands of gallons of water into the burning lumberyard and warehouse, Fontana gave the command post over to the chief from Fall City.

On the flat roof of the Sunset Motel, Hawkins and one other volunteer manned an inch-and-three-quarters hose line. The wind pushed heat and smoke down on them and then let up.

"Damn," said Fontana, coughing as he crawled across the roof. "You two okay?"

"This is the best fire, Chief. Absolutely the best," said Hawkins excitedly.

"Well, you're welcome," Fontana said. "Maybe we'll have another one in August. I'll see if we can't find some widows and orphans to leave homeless."

"I didn't mean it that way, Chief. I just meant . . ." Hawkins lost his concentration when a furnacelike burst of heat swept down on all three of them, so intense and hot and explosive that Tolmi threw down the nozzle and crawled in a mad scramble toward the ladder. Fontana picked up the bucking nozzle and aimed it at the heat in a broad fog pattern, bringing immediate relief to all three.

"I thought we were goners," Tolmi said bashfully, as he crawled back.

Fontana said, "That nozzle's your lifeline. Use it like an umbrella if you have to. Don't drop it. By the way, who was at the station when the alarm came in?"

Hawkins cocked his head around. "Me. Tolmi here. The medics. Jenny Underhill. And Sandusky had just walked in."

"Why didn't Sandusky act or drive?"

"He said he'd take the tanker. You know how he is."

"Okay. You two do your best. Don't let the smoke disorient you. Remember, the line leads back to the ladder. I'll send you some relief."

"We ain't gonna lose it, Chief," Hawkins said. "Not while I'm up here. And we don't need no relief."

Tolmi looked visibly relieved when Fontana said, "I'll send some anyway."

In the street, Roger Truax weaned himself from a group on the corner. "Should have had your regulars working tonight," Truax said, his breath sour with beer and gossip. "Saturday night? Yeah, you should have had your regulars at the station. This wasn't a fire for a bunch of volunteers."

"Which regulars, Roger? The ones who did seventy hours last week? Or the ones who did eighty hours this week? Everybody is exhausted."

"That's what planning is for, Mac."

"Thanks for the advice."

"No problem." His arrogance bolstered by the cool assurance that none of the responsibility for tonight's calamity would fall his way, Truax continued, "And Mac?"

"Yeah?"

"Robinson Jeffers got the crap pounded out of him by a hose stream. You don't know what happened, do you?"

"There's a lot going on at a fire like this, Roger. It's hard to see everything."

"That's exactly what I told him."

At the west end of the complex, two crews from Fall City had laid lines and a monitor in the woods and were wetting down the trees and brush on the far side of the buildings. Most of the blackberry bushes had already been scorched by the heat.

When Sandusky and the Fall City crew waggled their monitor stream away from the trees toward the flames, the water vaporized long before it reached the fire.

"Heeeey, Paco," said Sandusky, standing in six inches of runoff and mud as Fontana stumped through brush mashed flat by hose lines and firefighters. "Let's go pick up some meeeentaaally ill women."

"I need to ask you a few questions."

"Sure, Chief."

"You didn't set this fire, did you, Sandusky?"

"Me? Hell, no!"

"Did you set the Cove Road fire?"

"Hell, no. I was fighting it. Don't you remember?"

"Do you think this was an arson?"

"It had to be. It started out there in the lumber."

"Why would somebody start a fire out here?"

He grinned. " 'Cause they're insane."

"Have you ever thought about starting a fire, even though you didn't go through with it?"

"Chief, is this an interrogation? Are you interrogating me?"

"Yes, I am."

"Well, I never started any fires anywhere. But I know who did."

"Who?"

"Roger Truax."

"Why Truax?"

"Truax wants your job in a big way. He'd do anything to get it and to make you look bad. Shit, he loved it that you were standing around outside while your kid was in danger. He loved it that the first fire fatality this town has had in a hundred years came on your watch. I've been thinking a lot about him. Do you realize he doesn't have any friends? And the odd thing is, I don't think he knows he doesn't have any friends. Besides that, I don't trust the sonofabitch any farther than I can piss in a tornado. Have you been watching him tonight? He hasn't lifted a finger."

"He's had a little to drink. It's probably better he isn't doing anything."

"It didn't slow Mo down." Sandusky took off his helmet, removed a glove, and wiped his brow with the back of his bare hand. Salt from sweat had caked his face in thin layers, weathered his eyes, and chalked a line where his helmet strap had been.

Fontana stared at Sandusky.

"Damn, Chief. You don't think I set fire to the house where your kid was sleeping? Why would I want to do that? I'm telling you, it was Truax."

"If you could have made either of the rookies look bad at a fire, there would have been another opening and we'd have to test again for it. If they messed up at a fire where my own son was in danger, so much the better for your case. You knew exactly where to go with that hose line at the Sutterfields', as if you'd planned every step beforehand. What you didn't plan on was that Weed would be the hero. That might make you bitter enough to set even more fires."

"Jesus, Chief. I move by instinct at a fire. You remember how it was. I grabbed a mask and got the first bundle of hose and started running with it. I could tell by where the smoke was coming out I didn't want to go in the west end of the building. Then I got to that patio slider and saw how much flame was inside. When I was going by the patio door, Weed was at the top of the stairs. He said, 'I'm going in here.' I said, 'You don't have a hose.' And he said, 'The Sutterfield kids are in here,' and he just went into that inferno like a damn fool. He was lucky he didn't get killed too. I just kept going to the door where I could see I'd have the best chance of putting the fire down the fastest. I didn't really consciously remember the place until after the fire. Hey. Where are you going, Chief?"

"I'm going to talk to Weed. I'll be back."

"You believe me, don't you?"

Fontana didn't bother to answer. Stewing for a little while might do Sandusky's character some good.

THIRTY-NINE

♦

SHE SAID SHE'D KISS
MY DIRTY DRAWERS

Alone, Weed was working a two-and-a-half-inch hose line with a Wooster nozzle at the tip, had it looped around in a twenty-foot circle so that it came back under itself, a gimmick that allowed one man to handle a line that should have taken three men.

Weed sat on the T, aiming the nozzle from between his legs up at a corner of the lumber warehouse that was just starting to puff smoke, grinning as Fontana approached. From one angle it looked as if he had a thirty-foot pud, and he knew it. "Hey, Chief. This is bigger than anything I ever thought we'd see."

As Fontana squatted next to Frank Weed, a heavy mist from the two monitors west of them showered the area with sheets of water. Like a turtle, Fontana ducked into his bunking coat and under his helmet, but Frank, who knew he would soon be feeling the same heat as the firefighters up the line where the fire had already broken through, was content to get wet.

"You know, Frank, I think I've figured out who's been setting these fires."

"Really." Weed altered the spray pattern of his heavy, rubber-coated Wooster, tightening it slightly.

"Don't you want to know who?"

"Yeah, I do, Chief. Who?"

"It was you, Frank."

The tall, thin rookie sitting on the ground looked over at Fontana with a sickly smile. His teeth were spaced widely, and he had bags

under his eyes that made him look forty instead of twenty-four. "You're kidding, right?"

"No, I don't believe I am."

They looked at each other for a few moments, Frank trying to remain calm, although his brown eyes were jittery, tense, his brows lowered, jaw clenched. "Chief. It's me. Frank. I saved your kid. I saved that neighbor of yours."

"Frank, I need to ask you a few questions."

"Sure, Chief."

"Sandusky claims on the night of the Cove Road fire that when he was running around the back of the house with the hose line he saw you at the top of the stairs. He said you told him you were going in to search."

"I might have said something like that."

"He said you told him it was the Sutterfield house." Frank Weed turned from the fire building and looked at Fontana, trying to work out the implications of this line of questioning. "Frank, how did you know that was the Sutterfield place?"

"I never said that."

"He says you did."

"Well, I didn't."

"Then one of you is lying, right?"

"I just never said that, Chief. Sandusky's the one who went straight around to that door with the hose line. Nobody knew how he did that. Not that I'm trying to place the blame for this on anybody. Because I'm really not."

"There was something else you said the night of the fire that's been bothering me, Frank."

"What's that?"

"You said that west door was locked. I went around the hedge hoping to get a partner for you, and when I came back, you said the door was locked and you were going to try elsewhere."

"I don't remember that."

"You said it. Later, when I saw the Morgans kicking that same door in, I assumed it *had* been locked."

"Well, maybe I did say it was locked. So what? It was, wasn't it? It was all smashed in after the fire."

"It was smashed in because the Morgans will smash in anything they come across. But it was not locked. I looked at it tonight, and the dead bolt was discolored at the tip. Because it had been thrown back, only the tip had been exposed. If it had been locked, it would have been discolored somewhere in the middle. And I know why you said it was locked. You were in a panic. You knew there were kids inside, and the fire was getting out of hand. Fires do that, Frank. You wanted to get past me as quickly as possible, so you said the first thing that came to mind that would work. If you'd said the door was open but you didn't want to try that way, I might have argued with you." Weed didn't say anything. "And Rena Sutterfield tells me that they didn't know you and you've never been out to their place. Other than the night of the fire."

"So?"

"So how did you know it was the Sutterfields' and that the kids were inside, or which door to go in to reach them the fastest?"

"I told you, Sandusky's mistaken. I never said it was the Sutterfields'. How would I know? And you know what else? Those people I told you about who were talking about you behind your back? It was Sandusky and Truax. Mostly Sandusky."

"Listen, you stinking bastard, you looked the Sutterfields up in the phone book after you found out my kid was going to be there. You sneaked onto the property looking for a place to set a fire that would look like the arsonist we'd been chasing around for a month and a half, and while you were doing that, you found an open door. You went in and set the fire. Then you waited around until the response showed up so you could become the big hero. Just to confuse things, you even set it with a lighter you'd picked up from Roger Truax—probably took it when he wasn't looking. You threw it in the bushes hoping it would be found and throw any suspicion that didn't go toward the original firebug toward Truax. You were thinking the first arsonist would take the rap, but he had an alibi, Frank. He was busy burning down his own church. You guys are all nuttier than squirrel shit."

"Chief, why would I set a fire? I mean . . ."

"Your girlfriend was leaving you. From what I know, you got into the fire department thinking you'd be an instant hero and then realized firefighting is mostly work, drilling, waiting around, and that if you were going to be a hero, you'd have to arrange it yourself."

"Nobody's going to buy that, Chief."

"I know it sounds irrational. It *is* irrational. And that's what makes me so mad. How pathetic it all is. How senseless Lorraine's death was."

"I'm not sure what I said to Sandusky. That was a couple of weeks ago."

"Sandusky's sure. And I'm sure what you said to me, Frank, because I replay every second and every word of that night every time I try to sleep. You must have been wondering when all the little contradictions in your story were going to come to light."

"Chief. You're making a mistake. That was a busy night. It's easy to lose track of who did what. Or who said what. Besides, this is not a good time for a joke. Those guys over there are going to film me in a little bit." Weed gestured at a television news crew nearby.

"There's a new imaging system not many people know about, Frank. Recovers fingerprints that have been wiped clean. You remember the lighter we found twenty feet from the point of ignition at Cove Road?"

"Nobody said anything about prints."

"Cyanoacrylate fumes, radiography, laser fluorescence. Ain't science wonderful?"

"Nobody said anything about prints. Heather touched it. How do you know I didn't too? Just another fool recruit screwing up evidence."

"Heather swears she brought it straight to me. You know, Frank, you might be safer in prison."

"What do you mean?"

"Think about it."

"What? 'Cause your kid was in there?"

"That's right."

"I saved him. I got him out in plenty of time."

"Was the plan to save my boy and make me eternally grateful?"

"There wasn't any plan. What are you talking about? There was no plan. Chief, you're starting to make me nervous."

"Supposing you did start a fire, Frank? Why would you do it?"

"I mean . . . Well, let's just say, just for the sake of argument . . . I don't know. I mean, I never knew you could get fingerprints like that. If it's true that you had fingerprints, there wouldn't be any use in a guy arguing, would there?"

"Not with my testimony about that door and Sandusky's testimony about you knowing the kids were in there. No use at all." They looked at each other for a few moments, and then Weed turned back to the fire building. "A man should really try to keep his story straight when he's trying to kill kids and old women."

"Hey, nobody ever meant for that to happen."

"Tell me what you did mean to happen."

"Supposing . . . I mean, just for the sake of argument, and I'm not saying I did anything, but just for the sake of argument, if I had started it, don't you think I canceled that out by saving those kids?"

"Are you serious, Frank?"

"Well. Yeah. I saved those kids."

"And?"

"One of them was yours. I'm a hero, man. I've been in every paper in the state. I've been on four different national TV programs. I would think that would more than cancel out any kind of minor mistake a guy might have made prior."

"I'd be careful about calling murder a minor mistake. And you torched this lumberyard. You're going to be lighting fires for the rest of your life, Frank, unless we put you away."

Weed tried to maintain eye contact with Fontana, but he glanced away, stared at the flames, then looked down at his crotch, as if perhaps to certify that he was still a man. He mumbled something.

"What did you say, Frank? I can't hear you."

"I said I'm sorry."

"Sorry's not good enough."

"But I *am*. And I did save your kid."

"You can never make it right. The only way to even try is to shut the nozzle off, get up and walk over to Jennifer Underhill, and turn yourself in."

Weed was quiet for a few moments. "I never said I did it. All I said was I was sorry."

"You're only getting one chance."

"Then what are you going to do?"

"Take your wildest guess and you won't even be close."

"You know, Chief. You threaten somebody if they don't confess, of course they'll confess. Besides, you have the reputation of somebody who would do something ugly."

"Just tell me why, Frank."

"I never said I did."

"If you had done it, why would you have?"

Weed thought about it. "Well, to be truthful, with the other fires going on around here, I personally never saw how it could make much difference. I mean, if we fought ten fires in a week or eleven fires in a week. What was the diff?"

Radiated heat warmed their faces and sent steam off their boots and bunking coats, bestowing on Weed a sunburned look. Rain from the arching hose streams fell from a cloudless sky. On the horizon to the north, stars shone. A sliver of moon was bracketed by billowing black smoke.

"You going to do it, Frank?"

"Turn myself in?"

"Think about it, Frank. Think about the pressure you've been feeling. It's going to get worse."

"I knew if I saved somebody Sheri would kiss my dirty drawers."

"You didn't save Lorraine."

"The old lady? Well, sheesh, she was . . ."

"What?"

"Well, she was . . ."

"Old enough to die anyway? You lit a fire and she died, Frank. Under even generous definitions, that's murder."

"I don't get it. I'm a goddamned hero. Doesn't saving them mean anything to you?"

"Sure. It means you'll be a hero in the slammer."

FORTY

◆

I'M SEXY AND I'M DESCENDED
FROM HORSE THIEVES

To Fontana's surprise, Frank Weed shut off the nozzle, got up, and sought out Jennifer Underhill, speaking to her for forty minutes, confessing, but only after fluttering around the topic for a good long while, posing in a wide-legged stance reminiscent of Yul Brynner, while the fire ripped away in back of him, asking questions about mitigating circumstances, quizzing Underhill about a suspect's rights in granting interviews ("They can't keep a person from talking to the press, can they? Once they're in? I mean, if somebody wants to interview somebody in jail, isn't that his American right?"), and inquiring how famous people were treated inside the penal system. "I'd probably be pretty high on the totem pole, wouldn't you say? After being on *Oprah*?"

"I would think so," Underhill said gently. "I would think so." What she was really thinking was that it would be her first solo arrest since graduating from the state police academy.

Underhill handcuffed Weed and drove him to the King County Jail in Seattle, staying up most of the night processing paperwork. Before driving home the next morning, she phoned Fontana, awakening him from a dead sleep. "Good. You're up. Listen, what sort of ruse did you pull on Francis Xavier Weed last night? He kept looking over at you when he was turning himself in."

"He was under the impression you had his prints on that lighter from the Cove Road fire."

"You know there were no usable prints."

"I knew it, but he didn't." Fontana's voice was thick and woolly and hoarse. Last night during the final stages of the fire, the wind had died down and within minutes the town had been cloaked in a layer of smoke so dense he'd been forced to drive home at five miles an hour. Even with the house shut up, he could smell smoke inside.

"You were taking an awful risk. What made you think it was him? And what were you going to do if he didn't fess up?"

"Beat him to death with my portable radio."

"Uh-huuuh."

"I had him trapped in a couple of lies. He was starting to panic trying to figure a way out of it. The lighter was just the frosting on the cake."

Fontana listed his reasons for concluding it was Weed. While he spoke, he kept remembering the single moment in the dark yard at the Cove Road fire when nobody was around except Fontana and Weed. Weed had given him a quick, odd look, knowing all the while what Fontana had not known, that Fontana's son was upstairs about to die in the smoke with four other children, with Mary, and that Frank had caused it. The one person Frank wouldn't have known was in the house was Mary's mother.

"But I don't understand it," said Jennifer Underhill. "Why would Weed have said either of those things at the fire? Why did he tell you that door was locked, for instance?"

"Weed was in a panic. He'd set that fire hoping somebody would turn it in and then he would get there early and be the hero. But by the time it got turned in, more time had elapsed than he'd figured on, and the fire had gotten a good toehold. He knew exactly where they were because he'd scouted the house earlier. Any time he had to spend getting past me was just wasted. So instead of arguing about the door, or which door to go in, he just said it was locked, as if he'd tried it.

"And the same thing when Sandusky shouted at him. He said the first thing that came to mind to get Sandusky off his back, giving away what he wasn't supposed to have known, that the house belonged to the Sutterfields."

After a conference with the attorney his mother had retained, Weed recanted his confession, stressing publicly that he'd been coerced, that he'd never set any fires, and that he had no idea who had.

His rationalization for his former willingness to implicate himself was that Fontana had threatened him. As if that weren't enough, he came up with a bizarre story about accidentally having eaten some stew tainted with hallucinogenic mushrooms from the woods behind his apartment house.

However, using tips they'd received from Weed's girlfriend, Sheri, King County uncovered more physical evidence tying Frank Weed to the arsons. It seemed he'd kept souvenirs from each fire.

A week after Frank Weed's incarceration, Jesse Rothem was jailed for torching his house to collect the insurance money. After he was packed off by the officers, Kim Rothem threw all her belongings into a U-haul trailer and fled to Minnesota, where it was rumored she had moved in with a former boyfriend.

After Joshua Clunk was incarcerated for setting fire to his trailer, he managed to get space in one of the weekly tabloids claiming he'd had an affair with Aimee Lee. Clunk's allegations and photo made national headlines, which turned Sally into the butt of lewd jokes offered up by every radio DJ in the land. She braved it with the same quiet dignity with which she had braved everything else, without engaging a lawyer, without filing suit, and without feeling sorry for herself.

Except for some blistered paint and melted roofing tar, Hawkins and Tolmi had successfully defended the Sunset Motel. On the drive home that morning, Hawkins spotted a Doberman reeking of burned feathers and enticed him with the only food he had, a Tootsie Roll Pop. While the dog ate the candy, he unyoked the turkey from the dog's neck and sat wearily on the ground. After a bit, the Doberman tongued his face. Hawkins took the dog home and, over the strenuous objections of his mother, adopted it.

The night of the Wanamaker Brothers Lumberyard fire, Robinson Jeffers was taken to the local hospital for treatment of bruises and a dislocated finger. He told the nurse he didn't know what had happened to him.

Truax remained ensconced as the town's safety director, a post of limited duties, especially without floods, forest fires, earthquakes, or the biker invasions he kept warning Mo Costigan about. If his fling with the mayor had gone any further than their single rendezvous, Fontana discovered no evidence of it. Truax went to the city council and somehow got them to issue a silver badge for the position of safety director. He kept it in a polished leather holder, a gift from his wife, who didn't know his sole use for it would be to get through the Sun Country gate during alarms.

Having lost one recruit to the hoosegow, Fontana decided to pay more attention to his remaining rookie. She'd done well at the lumberyard fire, but the lumberyard had been an exterior attack. The questions about her had involved closed spaces. Fontana didn't know what to think. Was she a firefighter, or was she not?

One sunny afternoon in early August while her Porsche idled nearby, Fontana approached Mo Costigan with a file in his hands. Mo had blasted into the office in shorts, a white sleeveless top, and broken sunglasses she'd gotten free from her father's drugstore. She was on her way out of the building with an armful of papers when Fontana cornered her on the hot sidewalk.

"Mo, we need to talk."

"I'm in a hurry, Mac. I have friends waiting with a boat and an extra pair of water skis."

"It's about your recruit."

"*My* recruit?" She stopped cold and peered at him through the broken sunglasses.

"I've been going through her files. It seems as if the physical agility numbers from her initial entrance test may have been altered." Mo leaned close and glanced at the open file folder in his hands, brushing her cheek against his bare arm. "Look at her time for the hose drag."

"One minute and ten seconds? Not the greatest, Mac, but it's passing."

"But see what it's been scribbled over?"

"No."

"Look carefully, Mo. Underneath it says one-forty. One-forty is flunking."

"Is that what it says? Maybe it was a mistake."

"We tested everybody the other day. Heather could barely drag a charged two-and-a-half twenty feet. There's no way she could pass the entrance test today."

"She must have gotten weaker."

"The funny thing is, only one person checked this file out of the office before I did."

"Oh?"

"You checked it out, Mo. Twice."

"I guess those do look like my initials."

"You doctored these numbers, didn't you, Mo?"

"Of course I didn't do any such thing. That would be illegal."

"I'm not trying to hang you. All I want is the truth before somebody gets killed."

"I was somewhat involved in the testing process. You were on a much-needed vacation, if you recall. But doctor the results? I'm insulted."

"You don't sound insulted, Mo."

"Mac, we needed a woman. No woman passed. I mean no *other* woman passed. At the time we were the only Eastside town without a female in our department."

"This is why you've felt this special kinship with Heather, isn't it? Because you falsified public documents to get her into the department."

"I'm sorry if I gave you that impression, Mac. All I know is that Heather's been through almost eight months of probation and she's passed everything with flying colors."

"Mo, you weren't kidding when you said you were descended from horse thieves."

"Sexy horse thieves."

"You probably have relatives who started their own religions too."

"Only one."

In some ways, Fontana didn't want to know whether Mo had revamped Heather's entrance test. She would stand or fall on her own merits. He was peeved enough at Mo, however, to blurt out during a city council meeting that the mayor made most of her phone calls from the toilet.

Two weeks after the sidewalk tête-à-tête with Mo, Roger Truax, wearing dark glasses and a baseball cap with a fake ponytail attached to the back, entered the nude run at Sun Country. Somehow, during the highly policed run, Hawkins and Sandusky managed to snap a picture of him from the woods near the fourth hole of the Sun Country golf course.

By the end of the summer, as it was passed around behind Fontana's back, the photo became the most treasured item in the station inventory.

Fontana took Brendan and the dog camping at Mount Rainier, close enough to see a glacier from their tiny tent. A week later, after much begging and cajolery from the two boys, they went camping with Audie and his mother. During the drive home, Audie got his tongue stuck to a Popsicle.

Though he left turkeys alone, Hawkins's new dog began killing chickens.

Sandusky decided to test for Staircase's new position.

Several nights during the summer, Brendan woke up in a sweat. Once he related a dream that he was sitting on the couch watching TV with Lorraine and he looked over at her and she was on fire. Fontana talked to him about it for a long while and decided it was time to change the subject when the boy said, "If a werewolf was against a cannibal, who would win?"

Ironically, Robinson Jeffers won an award for his series on the arsons. Truax one day presented Fontana with seventeen pounds of meticulously sorted screws, asking him if he thought Sally Culpepper would be impressed. Fontana assured him that she would be, but when Truax ran into her in the store one day and offered to show them to her, she looked at him as if he were a lunatic.

The remainder of the summer dragged on in peace.